DEATH AT THE
BRIDGE TABLE

Death at the Bridge Table

Published by The Conrad Press in the United Kingdom 2021

Tel: +44(0)1227 472 874
www.theconradpress.com
info@theconradpress.com

ISBN 978-1-913567-97-2

Typesetting and Cover Design by: Charlotte Mouncey, www.bookstyle.co.uk
The Conrad Press logo was designed by Maria Priestley.

Printed and bound in Great Britain by Clays Ltd, Elcograf S.p.A.

A Brogdale Murders Mystery

DEATH AT THE
BRIDGE TABLE

ROBERT WHITING

In memory of my grandfather,
William Whiting (1880 – 1951)
archaeologist, master builder, avid bridge player and
first resident of Corners, 1 Brogdale, Ospringe, in 1923

Saturday 10th June 1933

The locations, properties, weather formations and extraneous events are real. The characters and their relationships are real, though their names have been changed.

The story is entirely one of fiction.

Chapter One

She noticed his hand first. It opened slowly and then released its contents: a pack of cards slipped from his grip and spread in a short, uneven row towards the side of the table.

It was his left hand, the one with the slightly twisted thumb and no nail in the index finger – the nail that had been lost following an accident in a factory where safety was not all it should have been. He had been twenty-three at the time; now he was forty-eight and had been a bridge player for nine years. This was the hand that held open doors as gentlemen do and which he had recently extended to the passenger door of his newly purchased car (the first he had ever owned), when he gave her a lift home after their game; the hand that guided her through the doors of houses, restaurants and theatres and the hand that comforted her when she was distressed. He always placed his left hand on her neck before he kissed her goodnight and it was the hand he held out as they parted, a sign of longing that they should meet again soon. For now, she watched his hand fully relax and fall gently to the table unfurled and without function.

It came without warning, the unrelenting thief in the night, stealing his life.

She watched his right hand follow the same ebb tide of his being; the hand of welcome to all he met. Tonight, after the thief struck, his hand was empty, there was nothing more to let go, no more clutter spreading across the green baize.

It happened in the blink of an eye but as she watched, his considerate loving life drain through his hands everything happened in slow motion. She wanted to cry for help, for someone to call for the doctor; she could not, she must not sit and watch and let the thief have his – for she was sure it was a man, a woman would surely never do such a thing – have his way. But she could not move. The horror of what she saw created such a weight on her shoulders that all she could do was to sit and wait for someone to come to her rescue; it was too late to rescue him.

And so she watched the all-consuming decline of a seemingly healthy man who only moments earlier had sat happily talking to her, chuckling at their mistakes during the game and those of their opposition.

She watched the man who was healthy enough to make love to her by the fading full moon's light.

She watched him fade into nothing.

Until he was gone.

Chapter Two

SUNDAY 11TH JUNE, MORNING

All of the places, people and events I describe in the Chapters that follow, existed or happened before I became involved with the events of that night. The properties and their locations are of possible concern or relevance to what followed but I had no idea at first which or what. It was the events, the sequence in which they occurred, who among the tableaux was directly involved and what lay behind the façade that the rest of the world saw that I needed to examine. I knew it would not be easy.

I was telephoned by Patricia less than 24 hours after the death of her bridge partner, Alan Broadoak. Upon my enquiring, she refused to provide any further information over the telephone save that it was a matter of some delicacy and could I please go down to help as quickly as possible. On further interrogation she twittered that a plain clothes policeman had been and talked to them and gone away, but she could be drawn no further on what had happened. She had always been scatty and of a melodramatic nature, so it was of no surprise that she gave so little away. In truth, she may have forgotten much of the relevant information on the spur of the moment.

It was a wonder to me – and to everyone who knew her – how she had ever managed to learn, let alone continue to play bridge for as long as she had. It was not just her considered inability to understand and play the game but also her everlasting knack of finding partners who would partner her more than once. She obviously had some attraction for them, hidden depths which only they had discovered albeit for some rather briefly, although exactly which hidden depths had attracted Alan Broadoak let alone the rest of them, those of us about her had yet to fathom.

Her telephone call was much as normal and indeed was of no surprise to me for they always followed the same pattern. She was in some kind of trouble (as little sisters are wont to be) and wanted help; the kind of help our father, Charles was either unable or more likely unwilling to give. There was a degree of inevitability in the manner to which I would respond: I had said 'Of course I will' and agreed to drive down to 'Arrive no later than sunset and yes for dinner if I could make sufficient time and yes, she could tell cook to cater for an extra one.'

The journey from my home in Bletchley to Corners, the family home in Faversham was a long one and the return trip was one I was not prepared to countenance in a single day. I initially agreed, therefore, to stay overnight and then, at Patty's exasperated retort, for as long as she might need my help. It was, she uncharacteristically snapped, a matter of some importance that could not be considered lightly or indeed be resolved in a matter of a few hours.

I packed unhurriedly and loaded my cases onto the car. The hot weather, the drought of the past weeks was continuing, and I intended to drive as far as I could with the top down.

My decision would require me to reduce the speed at which I travelled, but I had allowed more than sufficient time to reach Corners in time for dinner. My hesitance when speaking to Patricia had been solely to avoid any hysterics should I arrive later than we had discussed. There was no allowance for tolerance in Patricia's world and her behaviour was undoubtedly why Charles had become unable to deal with her exuberances however worrying or serious they may appear.

I had decided to travel through London rather through the surrounding countryside, I enjoyed the sights and I might even come across some old friends if I decided to take lunch at The Park Lane Hotel which was (and still is) currently the place to be seen. In fact there was never any doubt that I would stop at the hotel which served the best lunch and accompanying wine in the city. Only one of my acquaintances stood at the Palm Court bar when I arrived. George Hind was what I can only call a professional drinker and although he would undoubtedly deny it, his consumption of a wide range of principally gin based cocktails at the Palm Court let alone any of his other drinking holes outflowed any of my other acquaintances. We greeted each other in the current fashion of two cheek kisses – no doubt more enjoyable for the men – before he bought me two Bees Knees and after another of the same, we agreed to lunch 'juste à deux'. He was one of only a small number of my acquaintances who lived in Faversham and I thought long and hard about raising the subject of Alan Broadoak but decided against it, if for no other reason than I knew few details to discuss with him anyway. It was to my surprise that it was he who broached the subject.

'What's all this about Alan Broadoak?'

'Broadoak?'

'Don't play dumb with me, old girl. You're on your way down through this busy little city of ours less than 24 hours after his death, to a place you rarely visit; I call that too much of a coincidence. It must be dear Patricia who's called for you because Charles wouldn't give you the time of day unless he was forced to do so. I doubt you'll see him other than at dinner. Come on, spill.'

'There's nothing to spill, sorry. You know as much, if not more than I do because you have the benefit of town gossip.'

'It's too soon for gossip old girl and anyway, I'm hardly there much as you must remember. It's a pretty dull place to live, I think we're in agreement about that, otherwise you wouldn't live in some place in Hertfordshire.'

'Buckinghamshire'

'Buckinghamshire then.'

'Are you not enjoying the country then?'

'It's all hops and apples and growing things. It's not for me I'm afraid but my own Pamela likes it of course, she loves the place. We, or should I say she, doesn't see as much of your mother, Lavinia as she thought she might though. She's feeling a bit lonely truth be told, perhaps you could put a word in for her, could you, when you feel it's the right time?'

We bid our farewells, John to meet his latest floozy and I for Faversham. In the event the journey took more than five hours in all and I was regretting not having taken the train. However, I arrived at Corners a little after six o'clock easily in time for dinner to be greeted by our butler.

'John, good evening are you keeping well?'

'Well enough, madam and yourself?'

'Intrigued, John, intrigued.'

'You are later than Miss Whitten had hoped for; did you have a problem with the car, or perhaps with traffic?'

'Lunch was the cause of my delay, John. Lunch and the need to close the roof.'

He smiled. 'A bit chilly was it, madam?'

'Yes, anyway, I'm intrigued John, intrigued about my sister's telephone call and the reason for it.' I raised my eyebrows in the hope that he might be forthcoming.

'Yes, madam, so I understand. Miss Whitten has asked that you speak to her as soon as you arrive, I'll take your luggage up to your room and I am advised that you can leave your car here for the time being. We are not expecting any other guests for dinner.'

'Thank you, John. I presume that you are unable to give me any information as to the substance of my visit.' He shook his head.

'No, madam, I don't

'No, I thought not, it was unfair of me to ask and what have I said about this madam thing? Alicia is perfectly acceptable when we're alone.' He smiled as if to say that he had plenty of information, but he was unable to share any of it with me nor did he feel it appropriate to call me Alicia despite everything we had been through together.

It was unkind for me to have asked him; the secrets of life in the house were upheld by the staff in strictest confidence and it would have been inappropriate and in some instances embarrassing for John to relay things that were said and which should remain a secret from the world at large; even when that world was immediate family.

I had barely entered the hall before I could hear sobbing coming from the drawing room on my right. John had followed me in with my cases and paused only to nod his head in the direction of the sound before beginning his climb of the stairs. As I walked towards the drawing room door, the sound became louder and it was only when I entered the room that it stopped. Patty rose to her feet, came running across the room and flung her arms round my waist.

'Oh, Ali, thank heaven you're here. Now I know that we're safe and I can go to bed knowing that I shan't be murdered while I'm asleep.'

'Don't be ridiculous, Patty, you're overreacting again. Sit down and tell me why I'm here.'

In the best way she could, my sister relayed the information to me as it had happened so far as she could remember it and unusually her story was at least reasonably coherent. It was after making six spades doubled – she said – a simple case of Mr Broadoak having a heart attack.

'But he was your bridge partner, I thought he had just gone three down doubled in six spades rather than making it – or whatever it was I don't really care – but isn't that reason enough to have a heart attack or, indeed reason for you to be so upset at either his poor card play or his death. After all, he was only a bridge partner. Forgive me for saying so but don't all bridge partners die? Eventually?'

'This is no time for flippancy, Ali. A man has died and not from what they're saying.' She paused and looked sheepish, unusually calm and guilty. Not guilty of murder, guilty in the sense of holding something back.

'And?'

'He and I were lovers.' She looked away. 'You won't tell father, will you?'

'Your lover? Patty, my dear girl, you have a lover? Sorry, had a lover.' This is one revelation I was not expecting almost any other member of the family yes, but not Patty.

She nods slowly. 'Is that so surprising? Father's made my life murder since you left; he's living in the past and can't drag himself back here, back to me.'

'This is you overreacting again. It's not to do with father; you simply wanted to have sex with someone. You wanted a life, darling, testing the water I think we call it nowadays, there's nothing wrong with that. Not if that's what you wanted.'

'That's true I suppose. But it's mainly because I know that Father is having an affair and I wanted to pay him back. Silly I know when I've every right to see and hook up with whoever I want to and if he can find somebody else that's good isn't it because then we can live apart and I'm free. I wanted, somehow wanted to pay him back for treating me the way he did.'

'Who's he having an affair with?'

'Joan Saynor.'

'His bridge partner?'

'Yes.'

I had to laugh. I shouldn't have done so, but the look on Patty's face alone was cause for a smile and the whole situation was ridiculous.

'Are you saying that father killed Alan Broadoak because you and he were having an affair and because father and Joan are having an affair and you wanted to pay him back?'

'No of course not. I'm just telling you that Alan was my lover. We met in his flat and we had sex. I don't think we were

15

in love, that's for the older girls. We were lonely and then when we were together we weren't lonely and now he's dead and I feel lonely again, and I think perhaps I did love him after all and I can't believe that he died of a heart attack, I'm sure he was murdered but I don't know anyone who would do such a terrible thing.'

'But why did you ask me to come down? Why do you think he didn't die from a heart attack?'

'I was there, I watched him die slowly and painfully. I wanted to do something, but I couldn't move. When he needed me most I couldn't do anything. I can't believe it was a heart attack. He was so healthy; you could see that just by looking at him although it's true in the last few weeks he hasn't been looking as good as he used to.'

'We'll come back to that, but for now you've told me a bit about your relationship with him and you obviously wanted to tell somebody. Now that you've told me what do you want me to do? What do you imagine I can possibly do that the police and the doctor haven't already done?'

'I don't know but you're my big sister, you've always looked after me even when I didn't need you to. Now that I need you to look after me, I don't know how you can and nor do you. Just help me Ali, please. Alan was murdered, I'm sure of it but nobody believes me.'

Chapter Three

Corners stands behind me with its back walls smothered in a peaceful, late evening sun. At this time of year the two pairs of large, fully glazed doors are wide open, giving us easy access to the paved area at the rear and side of the house. The vanishing sun flows through the opening and seeps into the loosely woven, white carpet which is flattened in places where our family and friends walk between the house and garden. In the gardens, the lawns, in particular the croquet lawn, are smooth and as green as they can be and the large sundial stands majestically at the crossing of the principal pathways, casting a long shadow on its brass dial. Our gardener, Grantley has been out this morning cleaning the black and white star burst edges of the base, brightening the otherwise green and brown swathes of nature. A perfect house in a perfect setting. It used to be a perfect home.

Over the years, this area of Faversham has become regarded as no longer part of the town but more as a village – a settlement really, there are no shops. Brogdale is a collection of houses strung along one side of a narrow lane and Corners, the most recently built stands at 1 Brogdale Road,

I am not a great lover of Faversham a little over one mile to the North. After all, there isn't much to commend it, sprawling as it does as a caterpillar along the London to Dover road and its parallel noisy monster of the Southern Railway. The last house of any size in the lane – large enough to have servants' quarters – stands at the left corner where the lane meets the London to Dover road and the historically named Chapel House is a square property built of wholesome, locally made Cremer Whiting red bricks, painted white in a fair attempt to give it a typical modern appearance and this is where George Hind lives. I know little about George and even less about his family. I know just that we are friends who get together in Town and that he's desperately pleased he retained their property in Town for ready access to the theatre, social events and the occasional business meetings at his club.

While the clacketing and steam emissions from the railway locomotives and the noise of cars and occasional buses annoys many in the town, Corners had been wisely located and so none of the noise from the hustle and bustle of what might pass for normal daily life reaches this outpost of local civilisation.

Quite why my father bought the house is a mystery to the rest of my family and friends and indeed has never been established, although several views have been expressed after the events that were to occur during that weekend. There's no doubting the beauty of the location, the house standing as it does with hop fields to the North, West and South and a vast apple orchard to the East. Along the northern boundary is a farm lane, with deep furrows where heavy tractors pass and, across the track, behind a row of majestic poplar trees further to the west, beyond the hops is a large chalk pit. The pit had been closed now for several years but it makes for an interesting stroll if you've the stability and courage to risk the uneven nature of the track.

At the front of the property's grounds, at the end of a long drive boarded by carefully tended rhododendron bushes, a narrow lane with its source deep in the Kent Weald, winds its way past more poplar trees, northwards to the town. It trails past Corners, between the hop fields and apple orchards and – after the end of the poplar barricade – in front of a short terrace of six Victorian, red brick houses before arriving beside the large, detached Victorian Chapel House described earlier in these paragraphs.

I know it well.

That fateful Saturday night, there had been no North East wind. It had been a still, beautifully warm summer's day and all that remained was the late sun of an early June evening, dipping over the pale blue horizon.

This was the County of Kent at its finest.

So, let the story begin with a review of the events of that Saturday evening, then moving on to my involvement with the questioning of the familial and servant occupiers of my home. The aim, of course, is to establish whether Alan Broadoak died of natural causes or was murdered and if so unearth the culprit.

Chapter Four

It is one of the many customs of my parents – my mother really – to enjoy a few rubbers of bridge after their Saturday evening meal. They're not gamblers and it's not generally considered necessary for them to play the game for the benefit of financial gain, but they'd become accustomed to agreeing stakes at a modest oft used phrase of 'a penny a hundred'. The pecuniary level had been decided after our John had concluded his investigations into the stakes normally played for by George Hind and his cohorts. That, at a ha'penny a hundred, was apparently considered to be adequate for them but it meant that we Whittens edged up the bounty to something more suited to our alleged means. Even so, while the potential gains or losses were worth concentrating for in the spirit of winning the game, they were not so high as to engender violence instigated by the losing pair.

So it was that this particular Saturday, 10th June 1933, Father, Patty and their guests – Mrs Joan Saynor and Mr Alan Broadoak – arrived in the card room, replete of their evening meal and set for battle. John had prepared the table and left it with one of the packs of cards placed in a fan, ready for the draw for partners to take place. The draw was a tip to tradition, nothing more. Father always partnered Joan Saynor and Patty, Alan Broadoak. That night was no different. The draw was used merely to decide the dealer and for him or her to decide on their dealing pack.

The conversation at dinner had been convivial with no talk of religion or politics or foreign affairs and the subject under discussion as they sat at the card table, readying themselves for play, was whether the scent, the bouquet of the hop flowers was this year as equally pleasing to the noses of the ladies as to those of the gentlemen.

There was no expectation that they'd reach a decision and it was, as always at this time of the year, agreed to reconsider the matter when the hops were in full flower and practical evidence could win the argument. The locally grown East Kent Golding hop known for having a gentle floral, slightly spicy, honey and earthy aroma was grown to extend the cutting until autumn and was thus rarely in flower until July, which meant they had only a few weeks to wait before they could reach an end to their discussions and fall deep in concentration of the game. It was therefore agreed that for the time being and when the opportunity arose, subject to an on-site survey when the hops were in flower, the attractiveness of the scent was the same for both ladies and gentlemen. It always was.

Father was drawn as dealer and chose the blue backed pack of cards.

The game began.

Chapter Five

The first rubber had been uneventful and although Joan Saynor and Father had won it in two games, they were only one hundred and fifty points up. This was thanks to an earlier, reckless bid of three no trumps by her partner which with great conviction and subsequent success, sister Patty had doubled. Joan Saynor was a player of above average ability but despite her best attempts she ended the hand six down, making only three of the nine tricks required.

'I'm so sorry, Charles, Alan was simply too strong in his spades. There was really nothing I could do.'

Charles smiled and nodded gracefully; he knew otherwise, but it was bad form to criticise one's partner at the table and particularly so when she was your guest! This was not the first occasion he had wished their partnership arrangements could be changed, but however many faux pas Joan Saynor might leave in her wake and whatever the end result, he could deny her nothing and forgive her anything.

'Fear not, dear lady, these things happen. It is shameful that Alan was not sufficiently awake and therefore able to take control of the bidding. As a result my cunning little daughter took charge and was disagreeable enough to double you. I

22

hope it was nothing Broadoak ate. More likely as not, to be too much port eh old boy? I suppose that makes it my fault!' he paused, 'John?'

Charles signalled with a nod for John to refill Alan Broadoak's glass he managed a smile to his partner before continuing, 'We're still ahead and that's the main thing isn't it, Patricia?' He knew that she was far more competitive than he and that she made every effort to hide her emulous nature from her partner and the opposition.

'Not at all father, we're here to entertain our guests and all that that requires of us.' Patty's smile was not convincing.

'Of course, of course. My deal I think.' He moved the freshly shuffled, blue backed pack of cards from his left to his right so that Patty was able to follow the procedural cut prior to his deal. It was not long after the gloating at the end of the first rubber, that lady luck deserted the winning pair and despite valiant attempts to regain the lead, it was ten thirty before they, Joan and Charles, finally conceded defeat.

'Well, partner, I fear I have let you down yet again. I must fall at your feet and beg forgiveness once more.' Father is well known for his effusive manner and this sort of occasion lightened the atmosphere perfectly.

'My dear Charles, there is absolutely nothing to forgive. In the end we did not have the cards tonight and that's all there is to it. Next time – perhaps next week – I'm sure it will be our turn.' She fluttered her eyelids, flirting playfully in front of his daughter.

'You're too kind, Joan.' He gathered up her right hand, leaned forward and kissed it lightly before he looked up and smiled.

Uncharacteristically, Patty did not respond immediately to her father's flirting. She was aware of his affair with Joan Saynor and played along with their supposed indiscretion. While normally she was quick to pick up and react on any opportunity to do so, tonight her retort was a few seconds later and more considered.

'You never know,' still seated and as if in a trance Patty had said slowly, 'we may have different partners next week. There's nothing we cannot change if we so wish. Is there?'

Charles made no response other than to turn his head in her direction and nod slowly, as if deep in thought. 'We will see, perhaps Alan won't want to change. After your run of successes over the last three weeks is it, or four? He might refuse. Isn't that so, old man?'

They all turned to look at Alan Broadoak who, since playing the last card of the previous hand winning them yet another rubber, had remained silent during the lightly heated remonstrations. This was not unusual, Alan had always been a man of few words but pleasant enough and with a dry sense of humour that he ably demonstrated, invariably during meals. That is, all turned to look except for Patty. Throughout the gentle banter, she had been staring at her partner for a while now, watching him closely and with hindsight, they realised why she had been so slow to react to the flirting.

'What do you say, old man? Eh?' Having initially been looking at Alan Broadoak, Charles turned to look at the ladies and then back to Broadoak. 'Alan, old chap? Are feeling okay?'

Joan Saynor (who was relying on Alan Broadoak for a lift home) noticed his hand first. It opened slowly and then released its contents: a pack of cards slipped from his grip and spread in a short, uneven row towards the side of the table. Joan touched his shoulder but there was no response and it was clear that something was amiss. After only a few seconds and despite the lightness of Joan's touch, Alan Broadoak tipped gradually forwards and landed gently on the table headfirst, his forehead resting on the winning card of the winning final trick, the rubber winning Ace of spades.

The room fell silent.

Patty screamed. At least, it seemed as though she had tried to scream, but only a whimper leaked from between her delicate lips. The shock was too terrible to believe. Only a few moments earlier he had been playing in yet another contract of six spades doubled making all thirteen tricks and winning not only the rubber, but the evening's game with a substantial net score. It was, or at least Patty would have acknowledged, a time for celebration and although Alan Broadoak was not an optimistic, highly demonstrative gentleman she did at least expect from him a word of congratulation before a chuckle at beating their old adversaries yet again. Nothing had happened that warranted her partner's stillness of movement and subsequent dormouse-like position.

Without further comment, Charles took charge: 'Come ladies, it's very late and much wine and port has been consumed, I expect the poor chap is in a particularly strange sort of deep sleep, but all the same I think you should retire to the drawing room while I sort his situation out. John will find you both some brandy to steady your constitutions. There'll be some innocent, straightforward explanation for this, you see if I'm not right.'

Joan smiled at her partner and, steadying Patty, they left for the drawing room.

'Perhaps you should telephone the police, dear,' As she passed through the doorway, Joan briefly rested her unencumbered hand on Charles's arm. He nodded, sagely.

Joan Saynor led Patty into the drawing room and quietly closed the door behind her. Simultaneously, a light knock on the card room door leading from the main hall, heralded John with the guests' coats and when he entered, he joined Charles Whitten in standing, looking at Alan Broadoak. His silent pose was but a brief one before he quickly handed the coats to his master and then walked round the table to where Alan Broadoak sat, slumped and silent.

After a cursory, inevitably superficial examination, of the body and of Broadoak's surroundings, he looked at up at his employer: 'I think I had better telephone Dr Hudson, sir.' His voice was deeper, more solemn than usual and his face really quite severe. There was, however, just a hint of a little more, a suggestion that something was amiss, and that the situation would not be easily resolved. Charles had, by this time, walked to the large window in the south wall of the room. The sun had long disappeared over the horizon, but the final glowing shafts of light threw an eerie pale orange brightness over the south lawn.

'So that's that, is it? That's all we need to do.'

'It would seem so, sir. I shall telephone Dr Hudson immediately.' John walked to the door into the hall but before leaving the room he dutifully turned to his master. 'Will there be anything else, sir?'

Charles turned around, his back now shielding Alan Broadoak's corpse from the dying sun's rays. He looked at his faithful servant and paused before answering. He knew that look on John's face – it was more than the normal dutiful expression. They had been together since 1915 and he knew John's reaction to the body meant that he, John, suspected that there was something sinister about Alan Broadoak's death.

'Oh. Yes. Brandy for the ladies please, John they went into the drawing room and I expect you will find them still there. Mrs Saynor was comforting my daughter who has apparently been the most severely affected by the events of this evening. I think it best if you do not enlighten them of Mr Broadoak's demise, let alone the possibility that you clearly believe there to be something more to the situation than might first appear.'

Chapter Six

Detective Inspector Leonard Drabble (Len to his friends and acquaintances) had arrived at the Station only three weeks before the telephone call came from our butler. I later found out that he had been transferred to Faversham Police Station on post-war compassionate grounds and thus the reason for his move had been kept quiet so that he could gain and retain respect from his subordinates. It was unusual for a provincial station to have a detective inspector and none of the uniformed police stationed in Faversham was quite sure who should do what, but when DI Drabble heard there was a suspicious death in the town he was in no doubt who should be responsible and immediately took control.

It was 11.35 pm when DI Drabble arrived at Corners. He had not been long enough in the town to have yet had the opportunity or cause to make the drive to the outer reaches and to find such an imposing dwelling hidden behind a tall hedge was a surprise to him although he couldn't quite put his finger on why. On his arrival in the town he had thought it a small insignificant place where nothing ever happened and unsurprisingly, he assumed that was why he had been sent there, yet here was a major household potentially requiring deferential behaviour and care. Strictly speaking this was his return to the area but he had been a young boy when, after his father's death in suspicious circumstances he left to live with his aunt in Whitechapel. It was therefore no surprise to anyone who cared that he wanted to join the Metropolitan Police when finishing his general education.

He survived The War and emerged, without physical blemish, as a Detective Inspector. His father had not been so lucky, service in the previous two wars had taken its toll. Although details of his immediate past remained a secret, it was clear that the last thing he wanted was his superiors to be called in because of his inability to solve the crime without upsetting the bereaved. He was determined to prove his ability and justification of promotion by getting this – his first ever murder – right and he began by trying to assess the property in which they lived. It was too dark and misty for him to take in the full extent of the grounds, although the light from his car's headlamps along the extended drive was enough for him to know that they would be sufficient. It was inevitable that a search would be required, and it would help to be aware of the scale of area and locations where his men would have to tread carefully.

Drabble pulled the substantial, black iron ring on the left hand side of the front door and waited under the covered porch. He heard a bell ring somewhere inside the house and the door was soon opened by the butler, John Staples. Drabble introduced himself and John duly took him into the hall to await my father's response to his arrival. The hall is large but not ostentatious: the walls are lined with oak panelling and an oak staircase leads upstairs from the centre of the hall to the first floor. There are four doors leading from the hall and

29

he could only guess as to where they led – access through the house meant that he would find out soon enough.

On the walls between the doors hang a total of six paintings, large paintings such as you might admire in a public gallery. Upon inspection he discovered that each was a painting of one of the last six heads of the Whitten family. The entitled image of Charles Whitten was in stark contrast to the other five because of its more recent commission. The others went back to the late 1500s and the oldest was not surprisingly extremely dirty with so many years of dust and grime that the head of the family at that time was barely recognisable as human never mind any particular man. With hindsight it could be argued that to pay such attention to detail when the extent of his investigation had yet to be established was unnecessary. However, future developments might show the early assessment of the family line to be exceedingly beneficial.

'Detective Inspector Drabble, Charles Whitten, welcome to Corners, I am sorry that your first visit is in such unfortunate circumstances.' Charles Whitten held out his hand in greeting, a hand which was large and generally warm, but this particular evening was rather damp. Drabble had had no warning of Charles's entry to the hall and it surprised him so much that he was momentarily short of breath, but he soon regained his pose and turned to be greeted by what transpired to be his initial and principal suspect. 'Such things are meant to try us, Mr Whitten. I believe you are concerned at the death of a colleague, perhaps I might see him please and then we can talk.'

'Yes, yes of course. It was more John's concerns that resulted in him telephoning you rather than mine and in fact since Dr Hudson – whom we have known for many years – has been here, it seems that my daughter's concerns have been unfounded. It appears that my friend's death arose from nothing more than a straightforward heart attack after being three down in three not trumps or whatever it was – I confess that even I cannot remember what - and winning the evening, no more, no less. Mr Broadoak is in here, please.' He led DI Drabble into the card room where the unsuccessful contract had cost my father three pounds six shillings and four pence. 'Dr Hudson said he was going to contact the funeral directors to save us the inconvenience at this hour, to say nothing of the embarrassment of having a dead body in the house, even if it is one of my oldest and dearest friends.'

'Forgive me, Mr Whitten but you seem to be taking Mr Broadoak's death in a very offhand and almost relaxed manner. You say he was your oldest friend and yet he seems to be little more than an inconvenience to you.' Such was his concern that DI Drabble's eyebrows rose towards his hairline causing a few wrinkles to appear.

'Just my way, Inspector, just my way. When you've seen as many deaths and bodies as I have in my time, too many of those my own men and colleagues, it's somewhat difficult to display one's feelings and grief in a way others might expect. I can assure you that Alan's death is not considered – by me at any rate – merely an inconvenience and I'm extremely sorry if my behaviour might appear to demonstrate otherwise. My prime concern is to establish how he died and we have now done that, it was a heart attack; although Dr Hudson said he was prescribing something or other to thin Broadoak's blood in the hope of avoiding an attack he acknowledged that the death was unexpected certainly, but also occurred in a peculiar manner. There was no trembling, no cries of pain or exclamations, or convulsions, you see.

'He died silently, in complete silence and watched by his bridge partner – Patricia, my daughter – although of course she had no way of knowing what she was witnessing at the time. She said that it all seemed to be happening very slowly. I'm not sure what to make of that, but Hudson has given her a light sedative to calm her and help her sleep so you wouldn't have been able to see her until morning even if you felt she had in any way been involved in the murder. That is if you had thought there had been anything odd about Alan's death but as there is no suggestion of any funny business you no longer need to see her and I'm afraid you've had a wasted journey and so late at night too. Can I offer you a glass of something before you leave us?'

My father's expounding of the evening's events so far was unfaltering and, in the circumstances, somewhat surprising.

'Thank you, Mr Whitten but I won't thank you, not at this late hour nor while I am on duty.' My father's behaviour and the tenor of his voice implied such a high degree of nervousness as to suggest that he felt some element of guilt surrounding the recent death. DI Drabble had yet to see the body and he endeavoured to maintain an open mind, but father continued to demonstrate his guilt having taken up position between DI Drabble and the corpse. 'Despite what Dr Hudson has said about the cause of death, might I have a look at Mr Broadoak's body? Just for the record. I have to make a report of any and every time we get called out, I'm sure you understand.'

'Of course, Inspector, of course.' Charles Whitten stood back granting DI Drabble a clear view of the body which was still slumped on the chair and over the card table where his death had occurred.

DI Drabble checked the more obvious places where murderers normally attack their victims and there were no signs of any misdoings. 'You say there were just the four of you in the room at the time of death. Is that so?'

'There were just the four of us in here playing and John, my butler was in the room from time to time to perform his duties. There was nobody else in the house I can assure you.'

'Well, as you say sir there doesn't seem any need for me to start worrying your wife or daughter with questions or your other guest – what did you say her name was?'

'I didn't Detective Inspector, but it was Mrs Saynor, Joan Saynor an old school friend of my daughter and since she has joined us in the Saturday night routine a friend of mine too, now if that's all Inspector, John will see you out.'

At that moment, the door from the hall was opened and John, expectant as always, began to usher DI Drabble towards the front door. As the Inspector stepped into the hall, he rounded on his host who, as the action had been intended, was caught unawares.

'Just before I go Mr Whitten I should say that I may almost certainly have to return to ask you – and possibly other members of your family – further questions if anything raises an issue with your friend's death. It would so far seem unnecessary to have a post-mortem examination as both Dr Hudson and I are in agreement as to the cause of death, but somebody might challenge our findings for some reason as yet unknown.' With that, he turned again to face the front door and left.

John Staples returned to the card room to find his master

gone, Broadoak still in his place but now covered by a damask
tablecloth and the rest of the room just as it had been when
the rubber ended.

Chapter Seven

After he had ensured that the card room was locked securely, John Staples returned to his pantry.

Although he had not been specifically instructed to do so, he knew it was essential to ensure that the cleaner did not go into the room where Mr Broadoak remained at the bridge table. Like his employer, John had seen many men die, where the cause of death was well known and too horrible to contemplate. In some instances there had been so many bodies that the trenches were almost impassable until the bearers had removed the dead and dying.

Unlike his employer, John had witnessed many deaths caused by gas attacks, heart attacks, foreign fire and friendly fire. In some cases both during and to an even greater extent after the war, a death was put down to so called friendly fire and thereby covered a multitude of sins that were never investigated. Increasingly, deaths could more accurately have been identified as murder and increasingly those murders had been carried out by so called loved ones, often, women who could not cope with their man returning so damaged that he was unable to function as a real man. His physical and often mental state prevented him from returning to the life he had left behind to serve his country.

While their husbands had been away, friendships had developed with those in reserved occupations or those who had been boys too young to be drafted but who were now young men. Some so called friendships had formed with farm workers and labourers, some of them released into the local community from prisoner of war camps. Those friendships did not sit well with husbands on their return (or indeed with the wife and her lover) and steps were taken to relieve the new couple of the damaged men that had come home. John was aware of and experienced at first hand such relief being given to those whose husbands had returned from the trenches looking for solace but getting none and he remembered those instances in which he had helped friends and family when nobody else was available. Despite his best intentions he had become an undetected murderer.

John had fared well as my father's batman. His master had attained the rank of lieutenant colonel and despite his rank had treated John with somewhat more consideration than most of his compatriots. He was therefore pleased to accept the post as Charles Whitten's butler after de-mob.

Among John's many assets was an in-exhaustive list of his master's misdemeanours. Some trivial – schoolboy frolicking as one experiences at many public schools – others less so but in addition a few of which might be regarded as illegal. It was with some satisfaction that he had made my father aware of this list and particularly of the more sinister elements. He had given his word that he would not divulge any of the information while he remained in Charles Whitten's employment and that he would carry out all the normal duties of a butler but for a substantially increased level of remuneration.

He was an intelligent man with significant information and with expensive tastes, why should he suffer comparative deprivation while his master lived in such luxury?

Chapter Eight

I remember Frank Spillett well. After his father died, he didn't know whether to launch into a new profession or take the easy way out and carry on the family business.

Many years before, his father had been a successful private investigator and had built a substantial reputation during the pre and post war years. He was considered the epitome of Hercules Poirot but unlike the fictional, dapper Belgian detective with those hard working, intuitive little grey cells, Frank's father was the genuine article. His little grey cells were not intuitive and it had been hard work to get where he was by the time he died from overworking, always wanting to do just that little bit more than was necessary for his clients. It was on this principle he had gained peoples' trust and brought in the enquiries, many of which remained unsolved or because of his failing health had not even had a file opened on them. But it was too much and after two early warning strokes he died from a major heart attack. His family had been devastated but not surprised.

My father had always kept a fatherly eye on Frank and, indeed a somewhat lecherous husbandly eye on his mother Mary although he never let her know that and never made any passes towards her – not even after Frank's father died. So we knew that in his formative years, his 'what shall I do for a living' years, we knew that Frank had been sure of one thing, he was never going to do what his father did.

After Amos's death, one of the first things he told me – during one of our early talking times in a distant public house where nobody would know us – was that he couldn't bear the thought of sitting in an office, or pounding the beat, questioning questionable characters or helping abandoned women find their husbands. He wanted to do something useful, he wanted to use his literary skills, something – he didn't know what, but something like that and not a private investigator like his dad. His father had understood but he was disappointed that the family name would not live on and although he appeared to support Frank he was doing everything in his power to ensure that Frank would continue his own trade.

It was after his father's death that Frank discovered Amos had been close to completing a major contract. Out of respect for his father and the need for cash he agreed to complete the investigation which he did to the client's satisfaction and for which (I understand from my tell-tale sister) they duly paid Frank's invoice promptly. My father tried to persuade him to keep on the investigating business but when his encouragement failed, he talked to some of his business contacts in an attempt to find work for Frank but his efforts were unsuccessful and, indeed, unappreciated by Frank not least because the payment for the case had enabled him to sit back to consider his options.

My father demonstrably washed his hands of his surrogate son and because my father had little else to do at home, he simply sat back and watched Frank fail; my father was (and still is) good at sitting back and watching, it enables him to pick out other peoples' problems or errors in life so that he can 'help' them out. (My sister and I would naturally have preferred him to help us, but his disinterest in both of us did at least teach us how to develop our strengths - though Patty seemingly had none - and to deal with life's trials!)

That was over a month ago, Frank's father's death, the funeral and the whole mourning bit were behind him now, it might seem callous, but life had to go on. I was long away, first in London and then beyond to the pretty little town of Bletchley. I expect Frank continued to sit at his desk, pondering not so much the purpose of life, but what the hell was he going to do next. If nothing else he would have to decide what to do with Jennifer; she was his father's assistant, secretary, typist general dogsbody and his sidekick. We were never sure whether she might also have been his lover, but with hindsight this would never have been the case. She might have agreed to continue to work after Amos died because she knew a lot about the firm and how things were done; she might even have had her sights on taking charge and earning her fortune from local tittle-tattle leading to arrests by her very friendly policeman whose name remains a mystery to this day. There was stuff that needed to be processed, but he couldn't afford to continue employing her when there was nothing new coming in. However, Jennifer continued appearing to be a conscientious girl and continued sorting out the files and sorting out the little post that came through the door.

I had always had a bit of a soft spot for Frank, I'm not sure why because he's not my type, heavens, not now darling and from what I remember he wasn't when we were younger although we did spend time together just talking. Really. But now I needed a private detective with offices in the seedier side of town and with the seedy contacts that lived and worked there. Obviously, I thought immediately of dear Frank Spillett even though he always protested his lack of interest in the business.

I climbed the rickety stairs to his small offices above a flat (it could never be considered an apartment) and opened the door which in turn opened into what I discovered was the afore mentioned Jennifer's office.

He had presumably heard the doorbell ring in Jennifer's room next door and was not surprised that although he had said not to be bothered this morning, Jennifer knocked on the door. She was a slender, good looking girl and aged in her late twenties looked like a young lady waiting to break out into real life wearing slinky dresses, carrying a long cigarette holder, flattened hair and a look to kill. Her hourglass figure already caught every man's eye, but they had been scared off by her strength of character, an unshakeable self-belief and a high level of self-determination. The prospect of her being their 'little lady in the kitchen' would be destroyed within a quarter of the inevitable dinner he had taken her to. But she had learned to take orders from her employer: Amos was dead long live Frank; she knew it wouldn't be the same but straight away she didn't see a prospective husband but somebody who wasn't used to working for a living and needed to be taken in hand, to be controlled and prepared to take orders, if she acted fast.

'I'm sorry, Frank darling, I know you said not to bother you, but this sounds urgent. It's one of your father's friends – a Mrs Matcham – and it sounds right up your street. They were at the bridge table yesterday evening and one of the players dropped dead at the table. He seems to have been written off as a heart attack, but this lady seems to think different.'

Jennifer had taken control of the situation and that meant he didn't need to. Before Frank could reply, I pushed past Jennifer, who had introduced herself to me when I arrived, and stood in front of the desk. For a moment, nobody said anything although Frank stared at me, I liked to think that he was taking in my good looks – I stand a good six feet tall and almost as slim as Jennifer who was – as I may have already mentioned, although don't take this repetition as an indication of jealousy - extremely attractive, she looked more intrigued by what I was wearing - a rather drab tailored suit (unusual for the so-called modern lady) and a hat which suited more the times in a contrasting pale blue. The hat style is a trifle 'old hat' but I can't help feeling that it somehow suits me, Jennifer has no reason to be jealous and by the look on her face put it down to the fact that I'm in my mid-thirties and that she, Jennifer, was in her late twenties. I'm standing here trying to display strength and equality to Frank (who has remained seated) but can see that I'm not succeeding. I can see him looking me up and down, undressing me, wondering how we could be together – he's making no effort to hide it – but then realising it's not going to happen, even in his wildest dreams, that he needs to look no further than Jennifer and I will forever be simply a client.

'It's okay Jenny,' I can feel, almost see her glare, it seems that he never calls her Jenny when there are clients present; he probably thinks it sounds less than professional and actually I think he's right. He stands and walks around his desk, nodding to Jennifer as a sign for her to leave before he lifts my right hand and kisses my long slender fingers and perfectly painted, bright red nails. Despite the dimpled knuckles, I can see from the way his head moves slowly in a rocking motion and feel from the way his lips move almost sensually along my fingers and back up to my wrist that, although I cannot deny a slight tingle down my back, he's enjoying the experience far more than I am. There's a time and place and this is neither, it is getting ridiculous and although he doesn't know that I consider I'm spoken for, he needs to get a grip on himself. I can feel the damp softness of his lips as I pull away and let my hand fall slowly back to my side. He's still looking at me and I can sense he wants to kiss me; he's leaning forward now, and I must stop this before things go any further and get out of hand. I turn away and notice a photograph frame balanced precariously on a shelf that's otherwise loaded down with files; the grubby glass that protects the photograph shields a view of his father. I say: 'I haven't seen you since before –'

He seems shocked at the sound of my voice, by my speaking trivia, speaking about what he acknowledges is a grubby frame, speaking about anything that refers to anything other than making love wrapped in smooth silk bedlinen. By now I'm dreaming of the same but with almost anybody other than him. His response is vague to say the least:

'Um.'

'Since before Amos died and I'm so sorry, Frank dear, sorry that I was unable to attend his funeral, but I was unavoidably detained.' I look down at the floor and can feel that my light brown bobbed hair is moving only slightly – at the time, I felt that the modern cut would seem somewhat out of place with the rather drab clothing I wear, but what the hell.

'Um, yes, I quite understand, these things happen, to be perfectly honest I hadn't realized you weren't there until the leaving parade from the chapel.'

'And how are you? I always find that the best medicine is to carry on regardless and to throw yourself into work.'

'Yes, well we all have our different ways of handling things don't we.' Frank smiled 'How are you?'

'Oh don't worry about me, my dear, I'm tickety-boo, I think I am anyway, but I do have a problem.'

'Please, my dear Alicia, sorry, how presumptuous of me, Mrs Matcham, how rude of me do please sit down. No dear, not there - ' he calls to the outer office, 'Jenny please move the comfortable chair across for Mrs Matcham to sit in. Thank you. Now, Mrs Matcham, how can I help?' Frank returns to behind his desk and sat down, waiting for his father's client to speak. His nervousness, his almost 'ever so 'umbel' demeanour, is quite unnerving.

Chapter Nine

'Are you a bridge player, Frank?"

He smiles. 'Er, no not really. My father was an accomplished devotee but I'm afraid I can only manage the basics, why, is that the problem?'

'Not necessarily, but it would help you to understand the degree to which a player might become engrossed and deep in thought when playing what I believe they call a contract. If you were able to play then you would understand the principles of the game and just how important it is to win. It is said that to a devotee 'bridge is not a matter of life and death, it's much more important than that." I laugh in a casual ineffectual way that I am often told is infectious – though I am barely aware of how to laugh in any particular way – but a laugh with which he appeared to want to join in but managed to resist. He looks away at the ceiling or a noise from Jennifer's office – I am never quite sure – and then back to me staring unnervingly into my eyes.

Frank laughs for he has heard his father say the same. He could never understand the importance of each card, the significance of each bid, the inference and information conveyed by the bids and cards played as well as during the initial phase of determining the contract. His father had tried to explain it all and Frank made an effort to understand, but it was more important to him that newly elected Margate beat Guildford in the Eastern Division of the Southern League. He had no time to try to understand anybody getting excited about any other game, let alone a game of cards.

'My father believed exactly that and played every opportunity that presented itself. He told me that at the level he played it was no less important to him than football was – is– to me.'

'Your father was right.'

Our discussion, such as it was, was interrupted by Jennifer bringing in a tray of tea and biscuits. She put down the tray with more deliberation than was necessary and glared at Frank as an alpha male lion might glare at another male who was trying to take over the pride. Her objection to my appearance and presence is clear. He ignores her stare but would try to remember it for a more appropriate occasion when he had more time to take such matters in hand.

'Thank you, Jennifer. I've forgotten, do you take sugar Mrs Matcham?' I can almost feel Jennifer's eyes boring into his head, see the steam oozing from the holes in his skull, but I could be wrong and he's simply deflecting her hatred, that all he's thinking is that he wants me out of the way to see to Jennifer given half a chance. But then he knows that as soon as she's gone, we would soon be on first name terms, and me a lady. Frank is a very confused, very immature man who appears susceptible to almost any form of persuasion.

'No thank you.' I smile a smile that Jennifer recognizes, a condescending smile to her an encouraging one to Frank clearly something she would need to talk to him about once this tart had left.

Frank brought the conversation back to that of business. 'Okay, so we've established that the game of bridge is relevant to your visit. What you haven't told me is what the relevance is or why you're here.'

'I believe your father filed my family's cases under 'The Creek Killings', it was something that he had worked on some twenty years ago but for whatever reason, never completed. At least not all of them.'

'Twenty years?' Frank could not believe that I, the young lady sitting opposite him, my slender stocking clad legs elegantly crossed was old enough to be involved in such a matter so long ago. If so, I was wearing exceptionally well! 'But, forgive me Mrs Matcham, might I say that you don't look mature enough to have experienced my father at the peak of his career.'

'How kind of you to be so delicate. You're correct, I was a mere child at the time, and I remember very little. I was preparing for my Matriculation but I do remember that my parents were concerned to keep me protected from whatever was going on.'

'That must have been difficult.'

'It was a murder in the family or at least it seemed so at first I recall. Mostly they succeeded in keeping me concentrating on other things but of course inevitably something of what was happening seeped through.'

'Perhaps it would make sense if Jennifer dug out the file for us.'

'Perhaps, but I doubt you would find much relevant information at this stage and I think I should appraise you of the current situation. Once you are aware of my recently acquired problems, it may well be of benefit to review the background in the light of the current events. I believe they may be related, although how I have yet to establish. That is always assuming of course, that you are prepared to take me on as a client.' There was that smile again. How could he refuse to try clearing up something his father had left unfinished?

'Oh there's no doubt about that. My father's clients are my clients.' I would have thought that it was genuinely his turn to smile now but he refrains, preferring to simply nod and turn to look out the window briefly, before turning back to face me. 'May I ask where you live now?'

He turns his head when Jennifer, who had been standing by the office door, coughed: 'Is there anything else Mr Spillett?' She curtseyed, mocking his behaviour in front of their visitor. 'Would you like me to try to find the files for Mrs Matcham's murder?'

Frank glared, 'It is not Mrs Matcham's murder, it's The Creek Murders which my father was investigating and with which Mrs Matcham's father was helpful.' He pauses, looking back to me. 'I am so sorry.' Once more to Jennifer he says 'Yes, The Creek Murders file – please.' The last word seethed out of his mouth, Jennifer curtsies again and leaves, closing the door firmly as she does so.

'Now, once again, my dear, Mrs Matcham how may I help you?'

I take a sip of tea and sit back in the chair, clutching a small bag on my lap. In hindsight I can't help but feel that I looked helpless to Frank. I'm quite a bit younger than he but I've built a reputation on helping my friends and family for free. My successes must surely have reached his ears from his various sources and he should feel honoured that I appear to be going to ask for his help. (Conceit has always been one of my failings, but at least I admit it.) I know that his father had worked hard to keep my father's name out of the newspapers when the murders were reaching their height and to Amos's credit, he had succeeded. Although there were several suspects, they were all members of the local North Creek Gang which meant that the murders had never been solved in a public court and the murderers never brought to justice.

'I have been called down here by my sister Patricia Whitten. She is younger than I and often looks to me for help.'

'Of course.'

'Her current bridge partner – well I suppose her latest bridge partner – has died at the bridge table after making a rather difficult six heart contract or not making a three no trump contract I'm afraid I cannot remember.'

'Is the contract of any particular relevance to his death?'

'None that I am aware, no. What is relevant however – and the cause for my sister's telephone call and my journeys to her and now to you – is that my sister considers her partner's death to be suspicious.'

'She has called the police?'

'Oh yes and they believe his death to be a heart attack, a decision that is backed up by the local doctor who examined the body soon after the event occurred.'

'And how do you think I can help? I will of course if I can, but you must realise that I am not a fully licensed private investigator and certainly have little experience in such matters.'

'Please, Mr Spillett, let me finish. I will take responsibility for the actual and overall investigating and the announcement of our – your – findings or at the very least tying all the information together and any necessary talking to the police. I am here because of your father's reputation and more importantly his contacts who should be able to give you information of what's going on in and around the Creek, its boundaries and its gangs. In particular any new drinkers or drug dealers in the local pubs who might be involved in a murder at Corners. There must be no connection between us at all, if that is the case then I shall be of no further need for your service.'

'Well, I could ask around I suppose.'

'You will, of course be remunerated at the appropriate rates for your work. Shall we say two pounds ten shillings an hour plus expenses?' I look at his face trying to gauge whether my offer is acceptable. 'Or perhaps three pounds two and six hourly, I am not conversant with the going rate, again plus any expenses you have, of course.' I can see his face brighten.

'That's most acceptable Mrs Matcham. I shall do everything I can to help. Is there anything else you can give me that might perhaps help with where I can start looking?'

'Well, I'm rather hoping that you find someone or something quite quickly and while there are comparatively few inhabitants of Brogdale I feel that we – you – must look to the Faversham crooks for the murderer; at least I hope so or the options will otherwise to be too many to consider.' I smile at him.

As you will see throughout these chapters I am forever smiling. I'm not sure quite why; I imagine that it's because I enjoy my way of life so much. I'm so carefree and have so little to do. This – these – investigations are a dark relief to my normal lifestyle, but I still keep smiling, darling. What else is there to do? Life goes on.

'And please, if we are to work together you must always call me Alicia even if we happen to be in polite society. It is important they realise and, indeed believe that we are close business colleagues and that we, more importantly you, can be trusted. When, in the unlikely event that we are together amongst your local people you shall address me as Ms Whitten, rather than Mrs Matcham, so that your people are aware of the true relationship we have and the connection that I have with the family, if not the deceased.'

'Of course. I shall try to remember you in your various guises and I'm sure that when we are alone I shall always remember to call you Alicia and you must call me Albert.' He holds up his hand to pre-empt my inevitable question 'Franklyn, Frank, is my middle name and it fits in more easily here in this part of town where Albert would sound pretentious.'

'Then Albert, we will find Mr Broadoak's killers and, perhaps uncover some of your father's other bodies! Now, is it normal practice that we clients pay you a deposit, an advance payment to cement the contract we have between us? How much? Would seventy five pounds be sufficient - that's three and a half day's work?'

'It would – Alicia, thank you. I'll see what has been happening out there'. He points out of the grubby little window in what passes for an office. 'I'll let you know anything of relevance by the end of three and half days. Meanwhile, as I asked a few moments ago, is there anything more that you can give me that might perhaps help with where I can start looking?'

'I'm afraid not. His name was Alan Broadoak, a bridge player but not a gambler. He was a friend of theirs, of the Whittens at Corners 1 Brogdale Road but only until quite recently when a previous partner died.' I hold up my hand before he can speak. 'All perfectly natural I can assure you. He – the previous partner – died of cancer; he was full of it by the time he gave up the ghost. Anyway, Broadoak was a long term friend of Mrs Lavinia Whitten, my mother, and a good friend of my sister, Patricia.'

'When you say a good friend…'

'That is all the information I have that might be relevant to your part of the investigation, leave the inhabitants of Corners and the rest of Brogdale to me. One last thing, all this information and any that you might unearth must be kept in strictest confidence. Nobody must know. Anything.'

'Not even Jennifer?' The look on his face is one of utter despair, his eyebrows arch so high they nearly leave his face and his eyes open and close owlishly both raised in despair and resolved to failure as they looked down, apparently searching below his cheeks for consolation.

'Absolutely nobody, not even Jennifer. Just the two of us.'

'Very well, it will be difficult you understand – if I must carry out all the administration concerning the case myself – naturally, it will take longer carrying out basic research that I would normally expect Jennifer to do.'

'What you're saying is that the three day contract into which we have entered will be insufficient.' Frank nods, his face is one of uncertainty this time supported by raising only one eyebrow, his right one, and the lowering of the left corner of his mouth. He shakes his head slowly. 'Very well, I agree to a six week contract to be reviewed after three weeks. You are to supply me with a substantial interim report after the original three weeks.'

Frank nods his head in agreement. 'I normally take a larger deposit for such long contracts, to cover early incurred expenses you understand I would think that I could say fifty pounds for you.'

'But that's less than the seventy five pounds we have already agreed.'

'Of course, sorry I mean an additional fifty pounds'

Now he's pushing his luck and he knows it.

'No, I think, seventy five pounds will suffice as you say, the additional work is minor and consists mainly of filing and such matters.' I smile, this time one that is almost a sneer at the keenness of the businessman opposite. I've hired him because of his father's reputation but now I'm confident that Frank is every bit as good as the old man. Frank's rugged, simple approach to life and to business is encouraging, I was beginning to like Frank Spillett, to like him very much but he's not worth the risk of backing by an extra fifty pounds.

'Whatever you say Alicia.'

Chapter Ten

I return to Corners shortly before dinner and cause great consternation in the kitchen despite the fact that I know cook always overprovides. The eponymously named Pancetta Cook (who was also the housekeeper and principal cleaner) felt she was being overloaded with work and once again 'how could she possibly do anything right when things kept changing.' She was, as often portrayed in fiction, a tolerant person whose approach to life was that plans were constantly changing and that she must be prepared for anything without becoming flustered. She was, again as often portrayed in fiction, a rather short lady of ample proportions. She wore a mob cap and an apron when carrying out any, indeed all of her tasks and such was the range of her functions that they resulted in the stains and daily marks from her constant hand wiping accruing a russet hue not unlike her rosy cheeks. We all hoped that she washed the apron as frequently as she did the house linen, but none of us was ever sure and were certainly never going to ask.

Regrettably, Mrs Cook was not the unflappable individual whom my father should have employed when he and Lavinia moved into the house and everyone, members of the household and their visitors and tradesmen had to treat Mrs Cook with respect. Notwithstanding that we all understood the situation, today it was my turn to upset her. I like to believe that I am thick skinned and to be honest all I am concerned about is receiving something to eat in the relatively near future, when everyone else in the main household ate theirs, not whether Cook is upset about having to mind her place and get on with carrying out my instructions.

It isn't long before my little sister comes bursting through the door from the drawing room her arms outstretched as if a young girl at the end of term running towards her mother whom she hadn't seen for five weeks.

'Whoa slow down Patty, you'll slip on one of the hall rugs.'

The rugs had been deemed death traps as soon as they were bought from Childs the haberdashers in Faversham, but we were told that parquet flooring needs exposure to keep it fresh and in tip top condition. Fortunately, Patty remained in a semi-vertical position and grabbed me by the waist as soon as we were close enough to embrace.

'Ali dear, have you made any progress?'

There were no words of welcome or enquiries about my health, she went straight for it, straight to the reason for my being there. Patricia has never had any patience and it's essential that I endeavour to explain the basic principles on which I was operating, but now is not the time. I needed to take her to one side, in the drawing room probably, sit her down and then give her the facts of death. For now however I had to tell what little progress there had been on the first day.

'It's very early days, Patty, these things take a long time. One of the first things I must do is interview everyone who lives in the household and any that were here on the night of the murder whether as guests or tradesmen or staff. That's going to take a while.'

'Come on then, you can start with me, I'll tell you exactly what happened and then you can get on with someone else. Where do you want to start?'

'Patty don't be silly my dear girl, it's more complicated than that and even if you think you know everything, that won't be the case however much you think you know because you can only know what happened and was said while you were there, in the place it happened.' I pause for breath now after what can only be considered a complex and almost non-understandable question. It will almost certainly have knocked poor Patty for six. 'In fact I think I'll talk to you formally near the end of the list of people. You have already told me a great deal and I don't want anything you have said to colour my views of what happened.'

'Oh very well, but is there anything you've found out already? You know, any suspicious people walking the streets in long black coats with one of those funny trilby things on their head looking as though they are about to jump on somebody when it gets dark?'

'No, I haven't, and I really hope you're joking but I have spoken to a young man who works near the Faversham Creek who knows the local people and who can carry out initial questioning for me. Instinct tells me that he will discover nothing from the locals – such as finding the killer – but that he may well eliminate several of the likely candidates – such as those thought to be members of one of the larger gangs controlling The Creek – from our enquiries. It's also surprising what these types of downtrodden people can reveal when asked.'

'They won't have to come in here will they?'

'Who?'

'Well, the unseen and the unseemly tarts or street girls, they won't, will they? I'm not sure that Father will stand for that, in fact I know he won't.'

I laugh inwardly at my sister's horror that there is another world out there which might very well get embroiled in my investigations and that may have to come to and into Corners. 'They may want to visit me here, albeit unlikely, I doubt any will want to come anywhere near the place.'

'Right then, so when do we start?'

'We start with dinner and then you can help me draw up the list of suspects.'

'You've got some suspects already?'

'Everyone is a suspect, until I eliminate them.'

Chapter Eleven

During a more than adequate dinner I had reluctantly confirmed my agreement with Patty that she could join me in the drawing room. She was determined to help although I am convinced that her simple outlook on life combined with her simple brain will together be more of a hindrance than a help.

Patty has always looked up to me as her older sister. Our parents have long despaired with Patty and her failure to find an occupation or a husband. To be fair it was not entirely her fault. Her first love had ditched her for a younger more beautiful and more intelligent woman and it had hit her terribly badly. She needed my help and support and our relationship strengthened as she felt increasingly beholden to me. I could ask her for anything, and she would give it to me or organise it, in return if she was ever in trouble and asked for help I would provide it. We were as twins, joined by the desire to help each other.

But sometimes it just became too much!

To our parents it looked as though Patty was unable to do anything without my say so or support and that suited me perfectly. It meant that they looked on me as the stronger, more trustworthy and confident daughter, one who could never do wrong and knew exactly what to do when something untoward happened.

Suffice it to say that when my husband died while driving his Maserati undoubtedly too fast between Manchester and Birmingham, Patty consoled and helped me in return for the support I had given her. There were those who thought anyone who drove between those rapidly expanding industrial cities rather than by using the train deserved to die and there were those who thought he had been murdered by one or more of his unsavoury gangland colleagues. Some – though only a few - thought it likely that there was a mechanical fault and blamed his death on unavoidable circumstances. Either way, no blame was attributed to me and I was upheld by all, for the selfless sacrifice I had taken.

With Patty's help (and inevitable hindrance) I am determined to draw up a list of suspects, there can only be a few.

'Who are we starting with?' Patty asks, excited as ever.

'We're starting with the people we think of first. Not necessarily those whom we think are the most likely to be the murderer, just names. Okay?'

'Okay.' I can tell she doesn't mean that, she wants to rank them - accuse them, question them and get them arrested. I will have to be firm.

In no time at all, we have our list:

1. Charles Whitten (Our father and Joan Saynor's bridge partner)

2. Lavinia Whitten (Our mother and Alan Broadoak's erstwhile bridge partner)

3. Patricia Whitten (my younger sister and Alan Broadoak's bridge partner)

4. Joan Saynor (Charles's bridge partner)

5. John Staples (The butler)

6. Pancetta Cook (The cook)

7. Dr Gareth Hudson (The family doctor, pronouncing death from a heart attack)

8. DI Leonard Drabble (Local policeman, confirming death from a heart attack)

'Don't forget to add your name Ali, if my name is on there, yours must be too.'

'But darling girl, I was in London until today and you were all here, in Corners. I didn't get down until the middle of this afternoon, the day after he died. I can't see why my name needs to be added.' For once in her life, in her simple mind she's determined about something – I can see it in her eyes so there's no point in arguing. 'But if you insist.' She's nodding approval of my agreement as I add my name for the sake of peace and quiet. 'Right, is there anyone else missing?'

'William was somewhere in Corners when Alan Broadoak died, he's usually on his way home after being kicked out of a pub. But then on those occasions I suppose John would also have been out of the house while he was fetching him. But I have seen him in the house before he goes to the pub sometimes.'

'Oh yes, he's most likely to have been slumped on one of the seats under the Town Hall,' She's thinking now, I wonder if she'll reach the same conclusion as me. 'So I suppose they might both have alibis – that'd be a bit of luck – for them and us.'

'For us?'

'Well, it'd save us having to interview them.'

'Patty, I think we need to get something straight. You sound as though you're expecting to be involved with my examination of the suspects, but you're not sitting in on any questioning that I carry out. I've said that before, I can't have your story mixing with theirs.'

'But – '

'No! Now, is that the full list?'

My full list thus comprised:

1. Charles Whitten (Our father and Joan Saynor's bridge partner)

2. Lavinia Whitten (Our mother and Alan Broadoak's erstwhile bridge partner)

3. Patricia Whitten (my younger sister and Alan Broadoak's bridge partner)

4. William Whitten (older brother)

5. Joan Saynor (Charles' bridge partner)

6. John Staples (The butler)

7. Pancetta Cook (The cook)

8. Dr Gareth Hudson (The family doctor, pronouncing death from a heart attack)

9. DI Leonard Drabble (Local policeman, confirming death from a heart attack)

10. Me: Alicia Matcham (middle of three siblings and
     investigator of the murder)

'Ten, that's a long list Ali, even if we cross off, me, you,
William, Dr Hudson, DI Drabble and Butler John.'

'Now you're being silly. I'll start with the bridge players first,
tomorrow morning after breakfast. I don't think there's time to
speak to father now, that would only make him grumpy and
hard to question. But it'll give me a chance to sleep on the list
and the questions I need to ask before I get stuck in tomorrow.
And Patty – '

'Yes?'

'Don't listen through the keyhole while father, while any of
them is in here.'

She gives me one of her 'how could you possibly imagine I
would do such a thing?' faces. 'No of course not.'

On previous occasions when I've been about to question people
– and there been a few over the years – I've had a list of questions I'm going ask each of them in order to get a consistent
story, theoretically, the same story from each person. That way
I can make a direct comparison between the people involved
and see the differences to pick them up on next time. For this
crime I have no standard questions. This time I need them to
each build up the events and then I can draw up the list of
questions. And this is family. Not in the way that the gangster
films have their characters saying those words, here it's a simple
statement of fact, not an indication that I shall treat any of
them any differently. At least, I hope not.

Chapter Twelve

B reakfast has been a sober event and as if in anticipation, Cook seems to have made little effort. The meal is over soon enough and father disappears into his study for peace and quiet. I leave the dining room and go upstairs to collect my notes – I'm leaving nothing lying about for anyone – especially Patty – to read.

I have decided to hold all the interviews in the room where the game of cards was being played. I feel it will add some gravitas to the discussions and help to concentrate the minds of my interviewees. We shall see. John has agreed to collect father although perhaps collect isn't quite the right word!

'What's all this then?' Father has begun even before we've started and barely before he's opened the door, let alone closed it. 'I know you said you'd need to talk to all of us, but naturally I didn't think you meant me.'

He sits in his usual chair which is slightly higher than all the others in the room to give him some fanciful idea of superiority.

'Father, I need your view of what happened so that I can piece it all together. Please.'

'Oh. Well. Well, poor old Alan died, and I got John to call

Dr Hudson, then that new policeman chap - Drabble. That's all there is to it.' He starts to get up. 'Who shall I send in next?'

'No, Father no, please sit down. I need to know more than that – more detail.'

Clearly frustrated, he sits back into his chair, 'Well really, I know that baby sister of yours is convinced that Broadoak was murdered,' he huffs and puffs in disbelief before saying, 'go on then what do I need to tell you that you don't already know?'

It is clear that Patty's views have spread like wildfire through the household, I would expect nothing less. 'As I said, I need to build up a picture of what happened or was happening before the game Saturday night, what happened during the game and what happened afterwards in detail. When I have everyone's story, I can then put them together to see if there are any discrepancies.'

'And then what, call us all together and name the murderer like they do in Agatha Christie's Poirot?'

'No of course not and it won't be down to me anyway. If I get close to finding who killed Alan, I'll have to get the police in to finish it off. So, are you okay with all that? Can we get on, please?'

'Go on then.'

'Now, I want you to tell me what was happening with the four of you over, I don't know, the two or three weeks before you got together, what happened during the game and then after he died. Just tell me what you remember, please.'

'Well, nothing unusual I can think of. We played on the two Saturdays before he died. They were both normal. Joan and I won both evenings. The first three rubbers and plus 2100 up at the end. I remember your sister played particularly badly that night, she didn't put Alan into three no trumps which would have won them the rubber, instead Joan made a good three hearts and we cleaned up before poor old Broadoak could make things up. Then last week was a lot closer.' My father is supposed to be an intelligent man, he runs his own building business for goodness sake it must take some brains to do that surely and yet I get the feeling that he's hiding something from the family and now me, only time will tell.

'Father, I'm not sure that I need to know the detail of the bridge game you were playing or whether you were in hearts or no trumps and whether you went up or down and by how many. I just need to know the events, the feelings of the players, such as you can judge them and other people around the table.'

'But it was crucial in Christie's The King of Clubs and in Cards on the table as their titles suggest. It was crucial in determining who the killers were. Not only the actual cards but who was sitting in each seat and who was first to bid. I'm sorry Alicia, but if you want all the facts, then all the facts you shall have.'

'Right, I see what you mean, Father, sorry, go on.' I smile in apparent defeat. As a mere novice of the game I hardly know the basic rules let alone the meaning or inference of everything that any of the players do or say – or apparently don't do or say! I can't believe it's relevant here, but I must give him some rope to hang himself I suppose.

'Where was I? Oh yes, last week was much closer. We only won two rubbers last week but still won; only last week it was only by 200, I think. A close run thing and – you might find this interesting actually – that was because my Joan – silly old thing – my Joan went three down in three no trumps! Don't you see? Now, we'd just finished the game, the actual contract that finished off old Alan and believe it or not that was because she had forgotten that Alan was holding the Ace of spades.'

Does that actually mean anything? 'I agree that's some coincidence, but I don't see how it'll help us find out who killed him.'

'Maybe not, but you wanted all the details.' I'm nodding purposefully, trying to show my deep understanding of what he's saying. 'We noticed – well, your sister noticed first of course – that Alan had slumped forward onto the table. He always was a quiet man; a very personal man, but a reasonable bridge player I suppose. He wasn't married so a bit of a loner. I think he'd probably tried his luck with the ladies but some of us are luckier than others - shouldn't say that should I?'

He's smiling as he suggests his own, personal success in that direction and to be honest I don't really want to know, although my curiosity gets the better of me and anyway, I suppose I should ask, it might have a bearing on the case.

'Did he have a lady friend just before he died? Somebody we should contact perhaps?'

He hesitates, unsure about giving up such personal information and I get the feeling its sensitive, personal to him or, I suppose to me. Part of me wants to let him off and say that it doesn't matter but if there's that sort of problem with him telling me I am sure I should know. 'Father?'

He lowers his voice: 'This isn't easy, Alicia not at all easy, I'm not a gossip as you know, and you have to understand that I have nothing definitive on which to base or to confirm that what I am about to tell you is true. It may not be – and my God I hope it isn't – true and you must promise me that you will say nothing about what I am going to tell you to a living soul.'

'You must know that I can't promise that. Not if whoever it is, is a key person in determining the murderer. You have to understand that.' He nods and I can see that he does understand what I've said but it clearly doesn't change the fact that he is concerned about the person's privacy.

'Well, I suppose if it's unavoidable – Broadoak was having an affair with – with your mother.'

'WHAT?'

'Now perhaps you can understand my concerns.'

'But how long have – I mean are you sure – how did you find out – do you think…?'

Although I know about his affair with Joan Saynor and I suppose I'm not surprised – I wouldn't want to live with my father, but then there's rather a large age gap and I'm his daughter. I am, however, aware of his approach to life and to other people particularly, his pompous way of speaking and treating my mother. Even so I am amazed that she had the guts to have an affair. That's now three affairs within the family that I know of.

'No, no more Alicia. I can't tell you anymore.'

'Do you know if he had any enemies? If there's anyone who might want to murder him? Apart from you, of course.' He isn't smiling. That's something else about him. He has no sense of humour. Or perhaps he did murder Alan Broadoak.

'Enraged husbands perhaps but then he only seems to have gone after widows and spinsters.'

'Right, I think we've finished for now although I might need to ask you more questions later.' To be honest, I don't think I can cope with any more revelations; the fact that Alan Broadoak was having affairs with both my mother and my sister at the same time is about as much as I can stand.

'If you see mother could you ask her to come in please.'

'Humph.'

I didn't think he would, that sort of thing falls within the title of servants' duties, so I'm not going to wait and walk out into the hall.

Chapter Thirteen

I return to the card room and passing her in the hall, I ask mother to come in, I wait until she's sat down before I settle back into the far more comfortable winged chair I've chosen as the interviewer.

'Thank you for agreeing to see me, Mother, sorry it's all so formal but that's the way things need to be I'm afraid. I know it's difficult what with being family and all that but, believe me, if father can do it, I'm sure you can too!' It's important to relax her, but it looks as though I've failed, her face has turned as white as a sheet. 'Mother, it's fine, there are no problems, really. I just want you to tell me the story of what happened before, during and after Alan Broadoak's death, that's all. It'll be fine.' I lean forward, put my hands on her knees and smile in a further attempt to relax her and this time it looks as though it's worked.

'It's all right, Dear, it just seems so strange that you're going to be asking me what happened when it used to be me asking you. Do you remember when I brought you home from school just before the end of term, at the end of that terrible term when Mr Cattermole died? Everyone thought he'd had a heart attack and then some silly girl accused you of pushing him off the roof. It was obviously not true, but you were questioned by the police and I was called to school to be with you when they did and then I had to bring you home? When we got back here I sat you down in the chair I'm sitting in now and I sat in your chair.' She's away, remembering, what she would no doubt call the good times, I would call them something else! 'Do you remember, Darling? Do you?'

'Of course I remember, Mother. It was the worst day of my life. It was that term when I decided I wanted to train to be able to do some private investigating of my own, so that I could help members of our family when they found themselves in trouble the same way that I was. Then of course I'd started to work elsewhere as well. Once Oliver died and I didn't need to earn any money, I've been able to pick and choose which I do, a sort of modern day Sherlock Holmes or Poirot.'

I haven't mentioned Oliver before. He's significant only in that he was my second husband and only for a short while after Gerrard, he too died - I can't remember why or how - very suddenly and left me a large estate which I had to sell and as a result, more money than I could possibly cope with. I can and do live a wonderfully comfortable life but still charge my clients a fee so that they value my advice. Oliver is therefore most unlikely to crop up again!

'Sherlock who dear?' By the vacant look on her face I'm not sure whether she actually thinks Sherlock Holmes or Poirot are real detectives or whether she knows they're fiction and that she's playing a trick on me. I continue assuming the latter.

I smile. 'I shall never have as many little grey cells as Poirot.'

She laughs loudly and then winks at me. I'm still not sure. 'Right, Mother let's get down to this shall we?'

'What do you want to know, Dear?'

'Can you tell me what you remember about the last two weeks before Alan died?'

'Oh, that's easy, Dear. Two weeks ago we were all here and the rest of them played here as usual, in their normal pairings. There were, I think two rubbers and Alan and your sister won both of them. Handsomely as I remember. Then last week there were three rubbers and Charles and Joan won two of them. Alan and Patty won the last one with a big score Alan bid and made…'

She tails off and because as I know from father that this was when the last rubber was won by making six spades and winning the last trick with the ace of spades. I sit and wait. I can't prompt her it would make the whole process meaningless. I can see she's in agony and yet I can't help her, I really can't.

'Don't worry, Mother, we'll come back to that later. It'll be fine.'

'I'm sorry Dear, it's too painful. I wasn't playing of course so it's very difficult anyway, I only know what Patty has told me. She telephoned me just after he'd died. Just after she'd watch him die. I've always thought that three of the family at the table would be too confrontational, especially as one of them would be your father. I'm sorry.'

'Let's go back before all of that then. What do you know about Alan's social life – or work life if he hadn't retired. Was he married? Did he have a lady friend? Was there anybody who would like to kill him? Did he have any enemies? You know the sort of thing. Did you kill him?' I'm laughing now just so that she knows – or at least thinks I know – that she didn't. But she's on my list so I have to treat her the same way as everybody else at this stage.

She sits there shaking her head. 'Well it's really all a bit difficult, I didn't think you'd be asking me this sort of question.'

'Just anything you know about him, anything at all. Incidentally, is there anyone the police are contacting to let them know that he's died?'

'No. Nobody. I mean, I don't think so, he always told me that he was all on his own and that Christmas was the – was the worst time.'

She speaks the last few words more quietly and each word vanishes silently into space. She knows that she's given something away and seems to be hoping that I haven't spotted what's happened. To be honest, if I didn't have an inkling of what she was going to admit I might well not have noticed. But I do. 'It sounds as though you spoke to Alan quite a lot when he was away from the bridge table. It sounds as if he thought of you as a close friend.' I don't say anything more, hoping that I've prompted her sufficiently.

There's a palpable silence while we look at each other, wondering who's going to speak first.

'You know, don't you? You've guessed from what I've just said. I knew you would have picked up on that. You're a detective after all and a jolly good one too I expect.'

'Picked up on what?' I like to think I feign naivety quite well.

'That he and I were having an affair?'

'WHAT?'

That I do not expect. Her freely admitting to me that she and Alan were having an affair is one thing confirmed, I was prepared to do my best to sound just as surprised as I did when Patty had told me about her affair, or indeed when father told me about mother's affair but this means that neither she, nor Patty know that each other... not that they would know of course. They never talk to each other.

'You won't tell your Father, will you? He'd be furious if he knew. I don't like to think what he'd do. Please don't tell him Alicia. Please.'

'Of course I won't tell him. Don't worry Mother, if he ever finds out you can be sure that he won't have heard it from me. I promise.' I'll have more important things to worry about. It's difficult, getting my head round the fact that Alan Broadoak was having affairs with my mother and my sister is more than anyone should be asked to accept. No wonder he had a heart problem, but I have to put all that to one side for now and get on with the matter in hand – except of course that what I now know must put father at the top of my suspect list.

'Thank you, Darling. I know I can always trust you but, well, this is particularly special to me. You do understand, don't you?'

Of course I do. 'Of course I do, Mother, of course. To be honest I don't know how you've managed to put up with him for so long.' My observations are just as sincere as when I said them to Patty, but my brain is blown. I don't know how to deal with this.

She turns and looks behind her as if to check that father hasn't walked in on us and is about to cleave an axe through her head. 'Actually,' she whispers conspiratorially, 'it hasn't been as recent as you might think. Our affair has been going on for seven years.' She giggles like a little girl whose mother has just discovered that she reads in bed.

'Seven years? Are you having me on? Seven years? Good grief you sneaky old thing.' This has genuinely surprised me. Father can't have any idea that the affair had been going on that long, not a clue, he wouldn't have kept quiet or not done something by now if he had. I'm amazed at his lack of awareness, he's usually so on top of things, at least, things that affect him at work and yet this must affect him more than anything else!

'I know, I'm surprised that we managed to keep it going for so long. I think keeping it quiet is all part of the enjoyment. That and of course –.'

'That's enough let me imagine the rest. I really don't need to know about the details of your affair just that you were having one. And I'm sorry that it's finished this way. I'm sorry you couldn't have had more years together, even some out in the open.'

'Thank you, Dear, that's very kind of you.'

'Of course you do realise that this makes Father the main suspect for Alan's murder, don't you? If he'd found out about the affair I mean.'

'Well, yes, I suppose so, but do you really think your father would have killed Alan just because of the affair?'

'You obviously don't know him as well as you should - Father is capable of anything he sets his mind to. Even murder.'

Chapter Fourteen

I am finding interviewing my family harder than I had expected. They seem to think that I know all there is to know and that they can get away without telling me the full story. They can't understand that I want details – well perhaps not all the gory and glory ones – and I now realise I am going to have to have more than one extra 'chat' with them before resolving the problem for them; although none of them have actually said as much, they all seem to consider the murder of one of their bridge foursome a problem rather than a crime. For me that makes my questionings slightly easier and I can pretty much ignore the police – at least for now.

Keeping complete notes of the interviews is one of my major difficulties, what I really need is my own Jennifer, someone to take down what's said and then type notes for a file that she creates. But then, even if I could find someone I'm not sure I could trust her on the confidentially front so for now I'll just have to manage. Frank's bound to let her go soon, he's barely enough work to feed himself let alone pay her.

The card room is just the right size to carry out these interviews but although I've put the chairs together in a comfortable snug corner away from the table it still looks wrong. I stand up and look around the room to get a better feel for what's around me, for anything that might act as a sounding board to send my interviewing to listening ears waiting at one of the doors.

To my left is the table on which they were playing and where Alan Broadoak's body lay almost crouched on his chair and wrapped around the table edge when I arrived. The other three chairs had remained close to the table and its quite clear that none of the players had been hysterical at the time, that their rising had been a measured response to one of their number dying in front of them and possibly defacing one of the cards in the pack which I suspect was of greater concern than the loss of one of their number. When all this is over, I suppose it's possible that my mother might want to keep the pack hidden in one of her secret boxes where mementos of our childhood and possibly her own too are randomly concealed and shielded from prying eyes; I imagine too that there would have been an increasing number of Alan's writings and gifts given and received in love and now in memory of her lover, of happier times in secret places or in public, trying hard to keep their liaison énigme.

I'm going to check to see if the ace of spades remains in place and whether there are any signs of Alan's death on that or any of the cards still splayed in their fan; a spot of blood perhaps or a shard of skin or something that might give some idea of what killed him, if not who killed him – I'm not a medical sort of private detective and that's what we detective types have to do, we look for evidence. There is none that I can find, I relax as I straighten my back and look further round the card table meanwhile distracted by my thoughts of the players.

The table itself shows only little sign of wear and stands as a reminder of times gone by although I know for a fact that it's been re-covered twice and is already starting to show the normal St. George's cross design of wearing from where cards have been dealt, dragged and played at each side. The now usual oak lined walls are hung with paintings, much smaller than those in the hall and here of places rather than members of the family. They are almost entirely by unknown artists and of unknown locations, some if not all of them of favourite churches in the County. One that doesn't conform to the rest is an Arnold Helke seascape of smugglers bringing ashore their booty with another man, alone at the bottom of the cliff face. It makes me think of the murderer standing aside from the group, waiting and watching for the time to kill.

While I'm standing, admiring the small, quiet room, assuring myself that this is the most appropriate place to carry out interviews, I hear distant voices; there are two people (a man and a woman) coming closer in this direction and then they stop, their voices now raised in disagreement. Although I can't hear the beginning of their conversation, it's now quite clear. I hear the man speak first and instantly I know it's my father:

'I don't care; you have to hold your nerve. Answer anything she asks you honestly and firmly and don't let her get to you. Keep your damn voice steady.'

'I am trying Charles, but it's a very upsetting situation.'

'For you possibly, but for the rest of us it's an inconvenience. Nothing more'

'That's so unfair, Charles. You don't know how unfair you are.'

'You'd be surprised what I know you silly cow. Now, clear

off to the kitchen or somewhere else, I don't care where you go as long as you're out of my sight.'

'But, Charles – '.

'GO.'

He's really shouting, and I'm surprised that nobody has come from one of the other rooms leading off the Hall to see what's going on, but somewhat like me they stay hidden. They're not really scared of him but rather, scared of what the bastard might do to mother for whatever my mother's done or he thinks she's done. Whatever it is – despite what she says – it must be their affair but whatever it is, there's no call for him to talk to her as if she was a skivvy, it's beneath contempt. I want to go out into the hall and give him a piece of my mind and slap his face, but I can't. I need to be privy to such exchanges and to add them to my increasing number of information pages. There are bound to be more discussions out of my sight, anywhere around the house or in the garden and I need to be able to hear them. I need to be safe; I need to be sure that what they are saying to me is what they really think or know. There is one thing I hate and that's being lied to or not being told the whole truth as they believe it to be, because I genuinely need to know what's going on, especially if it involves me directly.

I can hear my mother's hurried footsteps as she runs towards the kitchen, then changes her mind and I think she goes towards the front door. I hear a door slam and wonder where she'll feel safe from him. They'll meet again if only at meals when they'll talk as if everything is fine, their exchanges being a sham that the rest of us feel would be better aired, but then…

My sister's whispering voice comes through the small gap left by the card room door to the drawing room not being closed properly. 'Ali.'

'Patty.'

'Can I come in?'

'He's not in here, if that's what you mean and mother's outside somewhere – I heard her go.'

She comes into the room and sits in the nearest chair. 'Oh,' she sighs heavily, 'did you hear their argument?'

'Of course I did darling girl – I heard shouting and swearing and mother crying.' I can't let her know that I heard all of it, or a large part of it at the very least. 'It'd be difficult not to.'

'What are we going to do?'

'What can we do?' I'm starting to get fed up with her simpering. What does she expect me to do, kill him off and then find somebody else to blame?

She pushes her clenched hands in front of her mouth as if to prevent anyone hearing, 'Perhaps he's the murderer and he thinks she knows and he's trying to get rid of her.'

'I think that very unlikely, darling. Now why don't you go and get John to fix you a really dry martini and then another one and then slouch off into the drawing room reading a magazine or a boring book so that you fall asleep and when you wake up you'll have forgotten the whole boring thing. The argument or whatever it was will be over, it'll be sorted out and we can get on with trying to find out who killed Alan. I'm sure that's what he would want you to do, don't you?'

She's crying now, I reckon the last few words have done the job. 'Do you think he would? If you think I should, Ali, that's what I'll do.'

I don't say anything further it would be pointless, she's hooked, so we hug and kiss and hug again and she saunters towards the hall, out of the room blowing her nose gently, discreetly into a handkerchief and eventually reaches his pantry and the lovely John's capable hands. I know that what I said to her sounds harsh, even patronising but you don't know her as I do. Trust me.

Chapter Fifteen

I've woken too early this morning so that even when I'm dressed – the process takes a while because I am particularly careful of what I wear and the extent of makeup I apply; these things cannot be hurried especially for a lady in my position – and ready to go downstairs everywhere is quiet apart from the distant clanging from the kitchen of saucepans with each other and a frying pan. I push my first cigarette of the day into its holder and light it using a match from the box on the hall stand. The first inhaling of cigarette smoke sets me up for the day but when I saunter slowly into the breakfast room I find that John has nothing laid ready for breakfast. There is what looks like a light frost on the grass between the patio and tennis courts but is of course heavy dew.

The wall clock strikes seven thirty and John enters the room carrying a freshly ironed tablecloth.

'Good morning Mrs Matcham. I hope you slept well.'

'John, I've told you to call me Alicia when we are alone, anything else is too formal, yes, I did thank you. I'm obviously too early for breakfast. Do you think Cook could rustle me up something if I go into the kitchen?'

'I'm sure she could, madam.'

Before I reprimand him again, he turns to my right.

'Good morning, sir.'

I smile at John, 'Thank you, John.' I smile and as I turn to go out to the kitchen I see him nod, seemingly relieved that I had picked up his signal.

'Good morning, Father.' For some reason I feel more antagonistic than usual towards him so that's it and he doesn't really deserve more. By the time I reach the door to the hall he's talking to John, no doubt making unreasonable demands. Mother is nowhere to be seen, I expect she's waiting in her room until she feels it safe to emerge either because he's gone or there are more of the family to protect her if he starts up again…

It's only forty eight hours since I walked into Frank's office, but I expect him to have an initial report. It takes me almost half an hour to reach his grubby little car parking area and, as before, I'm somewhat reluctant to park my Magnette so close to the less salubrious part of town, but I have little choice.

I don't bother to ring the bell – nobody answered last time and I don't expect today to be any different. I knock on the office outer door and walk in. Jennifer is sat at her desk and looks up as soon as I enter.

'He's not here.'

'Shouldn't he be here? It's his business after all.'

She laughs. 'It is but you wouldn't know it. He's never here before nine thirty at the earliest.'

I nod showing understanding of her plight. 'Right. Can I wait?'

Jenny looks at the clock. 'I s'pose, but it's a long time and he might not even be here by then. By ten I mean.'

'Could you 'phone him – perhaps?'

'Yeah, I could. Would you like tea? We don't have any coffee left; he says it's too expensive for a small office like this.'

'Thank you. Yes, while you 'phone him.'

She goes into a little kitchen; I hear running water and the lighting of gas. She comes back and walks to Frank's office door. 'I'll use his 'phone, so can you keep an ear on the kettle.'

'Of course, I'll make the tea if you're not back in time.' I've never actually made tea but how difficult can it be?

Jennifer has a soft voice, but she's been careless and hasn't closed the office door properly, she must have tracked him down and is trying to talk quietly to him.

'I know, I wasn't expecting her again yet either. I can't get rid of her and she's 'avin' tea now so get here quick. Not till then. Oh my god. Okay.'

I hear the handset returned to the cradle and simultaneously the kettle starts to boil, I obviously recognise what that means and I'm expecting her to take over, which she does. Some light swearing and muttering, and she returns with two large mugs of tea with biscuits on a saucer of their own. Such extravagance was surprising and I expect it was because Frank was going to be delayed and he wanted to butter me up.

'Thank you – no biscuits thanks. Although they are tempting.'

'A special treat, only because he says it's you apparently. He saves them for special clients.' I sit waiting for the tea to cool sufficiently so that it's drinkable. Jennifer starts to type again but then she stops and shuffles some papers.

'Am I making you nervous?'

'No, 'corse not, it's just that, well, I'm not sure what I can say.'

'Don't worry, why don't we talk about the report Frank's put together for me?'

'But -.'

'I know that he and I agreed he would keep all the information about my case to himself and not get you involved, but I seem to remember that typing and obeying instructions are not his strong points and I never really expected him to keep it from you.'

She smiles now, a pretty smile, and I can see why Frank likes her, it's obvious that he does from the way he looks at her and I can tell, I'm a woman. I know what men are thinking when they look at me, it's all part of our make up so I know what he's thinking when I see him watching her.

'Well, I suppose I can tell you a little bit of it.'

'I'd like it if you and I could work together so that you tell me when he's not going to be here and then I come in for a cup of tea and a chat. Could we do that? Just between us? I'm sure you're a lot better at keeping secrets than he is.' I'm taking a risk; she might tell Frank what I've tried to do while he's been away, but I suspect not. Here comes her reply.

'That wouldn't be difficult, Mrs Matcham. Well, yes I'll help you if I can. Just between the two of us like.'

'Okay, that's fab, so what's happened so far? Has he actually done anything?'

'To be honest, Mrs Matcham, not a lot.' She stops to blow her tea, dunk a biscuit - I'm a great dunker myself when I'm not in public - and to preen her hair. It's long and flows, shining over her shoulders. 'He's been to see one of 'is contacts down the Creek but didn't get very far. Another one of his old mates whose now at Shepherd Neame was a bit more helpful but -.'

'But what?

'Well, he hasn't given me the tape with what he was told on it yet, but he did ask me whether he ought to put some of the things he's found out on the tape for me to type and leave the rest in the file for now.'

'Sorry?' I find what Jenny has just said ridiculous, why did I ever employ this man to work for me when he's asking his secretary to do the work for him. 'Before you say anything, is there any chance that you think what he's asking you to do is somehow wrong?'

'Well it is certainly a bit strange; I keep thinking that when we have our chats as we are now, I can give you the full story. That way I'd be helping you even more.'

I see her smile she's preening her hair again, building her image into something she would like it to be and, with a bit more independent effort might be successful. She is making no secret of the fact that she's expecting to be paid handsomely for this undercover work and I'm not sure that I expected to pay her anything at all. I rather anticipated that her satisfaction would be in giving me information that her employer intended to keep from me. Remuneration might be forthcoming I suppose if rather tiresome. We'll see how much she gives me.

'True, I can see how that could benefit both of us, as long as he doesn't find out. Does he have any tracking devices in the offices? Some way of seeing that I or you have been moving the files when he's not here?'

She says, 'There's no way he could tell from the files, he barely even knows where they are in the first place let alone if you or I have moved them. Anyway, I've typed up an appendix which I'll put in his report for you with all the things he left out. If it's the sort of thing that helps you I can do it for every report. It's not a problem.'

I can see now that getting back at him is the driving force behind her deception which, in time, she will be able to black-mail him for whatever her demands at that time might be.

'Let's see how we get on shall we, see what the quality of information you discover is, yes?'

She nods and glances at the large wooden cased clock on top of the filing cabinets, then at her watch. 'I don't know why I'm looking up there, that thing hasn't worked in years. Right then, he's going to tell you that he hasn't gathered - that's a new word he picked up last week - enough information to fill a report and hopes he can get away with that.'

'Your shaking your head Jenny - you don't mind me call-ing you Jenny do you? - you can call me Alicia, all this Mrs Matcham is much too formal between us.'

'That'd be fine with me, though best keep it formal if he happens to be here at the same time!'

I continue: 'There's something he's not going to tell me, isn't there?'

'Not much, it's only Sunday you were in. Still, word is that whoever did it's local. Most likely a bloke. But that's as far as he's got.'

'I do believe I could have guessed that myself, Jenny. I'm looking for something he thinks is important that he's not telling me. Anyway, I think it's time I was going. Thank you for the tea, I shall call in again in a couple of days or so and we can have another little chat. Let me see, today is Tuesday, let's say Thursday shall we, about the same time unless he breaks with tradition and wakes early. You can let me know, yes?'

'Of cawse I can do that, sorry I couldn't help anymore.'

As I stand, I can see her face displaying any thoughts she might have had drifting away. It'll do the poor little girl good; it'll make sure she doesn't get ideas above her station.

My Magnette seems to be safe and sound. An urchin is standing next to the driver's door and opens it as I approach. 'Thank you, er…'

'Tommy, miss, they calls me Tommy.'

'Why?'

"Cos I usually smells 'a cats, miss. Tom cats, Tommy. See?'

I smell, imagining a rank odour and conceding that his friends had chosen wisely. 'You don't smell of cats today, Tommy.'

'No, miss, Mondays is barf nights - after Mum does the washing.'

I shudder at how revolting the water in the tub must be before my new-found friend climbs into it and the colour it is after his mother has scraped the dirt and grime from all parts of his young body. 'I'm very lucky to meet you today then. Tommy.'

'Nice car, miss. a Magnette isn't she? Red, good colour too.'

'Like cars do you, Tommy?' He nods furiously. 'Right, well, next time I come and park here, I want you to look after her for me.' A huge beam lightens his dirty face, it's seems that the now cold, black, smelly water hasn't reached his face this week.

'Yes, miss, I'd like vat.'

'Thank you, and if I give you one of my cloths and you make her nice and shiny by the time I come out, I'll take you for a ride in her.' It looks as though he's going to burst with pride.

The very thought of a ride in my car makes his job even more important to him.

He asks, 'miss, has your car got a name only you keep calling it a she?'

'Maggie,'

'Oh yeah. Maggie Magnette, that's right funny, miss.

He looks longingly at the car and I expect he's hoping for his first ride. 'Today it'll have to be a short one because I have to meet someone, okay?' He holds the door until I'm in and ready at the wheel before he runs around to the passengers' side. The next thing I know is that he's sitting, staring at all the knobs on the dashboard. 'Don't touch anything, Tommy.' He shakes his head and sits back, waiting.

I'm not going racing out to the main roads, just a trip round town so that all his little friends can see him if they care to look. As we near the end of Briton Road heading for Lower St Anne's after a short drive next to the railway line, a train comes slowly past pulling out of Faversham station on its way to London. Tommy waves madly at the carriages but nobody waves back, he's doesn't care, the mere action of it just adds to the ride. I turn the car down the hill towards the gunpowder works and back to his home. As we near the Creek I voice an idea that has come to mind, 'Tommy?'

'Yes, miss.'

'Could you do something else for me while you're not having to watch Maggie for me?'

' 'course miss if I can. You been good to me, I like that, what da wan' me to do?'

'A man was killed at the big house along Brogdale Road on Saturday, can you keep your ear to the ground and find out what everyone thinks about anything to do with the murder for me? It would be very helpful.'

'I've heard about that, we all have, word travels quick down va Creek, 'specially if it's somefin' that upsets the toffs. I'll see what I can do.'

'Thank you, Tommy. Do you want to hoot the horn?'

The noise is loud and tuneless.

Chapter Sixteen

I arrive back at the house to find it deserted. It's still searingly hot and even though they're still not sure it's murder, the police searching the grounds have obviously been allowed to step down because the cars and all the bicycles have gone. I open the right hand of the double oak doors and as I close it behind me the hall echoes as if welcoming me home with its attempt at a sort of warm feeling for my coming in out of the sun– or welcoming someone back to the house.

I am wearing soft soled shoes today (for a reason that escapes me), they make a light sticky noise across the parquet floor, John won't be pleased about that, not in this heat; the sealing they used to cover the floor is starting to soften and then presumably melt. Where is he anyway I would expect him to have come out of his pantry to welcome me and ask why I didn't ring the front doorbell? There's no sound from the kitchen now I think about it either, the entire house is devoid of life, just me, an echoing hall and a somewhat sticky floor. Cook should be here even if the family has debunked, it's fast approaching lunchtime and come to think of it that will bring the hoards back to safety. The lack of occupants does, however, allow me time to have an uninterrupted scoot round downstairs. I am confident there is nothing upstairs, there never was any expectation of anything by way of evidence upstairs so I shall leave that until later if I've found it necessary

In theory the only clues should be in the card room. It's quite eerie even though I've held three interviews here. I take short light steps towards the card table although there has been so much foot traffic since Alan Broadhurst was murdered it hardly matters. The cards are still lying on the table as they were when the murder occurred; if indeed it is where it occurred. We don't know yet at least I don't think I do, there are none of the usual weapons of murder by the table: no hammer, no knife and nothing with which to strangle him. The absence of any external force suggests poison as the cause of death which in turn suggests a female killer – women favour poison as a means of killing. The forensic pathologist has already been here so he should have removed anything incriminating but I feel I need to crawl on my hands and knees around and under the table just to check.

Charles always leaves cigar ash under his chair. We ladies dislike the ash, although the smell, the smoke is mysteriously attractive. He flicks the ash under his chair for the cleaner to remove later but in the circumstances she has been barred from the room until further notice. The quantity dropped on the ghastly night was excessive but then that's hardly surprising and to my untrained nose does seem to have been from his normal brand. I push through the disgusting stuff with an old pen I keep in the bag for just such occasions but there is nothing worthy of note secreted within the debris and I leave the pile of ashes strewn across the area under the chair.

The seat and back of the chair, the crease between them and

the fixings under the seat of the chair reveal nothing untoward that I can find except, except for Patricia's, well I'm not sure how to interpret what I find. My darling sibling Patricia (who one would think is far too young to have acquired any habits resulting in anything that would leave evidence whether unsavoury or not) has left some of her long blonde hairs on both the chair and the floor. It beggar's belief how they got there – well obviously from Patricia's head, but why would she be sitting there or kneeling on the floor.

I make a note to ask her how the hairs came to be where they are.

The rest of the carpet reveals nothing more than the normal grubby bits of stuff I imagine can be found on anyone's carpet when the cleaner has been unable to sweep and vacuum in the normal way. I didn't expect to find anything obvious like a needle or an Amazonian tribal dart but a little something more English – anything would have been helpful.

I have a quick rummage through the bureau drawers even though I know they would have been closed throughout the entire evening and as I close the last of them I hear voices in the hallway. Firstly Father's (inevitably) and then John's, the remainder are a jumble of Mother's, Patricia's and Cook's. William's is in there somewhere indicating that he had arrived before or during whatever caused them to abandon ship. His presence is of no consequence to me, I shall proceed with my questioning as intended, the content and severity of my questions might be more searching than I had originally planned, but then whose fault is that?

Father blusters: 'Alicia, my darling. We wondered where you had got to. Did you get very hot?'

'No, I only had to get from the car to the front door – no distance really especially when all the police cars had gone.'

Mother pipes up, 'That's good. Now then, I think Cook has gone to set up tea and buttered crumpets in the study if you'd care to join us. You can update everyone on your progress with poor Alan's death while we're all together.'

'But, Father I can't do…' but he's gone, uninterested in any protestations I may have.

'Ah, Ali there you are, you missed a dreadful thunderstorm but well, mother says it was just lots of loud noise anyway, but no rain.' Patty restores her form of sanity. 'We were all out in the garden for some reason or other and we were just about to start a game of charades when the sun came out and we had to come back into the house. It wasn't a real thunderstorm after all, just one of those that make the noise but there's no rain, when the sun goes behind a cloud of some sort.' Others will no doubt have welcomed the break in the stuffiness and lack of fresh air, but Patty simply wondered why there was no rain.

You may be interested to know that the thunderstorms continued and on 15th, only two days later torrential rain fell

'I expect you found it strange to find the whole house empty – especially the kitchen and with John gone too.'

'I did rather.'

'Still, I expect you were able to have a good old rummage while the house was empty, and you found out all our little hidden secrets.'

'Well.'

'That's fine; I haven't any secrets – especially not from you.

Are you joining us for crumpets even though it's baking hot and unfortunately none of us got drenched?'

'Tell the others I'll be there after I've changed and Patty,' she turns quickly, almost falling 'drenched isn't a very lady-like word. 'Even though I didn't get too hot', would have been much better.' She has no idea.

'Okay, don't be long – all the crumpets will have been gone by the time you get down there.'

'They won't and nobody will care anyway - especially if you're there.'

'Don't be silly.' She hangs her head in dismay and leaves the room to go and change.

If I don't hurry I shall have to arrive with my sister at the party and I'd really rather not do that when all sorts of things are going around in my head. If I precede her there won't be much time to answer questions about the investigation. It's all a question of timing. She'll turn up in a fabulously suitable gown (if wearing a gown of any sort to crumpets and tea could possibly referred to as fabulous or even suitable) and I shall be in slightly more plain attire. She will have high, high heels and appear eight inches taller than normal whereas I (and the rest of the family) will be in ordinary flat or at least much lower heels. She will be the talk of those around her, she with her brightened delicate lips, eye shadow and slinky dress, while I will be able to exist with my mouth permanently full of muffin, toast or cake (there's always cake) before I give my apologies and leave.

I have arranged to call on my father's bridge partner, Joan Saynor who has kindly offered to provide dinner – I gave Cook the relevant information at the time of the offer.

Joan lives in a part of Faversham I haven't experienced. West

I have never seen before or even imagined existed. She sees me gazing at the water, 'It isn't the Creek,' she almost twitters, '– everyone thinks it is, although it does flow from the Creek and is therefore Creek water, it's actually a large pond, Stonebridge Pond, full of all sorts of birds and that sort of thing.' The water is very still and now I look closer it is just like a mill pond. 'It was part of the gunpowder works water system but that's just closed down and left this wonderful view. Mind you, it was wonderful before the works closed down, just not, I don't know, not nice knowing what it was used for.'

'It's beautiful.'

'It is, but that's not why you're here is it. I can waffle on all day about the garden and the pond and the cottage and all sorts of nothing at all but first and foremost I'm a bridge player and that's why you're here. Now then, ask away.'

Mrs Saynor is a comparatively short, slender woman with short, light brown hair worn in the current crimped style above twinkling brown eyes. She is in a long, trimmed, V-neck pattern print dress which suites her, but I can't help feeling, is slightly overdressed for our meeting. However, there is no doubt that she is a beautiful woman in – I would guess – her early to mid-fifties judging by the lighter makeup than would be worn by a younger woman.

'I'm here, as you know, to hear your side of the story of Alan Broadoak's death. The police declared his death a heart attack, but some people – members of my family – believe that he was murdered and have asked me to investigate. Before you ask, I am not a professional detective, merely a member of the Whitten family who has investigated, resolved some question-able events for them.'

'You mean murders.'

'Yes, I mean murders.' There is no point in denying it she has obviously been filled in by someone in the family – possibly Patty but more likely Charles. 'Can you tell me how you came to be in the bridge group and how you came to partner my father, what you were doing during the two weeks before the fateful game and then your view of what happened last Saturday when Mr Broadoak died?'

'The first question is easy. As I said earlier, first and foremost above all else I am a bridge player. I have played for over twenty years now having learned and played with my late husband's mistress for the last ten years. That is, she was his mistress for twelve years and I partnered her for ten as an effective means of keeping an eye on them when they were seeing one another.' She looks quite evil at this point and I'm waiting for her to say that she murdered the pair of them and got away with it because of the inefficiency of the police of the time. 'I see that you approve of my actions.'

'I don't disapprove because I'm not aware of the circumstances and, to be honest, am not interested in them unless they have an effect on my investigations.'

'Certainly not; my husband died from natural causes at the age of 64 only a few weeks after his mistress was killed in a tragic motor car accident in Monte Carlo.' She raises the left side of her mouth, her incongruous bright red lips forming a sneer which fits the evil I had earlier seen in her eyes.'

'How did you come to play with my father?'

You will shortly discover that the name of Joan's husband was Duncan. He, like my own husband is mentioned only once and has no influence on the investigations into the murder.

'After Duncan's death some friends said that Lavinia – your mother – was looking for a partner to join her Saturday four. She then said that she had found it impossible to play with your father and sister also playing; three members of the same family was just too much, and she went off to play with another group of all ladies. She knew about my situation and introduced me to an old friend of hers, Alan Broadoak. It all became overly complicated because Charles said we should shuffle things round so that he wasn't playing with Patricia and so in the end Alan ended up playing with Patricia and I played with Charles. Charles is - was - a lovely man in his way but he did have his foibles; well, more irritations really, but it was his group in his house and so none of us, not least me, wanted to stir things up. But although I ended up not playing with Alan – lovely man though he was too – we've been the same group with the same partnerships for the last four or five years I suppose.'

'Until somebody murdered Alan Broadoak.' She barely flinches. There is no reaction other than the disappearance of her sneer. 'What about the two weeks before last Saturday?'

'That would be 27th May – yes –?,' I nod by way of confirmation. 'Let me think, in the morning I sat in the garden reading while Elsie made some bread and a cake. She served lunch at one o'clock punctually – I like everything to be at the right time – after that I put my face on, changed and drove to the Whittens. During the next week I had coffee with some friends or my special friend most mornings and in the afternoon read in the garden or tended the garden – yes I was probably weeding because Robert, my gardener was poorly, in fact he still is.'

That seems to me like a lot of time drinking coffee and sitting around in her garden, lovely though it is but of course I know that she's having an affair with Charles Whitten and I could really do with her telling me rather than the other way round, I'll have to work on that.

'You have a lovely garden Mrs Saynor, but don't you get well, bored with sitting out here just looking at it? Don't you like to go out in the evenings – to play bridge or just meeting a friend for a chat?

'Well, it's true that I spend a lot of time in my garden and yes I do spend time with my friends and occasionally I play bridge, but I don't see what that has to do with Alan's murder.' She's on the defensive now and is obviously not going to tell me on this attempt, so I pull back and switch to another, more obvious part of the questioning.

'And what about last Saturday?'

'Well you know, don't you, that's why we're here isn't it?' She shrugs as if that is all there to say, as if I already know. She claims to be confused. 'No, oh, or do you mean Saturday a week ago? Well I suppose we were doing the same thing as this Saturday when Alan was murdered, we must have been, we always do, oh no, wait a minute we couldn't play that Saturday because Patricia had to do something else so Charles managed to get tickets for a Noel Coward play at the Marlow Theatre in Canterbury – do you know it?' She ploughs on not giving me a chance to comment. 'He was very lucky it was very popular. So he took me out to dinner and then to the play, that was it and then this last Saturday, which is of course the one that you're really interested in, I had lunch with a friend and I went home to change before spending the evening together after a lovely dinner as always at the Whittens of course, with Patricia, Alan and Charles. If you must know I spent the morning at home and in the afternoon I went shopping in Canterbury after lunch with – oh, I can't remember, does it matter?'

'Not at the moment. Did you enjoy the play? What was it you saw they keep changing them so quickly, I've lost track?'

'Oh, now let me see…'

She has little choice, the only Noel Coward play seen playing anywhere at the moment is Private Lives, he hasn't written anything for the London stage for years. His latest is on Broadway but they can't get it on the stage over here so it must have been Private Lives; something so stunning I can't believe she's forgotten it or never went to the theatre which is what I expect. I only know all this rubbish because a friend of mine has been stage manager at the King's Head Theatre and is a chap in the know. 'It's that new one, you remember.'

I say. 'Private Lives perhaps?' She nods, furiously. 'You didn't go, Joan did you.'

'Well, actually no, I didn't, I'm afraid to say that Charles took me for dinner, and we sat talking for hours.'

'Are you saying that you're having an affair with your best friend's husband?'

She looks down at her hands which she is wringing so hard that her fingers are turning white and the red where her grip increases and decreases with the movement. 'It hasn't been going for long. I suppose it sort of started when he and Lavinia…' Now the guilt is starting to show.

'Tell me, have you had any contact with any of the bridge four during the last fortnight, that is, apart from Charles on the two Saturdays? Do you meet any of them socially at all?'

'Why do you ask?'

'I'm trying to get a feel for you all, that's all. You must realize that you are all suspects at the moment.'

'Well, of course, I see.'

'So, do you see any of the bridge group during the week? Mrs or Miss Whitten? For example?'

'Well, I suppose you'll find out sooner or later, but Charles and I have been having an affair for some time now. Longer than I led you to believe just now.' She looks away as if she's ashamed rather than excited at the goings on. When finally she looks up, she flushes, and her demeanour has changed. Now she's smiling and is clearly a much happier person, her whole body language is more relaxed and gives off an image of a relaxed, positive lady, appearing younger than her years.'

'Does Mrs Whitten know of your affair?'

'I doubt it, we have been extremely careful. You won't tell her, will you?'

'Well, Mrs Saynor, I think that's all for now thank you although as I'm sure you realize as with all investigations I may need to talk to you again.'

'Of course, and please, do call me Joan.'

She's less worried now as though the telling me her secret has made it easier for us to talk almost as if we are friends. We shall never be friends, but it makes it easier for me to talk to her, to delve into her innermost feelings, or at least let her think we are.

Chapter Seventeen

The plot, as they say, thickens. I suppose if bridge partnerships flourish through practice, experience and familiarity in one's partner's style of play, so it is that personal friendships are likely to extend beyond that of simply being friends. It is unfortunate that those extended friendships can sometimes become affairs when members of the same family are also the bridge opposition. Well to some extent you would be right, it's not a game I play with any degree of confidence or capability let alone from any competitive viewpoint. But I grew up in a house where my parents and siblings played the game until well into the dark of the night, while the rest of the world was either at war or playing the game with greater intensity. It's not surprising then that I have gained a fundamental knowledge of the game which will no doubt help in my solving of this mystery. Awareness of my knowledge has probably vanished from everyone's memory apart from that of my father. You will not be surprised to read that I shall not be spilling the beans until absolutely necessary even if at all. There are plenty of secrets here that another one will make no difference whatever.

It's time I had an update from Frank or preferably Jenny. I don't seem to have paid a visit to the Creek for some time although it was actually only yesterday, and Tom will be missing Maggie. The heavens open, pouring more rain upon us than we have seen for months. There is no doubt that the famers will welcome the water, if not so much over such a short period. I drive down Brogdale Road towards the main Dover to London road past the burgeoning hop gardens on my left and then the school playing fields on my right. The plush green is refreshing after the rather dull apple orchards where the blossom is long gone, and the apples have yet to fill out. The rain splatters on Maggie's roof and I hope that it remains waterproof until I can return to the dryness of a garage.

For a change I turn left and then sharp right into the beautiful Upper St. Ann's with its row of stumpy trunked horse chestnut trees green flowering white and dwarfing the houses that seemingly lurk on the left side of the road. I have to wait at the level crossing for a Dover bound train to pass and as it does I return the waves of little children each excited on their trip to the seaside. At last the gates open and I cross the tracks to descend Lower St Ann's, a poor relation to its sister road. The left hand side of the hill is planted with terraces of newly finished houses for the less well off and on the right as I decline is a solid red brick wall holding back the land on which has been built a substantial school building.

I arrive at the unimaginatively named Ospringe Road that leads to the outlying village of Ospringe where I turn right and drive past the local Gunpowder Mills on my way to The Creek. The gunpowder mills – or Chart Mills to give them their proper name – were built to supply armies during the Napoleonic Wars and have since been the largest ever UK suppliers of the dangerous powder. They're still producing low levels of their murdering wares but are due to be fully closed next year after the biggest explosion in the Mill's history which took the lives of over a hundred local men and women.

The road twists and turns until I pass the brewery and come to a stop outside Frank Spillett's office door. I have hardly cut the engine when Tommy is by my side with polishing cloth in hand.

'I thought you wasn't comin' miss that's what all me mates said but I knew you would.'

'Well now, Tommy I can't promise to come every day. It all depends on how busy I am up at Brogdale; you do understand, don't you?'

''Corse I do, but I just fwort you would today.' He grins from ear to ear and (with my gloves covering my hands) I ruffle his scruffy hair. 'I got some news for you, miss.'

He's excited about his find, so I hope it really is as exciting as his little face suggests.

'Yes, Tommy what's that?'

He looks from side to side to make sure nobody's listening as I bend down, and he cups his grubby little hands towards my ear. 'It's one of The Creeks Gang what did it, miss.'

'Well that's hardly surprising, Tommy is it?'

'No, but I knows which one it is.' He pauses as if for a round of applause before he stands and straightens himself up to his full height. 'I knows for sure'

'Come on then Tommy, spill the beans.'

'It's Franky.'

'Not Frank from up there?' I point to Frank's office on the upper floor, 'surely?' That would be inconvenient at best and awkward to say the very least if we have the killer as one of the investigation team.

'No, no, miss: Franky Blake - him who looks after Mr. Gouge's stuff nawf of the lines.' He lowers to his normal slouched height and grins, job done, he's done what I asked and if it's true he may have solved the mystery uncommonly soon. I can't be that lucky.

'Are you telling me that Frank Blake crossed the lines – somehow – walked up and across the London Road, up Brogdale Road and then walked up to the Corners card playing room, somehow got inside and then killed Mr Broadoak without anyone at all seeing him.?' Tommy nods his head. 'I'm sorry, Tommy, but that can't be true. I'm sorry, but it just can't be. There must be something your informant hasn't told you or that you've left out or misunderstood. Are you making some of it up? I wouldn't blame you if you are.'

I have never seen a young boy look so crestfallen – like a young man whose proposal of marriage has been rejected perhaps. I've seen a few of those – but never a young boy, or a small, older boy. It looks as though I have broken his heart. 'I'm sorry, Tommy, I'm not blaming you it's not your fault. Who told you all this? Who said that Frank Blake murdered Mr Broadoak?'

'Oh no, he didn't actually kill him, miss; but he found the stuff for the bloke what did. You know that poison stuff. Without that the bloke who did it, he couldn't have done the killing. So I thought that came out the same. Doesn't it, miss?'

Now it's my turn to smile. 'Of course it is, Tommy, of course it is. Now I see what your informant told you and what you mean. That makes much more sense – complete sense. Thank you.'

He sighs with relief at not having to think of a way of punishing his informant – although he must have a list of ready to use punishments as long as his arm. 'So, do I get to drive your car, miss? Like you promised?'

'Of course you can, Tommy but not on your own, your feet can't touch the pedals, so we'll have to sort something out when I come down from seeing Mr. Spillett.'

'Right, ta, miss.' With my still gloved hand, I ruffle his hair before heading towards Frank's outer door. 'He's ou', miss.'

'Is he?'

'Yes, miss. Left an hour or so ago. Miss Hudson's up 'vere though.'

'Thanks, Tommy.'

What a relief, surely Frank has finished his second report – although I never actually, formally received the final copy of the first one; as long as the second is ready for typing, or it's ready for him to sign off and send to me, I'm happy.

The stairs are, of course, still rickety and creak as much as the water that flows past the building, but then it was only the day before yesterday that I saw Jenny last so in fairness I couldn't have expected him to have done anything about them although in all honesty nobody who experiences them ever expects him to have done anything and always climbs them with care. Jenny is waiting for me at the top of the stairs displaying the second enormous grin I have seen today.

'Good morning, Mrs Matcham.'

'Alicia, remember.' She nods apologetically, 'Good morning, Jenny, it looks as though you have the second most important piece of good news I have heard this morning.'

'Well now, that depends what the first one was, doesn't it?

Tea?'

'Please. Go on then, don't keep me waiting until the tea's cool enough to drink.'

She retires to the kitchenette and re-boils the already hot kettle, puts out another cup and saucer and a plate of biscuits, these she brings into her office and as she places them carefully onto the desk looks across at me, smiles and leaves as the kettle conveniently boils.

'Sorry, won't be a tick.'

Sure enough she's soon sitting at her desk with the teapot brewing on its cork mat.

'Right, important news you said, good news, and all you've done is produce a cup of tea and a plate of biscuits that neither of us will touch because they look inedible.'

'Frank's not done the second report, at least he hasn't finished the first really, though why he doesn't finish it before he does something else – usually involving the pub – I don't know. Well, he hasn't actually solved the case of course but he's discovered established that, as we've suspected all along, that Mr Broadoak was poisoned and now, that Frank Blake from the Creek Gang provided the poison to the murderer. Although his informants are saying that he's only another link in the chain. They reckon that Blake passed the poison to the other bloke who they think passed it on to someone else. Frank's told me that the chain of men involved makes it harder for the police to find the actual murderer.'

'Yes, I can see that, in fact I've seen it before, so I know only too well how it's done. You'll be interested that a lot of what Frank has discovered is on the streets and that that was actually the first bit of good news I've had today!' I'm wondering whether it's worth spending vast sums of money on employing Frank when Tommy seems to be almost as good simply for the odd ride in my car. 'Any more? Nothing at all? Not even if it's simply a hunch or a hint from someone?'

'No, nothing I'm afraid, sorry.' She doesn't look sorry and I wonder whether it's because she knows something that Frank's told her not to tell me because after all he has learned of our tete-a-tetes or because she would like to tell me more but genuinely has nothing more of any worth to divulge. She seems a bit fidgety and I ask if she's okay. 'I'm fine Mrs Matcham, Alicia, thank you for asking.' I sense a rise in her voice a certain worry or concern.

'Are you expecting somebody, Jenny?'

'No, miss, thank you. It's just that working down in this part of town doing what we do and dealing with the sort of people we have to, I'm never quite sure who might come up the stairs; you know? A bag of nerves my little old mum tells me, perhaps she's right, I dunno.'

'You can't be worried when there are two of us. Surely.'

'No, of course not.' But she looks over to the stairs again and then at me as if looking for further reassurance.

'What's your mother's name?'

'Ada, lovely she is.'

'Well that's a very fine name, it comes from nobility a very important person or the first daughter in the family. Does that make sense?'

'Funny you should ask, she was the first daughter, three brothers two older one younger and a baby sister. Why?'

'Well, with a name like that in your family, you should be strong enough to look after yourself all right.' She looks at me is if wondering what the devil I'm talking about. 'I'm interested in family names and what they mean or where they've come from. Yours for example comes from the story of King Arthur and his knights. They think it comes from Lady Guinevere and means 'white waves' or 'fair one'. I don't do that much detective work but to know what peoples' names mean can sometimes help me in understanding why they do what they do – or don't.'

She ignores my answer to her question as she's more excited about what her and her mother's names mean; if she comes to think about it, the answer I gave, it might give her some insight into what my and Franks' occupations are all about.

'Oh, I'll tell Mum that, she'll be ever so pleased.'

She looks to the stairs again and I'm certain she's expecting somebody and would like me to go before they arrive. It won't surprise you that I can be evilly minded if I want to be and I'm intrigued as to whom it might be. So, 'Could I use your loo do you think?'

'Err, yes, of course, sorry. Do you know where it is?'

I point to a door at what could laughingly be called the end of the kitchen. 'Through there?' She nods. 'I won't be long and then I'll leave you in peace to type up the report.' The door sticks a little when I try to go in and closes with a thud – not quite a bang but not far off.

I have only recently closed the door when I hear a voice calling up the stairs. 'Jenny, it's me'. I wait for further information as this is clearly the issue that was worrying Jenny earlier. 'Jenny can you hear me'? I hear Jenny's footsteps across the wooden floor, presumably towards the top of the stairs, 'Oh, there you are. Has that bloody woman gone yet or is she still in the office?' Now, there are a great number of women in

Faversham and even quite a few in Frank's circle of friends to whom the gentleman could be referring but as I am a naturally suspicious person I fancy that he may very well be referring to me. I hear Jenny respond but can't hear what she's saying. I hold my breath hoping to hear more and gather that she's trying to quieten her visitor. I assume it isn't Frank – at least it had better not be!

'Ssshh – in there.' I can imagine her signalling in my direction and waving to the man – he is far enough up the stairs for me to be sure of his gender – to say nothing more. 'Ssshh' Again, I imagine him covering his mouth in apology and while I am finding the whole exercise fascinating I feel that I cannot reasonably justify my remaining in this little room much longer. I flush and having adjusted my clothing and open the door to find a young man standing cap in hand in front of Jenny's desk.

I say, 'Good morning, do I know you?'

'No, Mrs Matcham, this is Ronald a friend of mine. He's Frank's son-in-law.'

I turn and look at the boy face on. 'Mrs Matcham, pleased to meet you, Jenny's told me so much about you – none of the private stuff o' course – but about your little get togethers.'

'Yes, I gathered she'd told you about me from what you said coming up the stairs.' He looks guilty and apologetic but doesn't say anything. 'Goodbye Jennifer, no doubt we shall meet again soon.' I feel that one of us should react to what little Ronald said, there is no excuse for bad manners as my Great Old Aunts used to say and I use her full name as did Frank when he was displeased.

With that, I slowly walk down the stairs and out into the windy June afternoon. Tommy is standing there keeping any admirers away from my car and he is still smiling. I wonder if he has anything else to tell me; perhaps something Jenny wanted to tell me but had been told not to by Frank, in which case they are collecting secrets and she has probably told him about us getting together. Spies within spies, complicated but it can be much more fun, I wonder where Tommy fits in to all this?

I have achieved something this morning but neither of the pieces of information are crucial – as far as I know – nor particularly important but it certainly made the informants feel important which means that they will be keen to provide me with more.

Chapter Eighteen

I'm disappointed in my visit to Frank's office and am not my usual cheerful, vibrant self as I head towards Corners as I have so many times before. Even though I have chosen a different one of so many routes, the variation doesn't excite me as it usually might, not even the 90 degree curve left after swooping under the iron bridge followed by an immediate 90 degree turn right into The Mall then scorching up the tree lined avenue to the Dover – London road, an old favourite and breathed fresh air into my lungs reviving my get-up-and-go. I am consciously dropping the car's speed below the fourteen miles an hour abolished three years ago and if any of my friends see me, my reputation for a speedy, carefree driver will be smashed. A car hurtles past and the driver waves wildly, shouting something but I have no idea what it is, something to do with the new speed limit and people keeping out of the way I expect; everyone's talking about it – well all we drivers are. My journey along Brogdale Road is even slower because of a tractor chugging its way from one field to another. I pull into Corners and crawl along the long tarmacadam drive drawing to a silent stop outside a large flowering bush the name of which I forget.

I wonder if perhaps a wander round the grounds will revive

me and I turn right past the kitchen garden with its range of colours and mix of fresh smells from the herbs and flowers. As I approach the kitchen door I hear voices.

A woman's voice: I think it's Cook: '…well what if it is her it's none of our business, nothing at all. Still, makes you think doesn't it? Her with all that and nothing to do.'

Now a man's, probably John: 'None of its our business, 'Cetta none of it. Whether she has anything to do with it or not. You're sounding jealous and it's obscuring your thoughts. Now, get on with the baking or they'll be no jam for tea. They'll all be in soon wanting their crumpets. Now, no more talk of this, right?"

'I suppose, but wouldn't it mean that none of us would be safe in our beds. I've been closing my windows at night in case he or she comes for me in the night.'

'For goodness sake, Cookie.'

'But it could be any of them. They all got reasons to kill him and I know what some of them are. Mind, I don't have a reason, nor do I play bridge.'

'Well, what about you and Mr Broadoak? I heard that his wife wasn't too pleased about the outcome of a night of passion you and he had a few years ago.' John's voice has become deeper and he is speaking more slowly. I imagine him standing fully upright and that he has put on his stern voice.

'That doesn't give me a reason to kill him does it and his wife's been dead best part of two years so it can't be her.'

'But did he have any other lovers?'

'What like Mrs Whitten? I shouldn't think so, but if he did, she and Mr Whitten would have a reason…'

'…To kill him? They might.'

'I never knew that he and Mrs Whitten were…'

'I'm not saying they were or that Mr Whitten killed Mr Broadoak, I'm just saying that we have no idea what was going on and they probably have no idea about your dilly-dallying with Mr Broadoak. None of us has any idea and you mustn't go around spreading any rumours. That won't do any good for any of us.'

I hear John's footsteps as he leaves the kitchen, as must I, the last thing I want is for him to find out that I've overheard his – or anybody else's conversations.

I walk on as silently as I can in the hope they don't know that I might have overheard their chatter. It was an interesting conversation as many conversations are but contained little of really valuable information as most conversations don't, although the idea of Mrs Cook and Mr Broadoak together does conjure up some strange images. It is useful to know what the servants think of what's going on and will be interesting when I interview them later. John has obviously got the measure of the situation and made the point that Cook must keep her mouth shut. Spreading rumours might lead to far reaching rumours and – something might happen to her!

It has been rather dull skulking along the side of the buildings but now, having reached the corner of the main house I can see the evening sun spreading its rays across the sundial to the main lawn. It's a beautiful gold and even with the increasingly brown grass – badly in a need of a cut I shall ask father to speak to the current gardener – creates an, I don't know perhaps an ochre yellow coloured small field. The gardener, father and mother particularly would be horrified to hear me call their favourite lawn a field and perhaps its melancholy which is causing me to view it that way.

Is it my own melancholy I wonder that already I'm beginning to feel I should have refused to do this? To try to resolve a murder the police insist on registering as a death from natural causes and that only my imaginative little sister can believe otherwise – probably after reading too many Sherlock Holmes stories or some of those new Agatha Christie books – is a trifle soul destroying. It no longer excites me the way the original idea did and perhaps I should just say that I did it so that it can all be resolved, and I can go to prison. I need to pull myself round or up or together, I'm being ridiculous just as I used to be when I was a little girl and Patty and the family would tell me so; father might even give me a slap on my cheek as he used to do in such circumstances though he is unlikely to do so again.

I can see mother in the distance and we exchange waves as I walk along the north border which is edged by the grass at the front where I'm walking and at the rear by a thick privet hedge, beautifully, neatly trimmed by the gardener – Graham I think his name is, although that doesn't sound a very likely name for a gardener. Mother has never been sure about which flowers to plant in the north border and if I were a gardener I'd know whether her choices worked. I think she's started with roses of various colours then some sweet peas and cornflowers but whether the next clumps are hollyhocks, delphiniums, wisteria or clematis or, indeed, sprawling weeds, I really have no idea. I can see some iris toward the far end and I always think how morbid they are; a flower that so many people use at funerals as a memory to their loved one, or their mother's sister or the killer of a bridge partner is grown as a flower of beauty to brighten dreary flower borders.

I meander past the croquet lawn, hardly used and the tennis court never used and then over to the larger of the two summer houses where mother is sitting with her own 'crochet lawn' gently rolling in folds in front of her, a blanket for one of her aunts. A watery smile is all she can muster as she hooks the wool through the holes in a seemingly random pattern creating an obvious, clear result with all the questions about colour and design resolved for all to see.

'Alicia, darling, are you enjoying the peace and quiet of our garden? Grantley keeps it in such wonderful condition doesn't he? (I knew it wasn't Graham – although Grantley is somewhat the other end of the naming scale)'

'Yes, he does; although I do think he needs to slice the top off the grass to, to make it look tidier despite the awful colour. It's looking rather scruffy.'

'Do you mean the lawn, darling?' I nod sheepishly. 'Well perhaps he does although we do tend to leave such decisions to him rather. Perhaps I'll ask your father to have a word with him.'

'Mother we're living in a new age; employers can speak freely to their staff. This is the 1930s, you speak to him!'

Unsurprisingly she ignores what I've said, not wanting to have to cope with anything new in the world. 'Are you making much progress darling? I gather you have spoken to your Father and Joan. I expect that resulted in an interesting encounter.'

'You must know that I can't tell you anything about those conversations. I know this is only a private investigation, but I have to follow certain basic rules so that when it does get taken over by the police they will be able to see that I have done things the proper way.'

'Of course I do, but I'm sure you can tell me something.'

I shake my head in defiance of my mother's wishes for possibly the first time. I was always her favourite and I love her dearly, but this situation and its rules must be the same for everyone. 'I mustn't, I'm sorry. Once I start I shall have no reason to not tell anyone else something and then it will go on and on and when I question people they will already have made up the same story and I shan't get the truth of what happened.'

'In that case I shan't ask you again' She raises her hand and I feel that I have offended her, but it can't be helped. Strangely, she has renewed my fascination about the whole thing, and I must talk to some of the others, I must forge ahead with my investigation into the murder that happened almost four days ago now.

Chapter Nineteen

'John.'

'Madam.'

'There's no need to call me madam when it's just us I've told you that time and again. Alicia is perfectly acceptable.'

'I'm sorry, madam but I believe it important to maintain the dignity of my position and in any event, another member of staff or the household may enter the room and such familiarity would cause embarrassment.'

'Okay then, John,' he bows his head and it's ridiculous; I have known John since I was a young child and I can't remember when the changes from Ali to Alicia to madam occurred but whenever they were it's ridiculous. Still, I'm happy to maintain the formality. 'Please sit down, John I really don't feel very comfortable interviewing you as we are, I shall get a bad neck ache.' He sits opposite me and rests his left arm on the table with a degree of informality I find somewhat incongruous with his earlier comments.

'I expect you want to know what happened, madam.' He raises his eyebrows as if there's a possibility I should want to talk about something else or in the hope that I do.

'Of course, but I'll question you instead of you simply telling me. However, could you please tell me what you were doing over the two weeks before the death of Mr Broadoak.'

'That's easy, madam, each of my weeks is the same. As you may be aware I live in what is was rather gloriously named my pantry: I rise at five-thirty, wash, dress and go to the kitchen where cook has prepared me two lightly boiled eggs, some toast and a pot of tea. She prepares the items required for Mr Whitten's and the other breakfasts and at seven o'clock I carry those various preparations to the breakfast room where the Master and his family and guests are able to enjoy Cook's cooking and baking. I stand by the door to the kitchen ready to assist during the meal.'

'Whatever do you assist with?'

'A shortage of toast usually; occasionally milk, sometimes tomatoes but then at the end and when all of them have left the room I clear the debris and return it to the kitchen. '

'And for how many days a week?'

He sighs. 'Six, madam,'

'And what do you do during the day, John?'

His sigh is deeper now and he looks out the window which gives a limited view of the drive as if he thinks my questions are irrelevant. 'Much the same for lunch as for breakfast except, both meals are taken in the dining room at different times to breakfast of course. Dinner is the more – more complicated in a way, because everyone has to eat at the same time and unlike the other meals there are three, sometimes four courses. I have a little help setting up and clearing at the end of the meal but serving and coping with any questions or issues during eating is down to just me'.

'Between the meals.'

'Yes, sorry, I do odd jobs for Mr Whitten – since there has been no chauffeur, cleaning the cars that have been used the previous day is the most common job, I suppose.'

'How many cars are we talking about, John?'

'The family has five cars – although it's rare for all of them to have been used in one day – and then there are the guests' if there are any.' He's sullen now, making no secret of the fact that he wishes the whole thing was over and wondering what he could spend his time more usefully on.

'And after that?'

'Clean the silver, but not every day, it's something the maids used to carry out as are many of the tasks I now fulfil. madam, if I might make so bold?'

'Go on.'

'My duties are mundane and none of them bring me in contact with any of the guests – such as Mr Broadoak – other than at mealtimes or chance meetings elsewhere. I do of course have contact with you during our own fortnightly, private meetings on my day off and sometimes during the week.' Now he smiles, our relationship is aired at last.

While we are not having what might be considered by some as an affair, we do have a special, intimate understanding where I am teaching him the practical, sensuous aspects of marriage. This is not for our mutual benefit you understand, although many might think so; it is genuinely a teacher and well taught student whose experiences are sadly lacking. The least contact is on Saturdays when the catering needs are greater and for the weekly bridge session after dinner and there, as you know, is of course where the murder took place.

I am thrown by the irritated tone that John has shown in his answers, as if to say that I should know the answers and that there is no need for me to ask the questions.

He continues: 'I see that you are convinced it was a murder.'

'I can see no further explanation.'

'Why?'

'Because Mr Broadoak was a healthy man. He had a strong heart and had not even had a bad or stressful game of bridge prior to his death.'

'I see that you can play bridge.'

'Madam?'

'If you did not, you would be unable to say whether Mr Broadoak had had a stressful game or not.'

He says, 'I might also have been able to determine his frame of mind as to the bridge he had played by the number of alcoholic drinks he had consumed.'

'I see, well for the time being let's proceed along a different line of questioning. Was there any difference at all between the first and the second of the two weeks prior to the death? Either by you or seen by you, or known to you but which you did not witness?'

'Nothing, madam.'

'That was a very quick recollection.'

'Not at all, I had anticipated the questions you would ask, and I confess that that is one of them.'

'How long have you known the family, John?'

'I was Colonel Whitten's batman, madam. We saw a lot of action during the Great War and lost too many men. A lot of horrible things happened. He stood by me and I stood by him. I like to think we were a team clearing up the dead and learning to sort out the new, live ones. I lost count of the dead bodies we saw and now, now there's another one.'

He looks down and shakes his head.

'Mr Broadoak might not have died in the war, but who knows what he saw during the years that we're all supposed to put behind us, who knows what he saw, what he did or was forced to do and how he coped with it. It was a few years ago now, fifteen years and still those of us who were over there, in the mud and muck, in it fighting for our country and our freedom, still those of us have nightmares, regrets and memories of those we lost and those we served and won. Colonel Whitten was one of the good ones. I suppose he treated me well enough and despite his rank there were a couple of times when he saved me from death, no man can ever repay that sort of debt however hard he tries. Although he'd offered this job to Mr Broadoak first, when he had to go to hospital Colonel Whitten offered it to me, a job when I'd found it almost impossible to get regular work, I owe him a lot. I have enormous respect for that man. I cannot, I will not believe he had anything to do with this murder. Yes, murder. I have seen a lot of death and I know this is not through natural causes. This is murder.'

'That's quite a speech, John. I can see that you and Mr Whitten, sorry Colonel Whitten, have a very special relationship but I'm afraid I don't know him as perhaps I should – he is my father after all – and I don't have the same staunch belief in his innocence that you do; but what you say may be relevant and I can only hope you're right.'

'Thank you, madam.'

'I think we'll leave it there for the time being, but I will need to speak to you again. Soon. Thank you for your assistance so far.' A light smile flutters across his normally deferential face as if there is something more, something I have failed to mention or ask. There will be other opportunities.

He leaves, sweating after the effort he put into his speech, the effort he gave to try to persuade me not to accuse my father. Unfortunately, what he said has perhaps increased the possibility of a noose falling around his master's neck. If a man can go through what he and Charles went through all that fighting, killing, blood sweat and tears, killing an opposing bridge player would be easy prey.

Chapter Twenty

'Mrs Cook, or might I call you Pancetta?'

'Just as you please, miss; I been called a lot worse things in my time, makes little difference to me.'

'Pancetta it is then.'

'But most people call me 'Cetta.'

'Right, 'Cetta.' I sigh, this is already becoming tiresome. If establishing her name is this difficult, obtaining answers to essential questions will be like climbing a mountain. 'Cetta, you have been cook here for how long?'

'Ooo, well now,' I wait patiently, 'that'll be eight years since and now, let me think. I was with her when you's born so that must be what twenty-nine years 'first; how old are you, miss?'

'That hardly matters 'Cetta, but I'm thirty-one if you must know. So you've been a cook here for thirty-nine years.'

'That'd be about right, yes.'

'A long time then.' That's really all I wanted to know and I'm afraid that my inevitable next question might go on forever, but I do need to ask it. 'What can you tell me about Charles Whitten? What is he like as a man, how does he treat you and others about him? How does he treat John for example?

'Ooo, well that's a question 'n' no mistake. He's nice enough

125

to me, when he talks to me; Miss Patricia does most of the menus and the like. Mr Charles only come down if there's something special goin' on. Mr John his butler and Mr Charles – '

'Just a minute, 'Cetta; was there a special menu last Saturday? Was Mr Charles down here for that?'

'Well now let me see.' She seems to take forever determining whether my father has been down to talk about the menu which was less than a week ago. 'That'd be that special bridge day.'

'It would be, and do they always have a special meal on bridge days?!

'Mostly they do but usually Miss Patricia sorts out what they're 'aving, but not this time. I remember thinking it was strange, but I recognised some of Miss Patricia's favourites, so I suppose it didn't make any difference really. Now then, let me see.' I dread her pauses they are like the brief interludes in plays or music recitals; like having to wait for pedestrians to cross the road; all comparatively brief but so very annoying.

'The menu, 'Cetta, come along dear heart it was only five days ago.'

'Yes, it was Watercress Salad, then Duck stuffed with asparagus and artichoke – I never - 'eard of that before, in the end I had to ask Miss Patricia to find me some, ending with that new thing, what's it called, Pavlova. I know that 'cos I didn't have to stew up any fruit, it was that special. Then o' 'course there were cocktails flyin' all over the place: before during and after dinner. My Lord knows what was in 'em mind, I just left that to Mr John and Mr William. Does that help, miss?'

'It does, thank you. 'Cetta. I didn't know that my brother

was at the dinner.'

'Oh yes, miss. We 'avent seen him for a while now, he's usually in and out in darkness when we's all asleep o' course, I expect he just needed some more money from Mr Charles and Mr Charles found him something useful to do while he was 'ere. That's usually why he hardly ever comes out in daylight.'

'Thank you 'Cetta. I expect I'll have to ask you some more questions later on but that's all for the moment.' I smile, turn and leave the kitchen before 'Cetta drops any more bombshells for me to add to my pile of information.

I return to the shelter of my room to re-schedule what I now know:

Brother William has appeared out of nowhere and was at dinner if not playing bridge.

John and William were serving cocktails all the time as demanded by the diners.

Father was in the kitchen sorting out the menu with cook, presumably trying to ensure that whatever was eaten could have had poison added to it without affecting the flavour. Assuming it was poison that killed poor old Alan and, I suppose, that Father is the killer.

Patty usually played a part in determining the menu, but she didn't mention why she wasn't there - is that suspicious?

The meals before bridge were quite common so the arrival of different, trial, new dishes, like Pavlova, which had barely been seen other than in the most expensive hotels and restaurants, were by no means unusual and could also have had poison added to them without anyone knowing a change in taste, not if they hadn't tasted them before.

John sometimes visits the kitchen for no apparent reason.

Now what I really need to find is a poison.

Chapter Twenty One

It's unusual that William has ventured into the house for food on a Saturday and joined the family for an actual meal, albeit for an alternative motive. I shall need to have a meeting with Frank before I go any further, if only because I still have yet to receive any report. It's hard to imagine a report on the goings on the Creek area that doesn't in some way involve William, because that's where the pubs are. I also need an explanation for why he has yet to find anything for me and that he has not yet asked Jenny to commit it to paper.

I would have no objection to travelling through the town to Frank's office if the journey wasn't so increasingly repulsive and when I get there the degree of trust is so limited. Faith in somebody who is so hard to find and takes so long to gain such basic information gives me no confidence in the man, indeed the level of my confidence in the accuracy of any information he might find is, already, depleted.

I don't doubt that Maggie would enjoy a journey through the countryside for a change and a small detour is not without its interest for me. My levels of concentration are far less when driving than when I'm simply standing around at a party talking to people, thus a visit to Frank's wonderful little office could be a useful explanation for my disappearance.

The countryside route is really quite pleasant as it delays any contact with the major roads of the area. If I remember correctly – it's a while since I took this route – I turn right and pass some lowly council houses on the left with yet another hop field on my right.

It may please you to know that I have decided that after this one, I am no longer going to mention hop fields when I pass them whether they be ones we have seen before, or indeed as this one, where we have not. Continuous mention of the same agricultural feature must be as tiring and irritating for you as it is for me.

A short hill and a sharp turn right brings us into Vicarage Lane. A lane of a level of local beauty I had completely forgotten. The lane twists and turns with a few lonely cottages throughout its length ending in Water Lane which runs through Ospringe and floods regularly fulfilling its name. The Lane culminates at the ubiquitous Dover to London Road. In this instance we cross and head into South Road to soon be on the verges of Faversham and our destination. However, let me take you back in your short journey to the crossroads of Water Lane and the Dover to London Road. Here on the left, at the very junction stands the ancient Maison Dieu museum which has connections with Corners to which we may return as our story unfolds.

When I arrive at the street door of Frank Spillett's office I am surprised that my little car polisher and, more importantly, my little ear-to-the-ground informant is notable by his absence.

While we await his arrival I should note that I will no longer make reference to the condition of Frank's offices, his office doors or the creaky stairs. As so with the endless hop fields you must by now be tiring of their description.

At last I can see Tommy in the distance, and I climb out of the car being careful not to dirty the stark black of my long coat or more particularly the white collar and cuffs which ensconce the relevant parts.

'Tommy, I thought you'd abandoned me and that I was going to have to leave your little kingdom returning later for our conversation.'

'D'you mean you're sorry I 'aint 'ere miss?'

I laugh at his translation, at the hidden knowledge and understanding lurking beneath his rough, grubby exterior. There must be a great intelligence in that head of his, desperate to be released and used for the greater good, but which society subdues and keeps locked away.

'I do, Tommy, I do. Have you anything for me?'

'That's why I wasn't here when you arrived, miss. I was talking to one o' the lads in the North Creek Mob.'

'Was it useful?'

'Yeah, it was. He said that one of their bosses was asked to get poison a few weeks ago and one of the South Creek lot to hunt out what poison they needed; the killers, not the gangs themselves. He said that the killers are makin' it hard for them to be traced; word is that they're very clever and are puttin' down lots of false trails so that the police and you'll find it hard to follow. He also said that as far as he knows the police are doing bugger all and that they're leaving all the work down to you. Seems unfair to me and to my squealers too so, I'd get the old bill to start doin' their share or my friends might take it on instead. See?'

'You're right Tommy it is unfair, and I understand what you're saying – at least I think I do.' I hold up my hand as he takes a deep breath before trying to explain it all to me. 'I'll get hold of DI Drabble and sort out what they're doing. Even though they don't seem to be doing anything.'

'Begin' your pardon, miss, but it 'aint him who's doin' it no more.'

'And just how do you know that? Or indeed, how did you know it was – should have been – him doing it in the first place'

He ignores my questions as I suppose I expected him to do. 'This mate of mine told me that too. They don't trust 'im anymore 'cos he's getting nowhere, and they need someone who can. That's what my mate says anyhow.'

'Do you have a name for this new detective, Tommy?'

'Not yet, I'm workin' on it. Should 'ave it by this afternoon though.'

'I'll come back for it, if that's okay."

He nods and looks around and as he does so I see him change, I get a look at the real Tommy or whatever his name is. I'm beginning to learn who he is if perhaps not his name, I know who he works for, me and The Gangs but not who he's answerable to – if anyone. I know there is something about Tommy that doesn't sit straight and now I have another puzzle, another mystery if not a crime to unravel and all I know is that both are related. How and why I have no idea, but I must find somebody who does.

Chapter Twenty Two

'You've just caught him this time; he was just about to go out.' Jenny smiles because we both know that he was only about to go out because he had seen me arrive at the front giving him time to leg-it out of the back.

'Mrs Matcham, how lovely to see you; we keep missing each other and nearly did again. Do sit down, Jennifer, you'd like tea I expect?'

'No, thank you not this time. I'd far rather see the reports you have prepared for me, setting out who is involved, what they have done or what they have not done and why and then what you have discovered so that I can see how effectively you are using the vast sums of my money. Because of course if you are not making any progress the final payment will not be made. I don't believe that would be in either of our interests, would it?'

I pause to take breath and for Frank to come up with an answer that I know and he suspects will not be acceptable. If he is sensible he will already be thinking of an additional answer which explains why he didn't tell me that in the first place and so on and so on. However, I am ready for him at every level. What he does not seem to realise – although he should – is that I am, albeit an amateur, involved in and used to his field of investigation; I have used some if not all of the excuses or reasons that he will eventually accumulate in what I have confirmed to my satisfaction is his tiny brain and, I suspect, with greater aplomb and to greater effect.

I did, as I will remind him, employ him to dig around his seedy little area to obtain all the information that was available, and which will undoubtedly point the finger at the murderer if there is one. I acknowledge that without his help I would have failed but since appointing him I have acquired my friend Tommy who seems well appointed to provide all I ask of him at the cost of polishing Maggie and taking him and her for the occasional drive.

'Well, it's like this, Mrs Matcham – Alicia: men and women are reluctant to tell me anything in case the word gets back to the gang bosses who then take out their revenge on the grasses. It's not safe you see. So, it's taking me rather longer than I expected, and it's cost me more than I expected to get what little I have been given.'

'Frank, we go back a long way - at least, our families do - and I employed you based on the assumption that the quality of the service provided by your father had been passed down to you, his son. Clearly my assumption was flawed. We will go back to my initial instructions, for which you were as I recall paid handsomely. Firstly why have I not had an initial report from you telling me of your concerns and why the difficulties exist and how to get round the problem and secondly why haven't I had a second report giving me the information you have obtained and at what cost and what your proposals are for taking the investigation further and at what additional cost?'

'You did ask me to keep my investigations and findings confidential and even to type up the reports myself. As you will recall, I did say that typing wasn't my strong point and that it would take longer than if Jenny did it but still you didn't want me to ask Jenny out there,' he points to the outer office 'to type up my findings on my behalf. The typing and all the filing take time, particularly the typing, I don't know if you realise quite how much.'

'Mr Spillett, Frank, I hear what you say, of course I do, but I happen to know as I'm fairly sure you know that I know, that despite my specific instructions to the contrary, Jenny has typed up anything you have given her to type and she has similarly filed anything away that I instructed you to file. Your excuses are therefore both inaccurate and unacceptable. Unless of course, unless you have accumulated an excessive amount of information, sufficient to enable me to go to the police and ask them to make an arrest subject to them confirming that our information is sufficient for them to charge one or more people for the murder of Mr Alan Broadoak, If, however that is not the case, then I shall expect you to tell me why I should continue to employ your services, or rather the services of Jennifer and yourself.'

'Yes, well Mrs Matcham, Alicia, I agree that I have broken your confidence with Jennifer for all the reasons I gave you at the time you first employed me. In the first instance I did identify a number of people in the area of The Creek and beyond who I should be speaking to and who, particularly were not connected in any way to either of The Creek Gangs. That took much longer than I expected because for obvious reasons I had to protect those people who would be passing information. Once I had that network of people sorted out, I then began collecting the information we need. I am now about to give Jenny a report to type and to send to you for reading. When you have read it, I think you will see just how much I have been able to get from my sources and how much closer we are to finding Mr Broadoak's murderer. And I am convinced that he was murdered, although I have to find out why which will in turn of course, help me, sorry us, to confirm who the murderer is.'

'Well, Frank, I must congratulate you on what you say you have done. If you have made so much progress I would have expected at least three reports. I have none.'

'But – .'

'No buts, Frank, I need those or that report, and I need it within twenty four hours, because it is very important.' I lean forward at this point because I know that that has a greater impact and shows superiority in strength than sitting back in a rickety old chair. 'Right?'

'Of course.' He looks down at his desk and the array of paper strewn across the badly scored leather centre panel.

'And this time don't rely on Jenny to give me the information over a cup of tea and rather dry biscuits.' He smiles and that is not the right thing to do, it infuriates me. 'Do not smile, Frank. You do not have time to smile. You GET MY REPORT DONE or I shall have to speak to my other, out of area informer.'

I get up and walk towards the door, as I slam it shut I can almost hear Frank scribbling the words on a sheet of paper for Jenny to read and type sooner rather than later. She's smiling as I pass her desk and I wink as a spoiled cat winks when it finds the cream.

Chapter Twenty Three

Now, I think it's about time I spoke to the rozzers, as I believe Tommy thinks of them and although his informant thinks otherwise I suspect that DI Drabble will be still in charge.

Faversham Police Station is located in a short leafy lane which goes nowhere else except to the Parish Church – which may well feature in our later chapters – and provides one of the outer walls to the town's local brewery. The police station is of a stark brick construction which represents the strength and centre of control that the Police should display. Parking unfortunately has yet to be created other than for the force's own vehicles and I am forced therefore to pull up against the footpath in the somewhat narrow road and hope that there are no emergencies which would require police vehicles to leave at great speed. At the enquiry desk I am informed that DI Drabble is in his office and a lowly constable disappears to see if the station head would see me.

He would and I am shown into a brown office, brightened only by DI Drabble's bright blue suit. His smile was welcoming and his welcome cheery, too much so that I was suspicious of his motives for seeing me or that he was searching for information and believed that such behaviour would make it easier for me to 'spill the beans'.

'Mrs Matcham, good morning, how are you?'

'I am well, Detective Inspector, thank you.'

'Please sit down, what can I do for you? Sorry, tea, coffee?'

'Coffee, thank you.'

He starts with a statement of rather quaint antiquity: 'You will remember that there was and remains some doubt about the manner of Mr Alan Broadoak's death at Corners in Brogdale Road.'

'Indeed I do.'

'Mr Broadoak clearly died from a heart attack which was confirmed by Dr Hudson and accepted by Mr Whitten. I seem to remember that their Butler – Staples, I think his name is – and one of the daughters – your sister presumably – suspects murder. I think Mrs Whitten followed her husband's belief.'

'I am impressed by the detail of your recall.' Drabble shrugs as if to say that it was nothing and that he is a very efficient police officer.

'You are correct and Miss Patricia Whitten has asked me to investigate Mr Broadoak's death just to get a second opinion you understand.' He may be many things but DI Drabble is not stupid.

'You mean for you to see if he was murdered and by whom.' There is no animosity, argument or implication of obstruction. 'I have the file here, now let's see.' He opens the file and mumbles as he looks through what the paragraphs hold. I stare around his office which leaves no sense of warmth or welcome. There are one or two papers stuck to the wall behind him and a cabinet which presumably held other files or perhaps his lunch. The electric light is old and has not been brought up to fashion, but then no aspect of the building that I've seen has been either. At last he has finished bringing himself up to scratch with the case. 'It all seems quite obvious, Mrs Matcham we cannot believe that it is anything other than a heart attack although I know it will not necessarily be good for the household's image.'

'I'm afraid I can't see how their image is affected but at any rate it's not that that I am concerned with Detective Inspector, it's whether however unlikely Mr Broadoak was murdered. I'm not sure what makes you think that its heart attack. That has never been a possible outcome. So, back to the murder.'

He says, with some disbelief in his voice: 'Why should he have been?'

'Mr Broadoak was a very healthy by all accounts man. He had worked hard at making sure that he was, and he led a perfectly healthy and active life. This has been confirmed by his friends and in particular Mrs Whitten and Mrs Saynor with whom he played bridge every Saturday. Mr Whitten and Mr Staples are less convinced of this and agree with the heart attack verdict.'

'And?'

'From what I have discovered so far, I too am convinced that he was murdered.'

'Why do you think that? Are you saying that I should have looked into his death further and that I am derelict in my duty?

I shake my head denying any such thing.

'I believe that you have some experience in such investigations because I have spoken to some of my colleagues and they confirm that you have had some success. For that reason only

I am prepared to allow you to continue without charging you with impersonating a police officer.'

'Thank you Detective Inspector. Of course, once I have sufficient evidence I shall pass everything to you in order to make the arrest,'

'Of course you will, that was never in question; so what are you here for?'

'To keep you up to date,' he raises his eyebrows disbelieving that part of my answer, 'and to ask if you already have any evidence that will help me in my enquiries.' At this he laughs having fully expected to my asking this.

'Okay, Mrs Matcham, here is our file; I am going to make us a cup of coffee and to talk to one of my constables about another case. You must note that I cannot let that file leave this building.'

There is a twinkle in his eye, a feature I have never seen in my limited dealings with him. 'I understand, Detective Inspector,' and as he leaves his office I begin searching through the few papers and records he has gathered so far. There isn't much and little that I haven't got already. The coffee never arrives although DI Drabble does.

'Thank you Detective Inspector, I shall leave you in peace.' I get up and walk towards the door, as I open it I turn to look at him again, 'Just one more thing, if I may,' he nods and smiles again aware that I am adopting the frequently used ploy to unsettle an accused, 'I have heard that you had been removed from the investigation and replaced by another DI because the case was really closed. Is that true?'

'You are not the only one who listens to rumours that are untrue or that are red herrings, goodbye, Mrs Matcham.'

I leave his office feeling that a degree of support is available from the police or at least from DI Drabble which encourages me to carry on. He also believes that Broadoak might have been murdered but has no idea how to prove it or by whom.

I deliberately asked him nothing about who Tommy was, in case he would want to see him to give authority to carry on, Tommy would never do that however much he trusted me. I have nothing to go on other than there is something odd about him, more to him.

I leave the police station and decide to wander along to the Church for no other reason than that it's there. Before I get hardly any distance at all a boy leaps from between two of the bushes that are trying hard to disguise the police station and bar my way. As if I couldn't have guessed, it was Tommy.

'What are you doing up here, Tommy?'

'I could ask you the same, miss you wern' giving me up was you, not telling where I was or what I was doin"

'Of course not. I was trying to find out if they had any information that's useful to us.'

'An' was 'vere?'

'No, not really.'

'Well I got some good stuff.'

'What, who killed him?' I laugh knowing this is impossible.

'No, but I knows who the bloke from outside was what gave the poison to the bloke in the South Creek Gang.'

'So?'

'We know who started the whole fing off don't we? We can get how the poison got into the bloke what got killed.'

'But we don't want that, we want the name or names of the people who started the whole thing off. The people who asked

142

this bloke –as you call him – to get the poison in the first place. Whose idea it was to get Broadoak killed that's what we want to know and why they wanted to do it, although it's true that we want all this other information as evidence when the police charge the original killers and the way we're going we shall never know how long that will take, if of course it will lead us to the person who actually killed him even if we don't know how and we ever find them.' I've given poor Tommy one of my outbursts. Long sentences which make perfect sense to me as I'm saying them, perhaps less sense when I think of them afterwards and absolutely no sense to most people who are listening especially a poor young boy who's only trying to help.

'Yes, miss.' He's agreeing but doesn't really mean it because of course he can't possibly understand.

'Don't look so disappointed, Tommy what you've got is brilliant and very useful, as you say we know where the poison was going. Do you suppose it's someone down in the Creek? Could it be one of your mates?' I pat him on the head so that I hope he knows I'm joking. He looks up and grins so that I know he does. 'Come on, I expect you'd like a drive in the car, yes? Hop into the passenger seat and I'll take you home. He's up in the seat before I can open the car door and drop my brief case onto the back seat. 'Hold on, Tommy. We'll go round the long way if you like.' I'm turning the car round as he suddenly ducks down and drops into the foot well in the front passenger seat.'

'What is it?'

'They'll catch me, and they mustn't. I'll be in trouble if they catch me, quick, miss, we need to go.' I turn the car as quickly as I can, but the lane isn't very wide, and I need to take several attempts before I'm successful. There are now two constables standing outside the station smoking and chatting and watching me. Fortunately neither of them offers to help and I think I can guess what they're thinking but today I don't care.

'Okay, Tommy, off we go. I sort of lurch beyond the police station to the end of the road and turn left away from the busy high street past the village green, under a narrow iron railway bridge and out into the fresh green countryside. We stop and take deep breaths, certain that we haven't been followed and Tommy clambers back into the seat. 'Do I want to know why you were afraid of the rozzers? No, thought not.' I give him one of my disapproving but understanding smiles as I look at him over the top of my sunglasses. Come on, Tommy let's enjoy ourselves for a little while. The murder can wait.'

His eyes light up.

Chapter Twenty-Four

Another day, another interview, I really don't think I can call them interrogations, they are too friendly. What I really need is to be able to speak to Alan Broadoak, but in his absence my mother seems to know him as well as any other and she might be persuaded to spill a few more of those good old beans.

I find her in the summerhouse again, it's her favourite place. The grass is still glistening after the early morning dew and everyone wishes that they're more raindrops soaking the ground. Anyway, I walk along the path round the edge of the grass and disturb Patty who is deep into one of her favourite books on the life of Emily Pankhurst. She tells everybody who cares to listen, that she finds Emily's references to the war inspiring against the loss of her father and two brothers in the conflict. Patty looks up and smiles, knowing my understanding.

Mother looks up anticipating the purpose of my visit. 'Hello dear, have you come to persecute me about the murder?'

'Not persecute just ask I hope.'

She smiles. 'Fire away then.'

'I wanted to talk to you about Alan Broadoak before you married father and afterwards. I know that Alan was only fourteen when you and father were married but I hear that he – Alan that is – was already a bit of a ladies' man – well girls' man I suppose – with rumours about him getting some older girls and young women pregnant. Do you know anything about that? It can't be true surely.'

'Well, yes I suppose the rumours could be right. A good friend of mine from our schooldays – Fanny her name was – always had lots of boys around her. She was a beautiful girl now I come to think about it and clever too. Of course we were a lot older than Alan but that didn't stop us. They seemed to spend more time together than either of them did with anyone else.' She pauses, reminiscing about her schooldays the good and the bad, 'He was a big boy for his age tall, strong, confident -', there's a twinkle in her eyes, a twinkle of jealousy, '- and she was as I say, so beautiful, a good looker in her late twenties – just about twice Alan's age, about his height. They looked suited for each other and they certainly set tongues wagging.

'Just like the rest of we normal girls I kept on the lookout for men of our own age and I was out to enjoy myself. I'm afraid there were plenty of men, even some foreigners during the early couple of years into the war – we're talking the Boer War now of course – and most girls, a lot of my friends had to take what they could get.' She laughs reliving those heady days and a misspent youth. 'But not me, I was already spoken for as they say.'

'Were you? To whom?'

'Now, did you know that your father was married before we got hitched?'

I certainly did not know! 'No, I certainly didn't and I don't suppose Patty does either.'

'Well he was, to Fanny as it happens, and he and I were

having an affair until –'

'Until when?'

'Until she died. Fanny, poor girl, and she was only twenty seven – same age as me of course, lovely girl and nobody deserves to die that young, the cancer went right through her –', She pauses again, and a few tears ease their way from her eyes. 'but it did leave your father free and we got married two years later and you were born just short of nine months after that.' She looks me in the eye and raises her eyebrows. I know why of course but there's no sign of guilt on her face.

'And that was it?

'Not really, I confess that Alan and I had an affair that began when you were only five and lasted for four years and ended when he had accident in the factory and at about the same time I was carrying Patricia.'

'And?' God this is hard work.

'More a 'but' really, Alan and I started up our affair again which we carried on and off over the last twenty years, stopping and starting every few years until last weekend when he died.'

'Even though he and Patty were having an affair for – I don't know - the four years.'

I unashamedly nod, but then I'm a widow myself so what's wrong with that.

'There's no excuse for him sleeping with mother and daughter although I expect that it's not unheard of in these enlightened days, I still find it hard to believe. During my early married years I knew he'd been sowing his seed around and about and that didn't bother me, not to start with but over the years we got more struck and then, ten years ago we agreed to keep our relationship special. Just the two of us. And it lasted ten years.

A record. We were talking about my divorcing your father, but Alan died before I could talk to Charles.'

'Quite the philanderer.'

'That's not what I called him. He was a lovely man.'

'I'm not surprised.'

'He was a really lovely man, Alicia, whatever you might think of him. He was an upstanding gentleman trusted and loved by many around the town for his quiet understanding and reliable privacy for one's secrets. He was gentle and kind to everyone he met. And he was fantastic in bed.'

'It sounds as though father has a number of reasons to kill Alan though, doesn't it?'

'Assuming he knows, I honestly don't think he does. We were very careful. And don't forget, Charles is having an affair with Joan Saynor – you did know about that, didn't you? – so he has no reason to get up on his high horse to start talking about morality.'

'So he does know, and their affair is his way of paying you back.'

'Are those all of your questions dear?'

'And more I didn't even think I would ask!'

She's looking at me with mournful eyes now, the twinkle has gone, the sparkle has left her life and she doesn't know where to go from here.

Chapter Twenty Five

I have been making comprehensive notes of my interviews and when taken together I am, so far totally confused. There are too many affairs and marriages involved for either me or, I imagine, anyone else to sort out. What I need is not only to speak impossibly to the dear departed Alan but also my father. If only I was having an affair with one of them or, indeed had had an affair with one of them it would be easier for me to understand the intricacies of the events. One thing is certain and that is that Alan Broadoak was unreliable both as a lover and quite probably a husband – although nobody has mentioned a Mrs Broadoak, we all seem to have assumed that one does not exist. On the other hand perhaps there isn't one which would at least explain why Alan was so free with his affections.

I am telephoning Dr Hudson at his London rooms now, to discuss Alan Broadoak's death.

'Ah, Mrs Matcham, I thought I might hear from you at some point. Of course by all means come to my office – unless you would prefer me to come to Corners.'

We agree that we would meet at his rooms at eleven o'clock

by which time we would each have our papers in order to save time during our discussion. Although the timing of the meeting means my catching an incredibly early train – within the next quarter of an hour – I am not entirely sure what I can gain from him except to discuss the deceased's' death but after previous discussions anything could emerge.

I am greeted by a nurse who, by her manner and movement between the rooms is also his secretary and comforter when the need arises. She is quite pretty with a well-formed body and long light brown hair tied in a bun at the back of her head. As seems to be the way of the ladies in Town she is considerably younger than Dr Hudson and one of them will undoubtedly be having an affair with other men and women no doubt some of those I have been interviewing.

The office clock strikes eleven as the Secretary knocks on the red mahogany door with a brass plate announcing the occupant as Dr S B Hudson GP. She doesn't wait to be called and opens the door. Dr Hudson is sitting at a large double sided oak desk in a substantial office, the walls lined with bookshelves weighted down with the encyclopaedic tomes of his profession, their spines show very little signs of use and my eyes are drawn to each in turn rather than to my host who rises immediately to welcome me.

'Mrs Matcham, what a pleasure it is to meet you, I have heard so much from your father. Please – do sit down and we shall talk.'

With a flourish he indicates the chair in which he would like me to sit; it is opposite another in front of which he stands and speaks to the secretary.

'Evelyn, can you bring in some coffee please for our guest

– he turns and smiling, raises his grey bushy eyebrows asking for my acceptance – yes, coffee please and my usual. Thank you.'

He refers to her by name but it's irrelevant to my enquiries and I have forgotten it seconds after its used.

'Dr Hudson, thank you for seeing me at such short notice, you must have many patients lined up to see you either here at your consulting rooms or at their homes.'

'Mrs Matcham, I am at your disposal for as long as you wish and my patients are of such insignificant wealth that none is particularly bothered whether I delay our consultation or not, I am the only doctor within three miles of here. They haven't any choice who they see!'

'Thank you all the same.'

'How can I help you, Mrs Matcham? You're here about Alan Broadoak's death I assume and well, it's quite straightforward, as you know. A heart attack plain and simple.'

'I thought originally you had agreed with DI Drabble that it was a heart attack. We now have strong evidence that it wasn't a heart attack but murder which puts a different picture on the whole event.' I stare at him, trying to see a reaction of the mistake in the cause of death, but there is none. Nevertheless, I file the information away as yet someone else who is an unreliable recounter of the truth – assuming I ever get to the bottom of what that actually is.

'Well yes, it would, but how and why do you think that and presumably Inspector Drabble agrees with your suspicions does he? And anyway, I'm interested why you're investigating instead of the police.'

'He does now. So I'd like to talk to you about his – Alan

151

Broadoak's – medical history and then what could have killed him and how it was administered. Then we can try to work out what actually killed him. And I'm investigating because I'm a member of the family who's found out things that the police – in Brogdale, Bletchley and London – have been unable to do.'

'Right, I see, well normally of course I wouldn't be able to talk to you about anything personal, but as he's dead I can't see any reason why I shouldn't.'

'Good, thank you. Can we start with his medical history then? Had he been a healthy man?'

'How far back do you want me to go?'

That's a good question because I'll have to guess what's sensible and I could easily miss something that I/we later find out is critical. 'As far as you think is necessary. Has he lived here all his life?'

'I'm afraid not. He's only been my patient for the last twenty-five years so anything before that and you'd need to speak to let me see – ah yes a Dr Christian Sheppard in Harley Street.

'Okay, well we'll just go back twenty-five years then.' He's ruffling through the papers sighing and frustrated. Every few minutes he looks up at me, wishing he'd never agreed to such a time consuming exercise. He has no idea what's coming yet. 'I'm only interested in any major problems.'

'Of course.' He sits back on his heals holding a small pile of papers of varying sizes and colours. 'I think this is the lot, would you like me to just give you the bare bones of the different problems or would you care to read through them yourself.'

'I always find doctors' writing hard to read. Would you mind?'

He sits back in his desk chair.

'The first problem he wanted to see me about was twenty-two years ago when he had minor chest pains. I prescribed less work and more exercise.'

'But no drugs.'

'No. He came back to me with more pains of the same sort and we talked about his life, what he ate and drank mainly. I told him to change his diet and reduce his drinking. That seemed to cure him because I didn't see him again until the beginning of -.'

'But no drugs.' He looks at me sternly as if questioning his prescription and my interruption.

'As I was saying - In 1914 he came to me for evidence to get him out of the conscription and out of the war – not even a commission. I can tell you that I wasn't particularly happy about that and said he was fighting fit. That he must go and fight for his country. I suppose he must have done, because he didn't come back until 1916 when he came in because he had shrapnel in his left arm and left leg. It took the military hospital a while to sort him out on a basic level – it's all they could do with the limitations to their available care. Then he came back here for more hospital treatment before he could walk or use his arm properly. Even then he wasn't much use to anyone; he was still in pain and still couldn't think straight.

'When Charles Whitten came back he took him on as his butler. He'd been Charles's batman during first two years of the war and apparently saved his life on a couple of occasions. There were one or two minor problems which had started during his time in the trenches - this was before he took his shrapnel and was shipped out. Charles felt he owed him a favour but soon discovered that he was little more than useless as a butler so was pleased when Broadoak inherited some estate or other and had to leave. The new chap is much better I gather.'

'Didn't you get any information about his war injuries from the army hospital? You didn't mention any visits or problems, major or otherwise while he was working for Mr Whitten. Were there none at all?'

'Easy one first, he did come and see me about the minor problems of – of – some discomfort he'd suffered in the early months of the war flaring up again, but they were soon sorted out. I was supposed to get the army information after the war, but you know what it was like, absolute chaos. We were lucky to get him back, but the papers got lost somewhere along the line.'

'And again doctor, nothing since then?'

'Nothing major, I fixed his leg as best I could and helped with which exercises he could do. Then, in 1929 he contracted pneumonia which I treated with leeches – the accepted treatment at the time and now actually. It only lasted a few weeks.'

'A few weeks?'

'Now that I look it was just over two months.'

'What did you prescribe?'

'As I said, leeches and towards the end of the infection I gave him morphine to kill the pain.'

My medical knowledge is not deep, and I don't have any information as to whether what he gave Alan Broadoak was appropriate. I shall have to investigate. 'Anything after the pneumonia?'

'His heart was giving him trouble again and as far as I could see, his lifestyle was the best it could have been. So I prescribed more morphine.'

'Did he become addicted to the drug?'

'There was a risk, but I had no evidence that that was the case. In any event I also prescribed Potassium Chloride to reduce the risk of a low blood pressure which in itself is a side effect of the morphine and one drug tends to reduce the chance of addiction in the other.'

I felt that the problem had been dealt with rather dismissively. It was not a risk, possibly not, but it's something that might just have affected the means of his death. I shall make further enquiries elsewhere.

'So you remain satisfied with the cause of death? A heart attack? There is no chance in your view that it could have been murder? If he didn't die of a heart attack, then would you agree the most likely cause would be by poisoning and, if so have you any idea what the poison might have been?

'I remain satisfied with my original diagnosis, as does Detective Inspector Drabble I believe.'

'He was, but he now accepts the possibility that the cause might be murder and has agreed that I can ask some questions to see if that were the case. If for the moment we accept that it was murder by poisoning, which poison do you think is the most likely the murderer would have used?'

Chapter Twenty Six

My attempt to get further information from Dr Hudson failed with little ceremony following the inconvenient entrance by his secretary:

'I'm sorry, Dr Hudson, Mrs Matcham, but I have just received a telephone call from the daughter of one of our most important patients to say that her mother is suffering premature contractions and that in view of the problems she has experienced during previous pregnancies she feels that it would be beneficial if you would please visit her immediately. I heard a cry while we were speaking. It was a horrible scream really; one as might be heard when attacked in a dark alley in the middle of the night, so it appears that you really must leave as soon as possible.'

'Thank you, Evelyn and please there is no need to dramatize what you heard, I'm sure that Mrs Matcham is aware of the cries that expectant mothers emit prior to giving birth. I'm sorry, Mrs Matcham but you need to excuse me if you understand that Mrs Illingworth's needs are far greater than discussing Mr Broadoak's death any further.'

'Certainly doctor and whilst I have no personal experience of giving birth, I have been present in a house where such an event has occurred. Please, we can perhaps take up our discussions in the near future?'

He appears to have lost interest in my presence and is busily packing his bag with the special equipment required for this particular consultation.

I continue, 'I can see that there is no point in my waiting for your return and will contact your secretary later today to arrange another appointment.' I turn to look at Evelyn who in turn looks at her doctor with owlish eyes and then back to me before smiling and nodding in agreement. She is so, I suppose so perfectly suited as a doctor's secretary. I imagine she presents much needed comfort to visiting patients and I wonder what my reaction would be should I have been ill. I am hopeful of a meeting sooner rather than later. Dr Hudson has disappeared before I have finished speaking to him.

Evelyn pre-empts my request: 'Perhaps you can telephone tomorrow to make another appointment, Mrs Matcham? I shall need to consult doctor's diary before we speak, and I am rather busy at the moment.'

I find it hard to imagine that her chores can be so immediate that we cannot arrange my meeting straight away while I am here but she is clearly someone who wishes to be in charge of the smallest of additional tasks, so I agree. 'Of course, thank you. I hope Mrs Illingworth recovers from her, from her…' I have no idea what to say in these circumstances, recovery sounds as though the child is unwanted, and it is not for me to assume that to be the case.

'Thank you, I'll pass your concern to the doctor.'

She won't, but I felt the need to say something and the matter passes irrelevantly into the clouds. When I leave the rooms I am aware that it is time for lunch, and it seems a waste not to eat at my club. Handsomes seem to be at a premium but one appears at the distant Regent's Park end of the road and as I walk towards him I begin hailing him in the hope of preventing anyone else grabbing his fare.

'Park Lane Hotel, please.'

'Madam.' He nods and I'm somehow comforted by the clip clopping of the horse as we run down Harley Street towards Cavendish Square and then Park Lane. No doubt following my dismounting, the 'cab will proceed to the busy Victoria Station as if for my train to Faversham after lunch. But not yet. It's a pleasant enough journey, watching the different cars trundling past among the horse drawn Handsomes. During my brief fare and though I am in love with London, the roads themselves are dreary places, the pavements provide some relief with a few ladies walking short distances wearing shawls of blue and brown. Cavendish Square is a splash of a sort of green, the trees in full falling brown leaf and other peoples' clothing being of bright yellows, greens and brighter shade of blue. Hyde Park too is pleasant enough although we only pass a short way along the road before stopping outside the Park Lane Hotel.

'Good afternoon, Mrs Matcham what a pleasure to see you again, are you joining us for lunch?'

A warm welcome by the Concierge at such a place is so comforting. 'Good afternoon, yes, I am. Is Mr Hind in the bar by any chance?'

He smiles, knowing that Mr Hind is invariably at the bar during lunch.

'I believe so madam.' He ushers me to the Palm Court where I can see George Hind resting at the bar drinking one of his many favourite cocktails – he drinks such a variety that I can't see how he can call any of them his favourite! He waves and I return his welcome. As I walk demurely towards him, threading my way between the tables I nod and smile as I pass the odd couple or individual I've seen or to whom I have spoken to on previous occasions, though none of them can be considered more than mild acquaintances. The pianist is softly playing his routine which although we have all heard it before continues to act as a soothing background to our drinks and meals. It seems an expedition to reach George and thankfully he has already ordered my genuine favourite cocktail: a Bees Knees. The second went down particularly easily, the first having washed away the dust from the journey and the third was strong enough to dull the hubbub around us and smooth enough to return me to the relaxed mood I was seeking.

'My poor, dear girl you look frightful.'

'You are the best friend a girl could possibly want, George! Such flattery and adulation.' I laugh and realise that what he said is just what I needed – to make me laugh. 'Thank you, George. If the club rules permitted, I would most certainly buy you a drink, darling.'

'Generous to a fault, sweet lady. You never change.'

'You would be surprised, George but I'm sure you wouldn't want me to if truth were told, would you?' He smiles as I continue, 'but if you were to want a different me, what or who would you choose?'

'I can't imagine you as anything but yourself, your beautiful sparkling slender bundle of fun, so having cleared that up may I top up your sparkle?' He waves at Jamie our lovely barman who doesn't need any more asking – he knows exactly what we need

– and in no time at all each of us has again been furnished with large cocktails – do you know, I forgotten which one it was!'

George goes straight for the jugular: 'Now then, darling, tell me how your investigations are going.'

'Is that all you want from me? Not how are you Alicia? Did you have a good journey? Who were you seeing in Harley Street? Why come all the way to Town? How are your family? But no, all you want to know is who in my family is a murderer!'

'My dear, Alicia I'm so sorry. Which of those questions would you prefer to answer? Because I do of course wish to ask all those questions too, but it seems that to ask the general question I did, your answer would answer all of the others without necessarily complicating the actual content of your answer?' He leans closer and places a gentle kiss on my left cheek.

'I'm teasing you, George, you're right of course it would and will, all I need is another Beesy Thingy followed by the smashing lunch you're about to buy me and during which I shall shower you with all the details.'

'So, this is going to cost me lunch as well is it?' He never doubted it and would, I'm sure, be distraught had I not accepted his predictable invitation.

'I'm sure you wouldn't want to have your lunch paid for by a lady. That would be most improper. Anyway old thing you're rolling in it, you won't miss another few pounds will you?' He sighs, a friendly sigh and smiles lovingly all the time knowing that I will never marry him if only because he is already married but that he will do anything I ask of him without question. He turns and raises his hand towards the waiter asking to be shown to our table, already booked in his name and which by the time we reach it is now re-laid for two.

The view of Hyde Park is spectacular from this table, the table he commands every time I share lunch with him and no doubt the frequency of his lunching here is also a major factor when he invites another of his beauties to lunch. I could never be accused of being naïve in that regard. We look at the menu and as always I suggest that he orders for both of us. That done he takes a deep breath: 'Now then, darling, I ask again – tell me how your investigations are going?'

'Before I tell you, what have you heard? Even though it's only a few days ago I know you've been down to Faversham since we met here last, so you must have heard something. That cook of yours has ears like an elephant and picks up all the gossip that's going.'

'How dare you cast such aspersions on my poor cook, although she does rather look like an arachnoid I bagged last year in India – '

'You did no such thing and I think you mean a pachyderm if you're trying to be clever and accurate. Arachnoids are rather spider like and therefore generally very small.' What an idiot, he's trying to be clever and it doesn't work, at least with me, and it's pointless anyway when we're talking or trying to talk about a murder and one that's not been a frivolous matter by introducing flippant disagreements on his use of the wrong words.

' – quite but it's true that I have heard rumours about the odd affair mainly because I gather both our cooks have had one or two as well. Now, that isn't good for your family as a whole, particularly if some of them didn't know others were having affairs. Apart from that I've heard nothing and while everyone in our circle does 'it', it's of course quite juicy enough for a member of the Whitten family to be called a gossip.'

'Georgie, darling I'm afraid that makes no sense at all so I shall tell you. Our cook has an incredible imagination poor old thing; I think she must be referring to her younger days and wishing she could have them again. Even if there were any affairs at Corners I wouldn't be able to tell you, that sort of thing is very personal, and you know that. Anyway, as you say, there aren't many big houses where there isn't something going on is there? I've been asking lots of question of lots of people and so far haven't really been able to be sure of anything. I had a good journey thank you. I am well and do my best to look attractive. My family is as well as can be expected after one of their friends has been murdered while playing bridge. I have come to town to spend some time with you of course and to visit Harley Street.'

'Harley Street? You must have encountered the definitive Evelyn then, my word…'

'Nothing exciting or scandalous, I wanted to talk to Dr Hudson about Alan Broadoak he is, after all, the family GP. After all, he was the one who very quickly pronounced Alan Broadoak dead so there were obviously some questions I needed to ask him. Unfortunately, he was called away to an emergency that arose with one of his patients and we were unable to finish our discussions and -.'

Somewhat irritatingly, he completes my sentence for me: '– And anyway even if there were any affairs at Corners you wouldn't be able to tell me, that sort of thing is very personal, and you know that.' Yes, I know but you can't blame a chap for trying, can you.

Now he's being sarcastic but anyway as he knows, he's the last person to whom I would give any personal information to and he knows it. It's a cat and mouse thing and all part of our banter. We eat our first course in almost complete silence, and it wasn't until the roast beef arrived that the eating speed dropped, and the conversation returned.

'How is your family, George? You hardly ever mention them, and you seem to know a lot about me and mine whereas yours, you have kept a great secret. You have a wife who is she and two children of course.?'

'My life is as sacred to me as yours is to you.' He laughs. 'But I see no reason why I shouldn't confirm that what you say is true, Pamela, Frederick and Cassandra in that order. My wife's age is of course a closely guarded secret the children's ages are fifteen and thirteen, regrettably our second child, Samantha died at birth and we – Pamela particularly – are finding it hard to come to terms -you understand.' He looks at the table as a display of reverence but recovers quickly to carry on. 'They have a nanny of course, Matilde, whose age is unfathomable, but who has been with us for fifteen years. My age is also a closely guarded secret to all except my beautiful Alicia.'

'You poor man, I had no idea that you had been through so much pain. To lose an adult member of your family is bad enough but a child – let alone a baby is a tragedy beyond belief.'

I place my hands on his hips, lean forward and in an almost certainly unacceptable action within the club kiss him lovingly on the lips. I squeeze his hands and sparkling goblets of tears appear in his eyes. Our waiter arrives and is about to unleash the reprimand but as he opens his mouth, I put my index finger to my mouth and nod towards George so that he can see that the encounter is one of distress and consolation rather than anything of a sexual nature. Despite his obvious distress,

George dries his eyes, sits back in his chair, smiles and blows me a kiss from the palms of his hands. He nods and I continue:

'That's a lot of information all at once and more than I could have hoped for and pretty much all of it irrelevant to my investigations. What about your mistress?'

'Which one?' He's laughing again now. 'Really, I only have one who's name, age and location will be another of my closely guarded secrets.'

'And the other? I imagine there is another after Matilde left – I assume she was the mother of one or both of your children? Is your wife infertile and Matilde was happy to oblige? I'm sure she was a beautiful girl which made her duty much easier and the French are so romantic.' He flushes confirming my guesses. 'I don't mean any of that as a criticism of course pure speculation to avoid you any embarrassment.'

Droplets now of perspiration are forming on his forehead. His breathing is becoming more laboured and he attempts to stretch his collar to release the pressure on his throat to make it easier to breathe; his eyes are moving rapidly from side to side as he carefully avoids my gaze. As his cheeks redden I feel I should help him a little more because I don't want another death on my hands even if it is of one with whom I'm having lunch. He asks for some water and then some champagne after which he seems fully revived and indicates that he wants me to continue listing what I know!

'Are you sure you're okay?' He nods. 'I know that she lives in Ashford at the edge of the town away from prying eyes. She is very discreet and has only a few clients of which you are one. You visit her no more than three times a week although have been known to squeeze in an extra one if you're having a difficult time at work. Pamela, your wife knows nothing about her – or least you think that she doesn't – and nor does your other mistress. Ashford Eliza knows about both of them if only because you shout their names during frenzied bouts of sex. That's all you use Ashford Eliza for, isn't it? Sex. Sex on Mondays; sex on Wednesdays and sex on – '

'Yes, yes, all right. I have a mistress and – and Ashford Eliza if you will. Now, can we get on?'

'I am just helping you out with how much about your family I knew, and I now know. You need to be careful not to even suggest threatening me because I can be a nasty enemy.' I love George in a strange sort of way. He's not a replacement father figure or anything like that, but he's sort of cuddly loveable and great in bed. And I may need him to do me a favour at some time, so I want to keep him sweet.

'How did you find out about the girls?'

'I'm a private investigator and I investigate private people who might have something that will help me solve a problem with my clients. For instance, you live at the end of Brogdale Road barely half a mile from Corners so I am compelled to find out what I can about you and the others who live at the intervening homes of Laetus, Wilberholme and so on.'

'I can see what you mean but you have summed up my family from top to bottom in a matter of days and I haven't even seen you around my house – any of my houses.'

'More than two?'

'Well, yes but no more mistresses.'

'Very well now, where were we? Ah yes, you asked me why I went to Harley Street and I said to see Dr Hudson and you asked what he'd said; I told you nothing.'

He is still breathing heavily but the sweat on his forehead has vanished and his cheeks are now the normal pink shade of whatever colour heavy drinking men's cheeks are. We've finished our main course and await our pudding: the apple pie here is simply divine.

I say, 'Well, the situation is still the same; I can tell you nothing about my investigations except that they are progressing and that even if there were any bits here and there which might be of interest to you, I wouldn't say anything – couldn't say anything – so does that mean we don't have anything to talk about?'

'Well young lady there must be something I can do to help. What about I keep a look out for who goes in and out of the house? Of the road junction? Something like that.'

'Yes, George, of course there must. I'll let you know.' And I must, he's such a darling.

I can feel his hand on my knee, made easier by the fact that he has moved so that we are sitting at almost ninety degrees to each other not facing each other as most people are and as many others would be. I can now easily stare at the rest of the diners and although it feels as though they are all looking at us wondering whether we are father and a daughter or old man and floozie I really don't care. Even if that is what they're doing, it's none of their business. We look at each other, creating our own special space and smile as we wait for the apple pie. The restaurant slowly quietens as the waiter places our food in front of us and then disappears leaving us alone. George removes his hand from me knee and we eat. When he's finished I feel his hand on my knee again and moving gently up my leg towards my thigh. I turn to look at him now and we both smile. Our

166

game is over, and he hails a passing waiter for his billet-do to sign to have the amount added to his account.

'Thank you for lunch, George I have so enjoyed it as always and you are so generous. I look forward to our next, longer lasting get-together.'

'The pleasure is all mine my dear. All mine. I shall see you to your car – unless you came by taxi in which case...'

'By handsome, thank you and then to Victoria'

The waiter appears as if from nowhere and holds my chair, gently moving it back so that I may stand. He now moves round to do the same for George, we leave him and George turns round to give the man a tip for his discretion if nothing else. Out of the corner of my eye I see the waiter bow, an enormous smile spreading across his face and I know that George has been his customarily, generous self. George walks me to the next cab and we both get in. It is my cab and I insist on giving instructions; this is the time of women's independence; we are the workers and managers of the future so the least he can do is let me decide where we are going. A wind has sprung up and as we turn left on to Park Lane I feel it ruffle my hair. It gets stronger and I am considering raising the top when I realise that it's George's hand playing with me.

'You know, you really are stunningly beautiful.'

'Thank you, kind sir.' I bow my head in actress accentuated fashion to a compliment. I glance left and smile, while somehow keeping my eyes on the road.

'Everything about you is perfect from your head right the way down to your toes. Stunning.'

The cab turns right into a cobbled roadway, a select mews lined with stylish cottages where nobody lives. They are cottages for those with money who need to stop in town after meetings; to keep as their place in town when they want to enhance their standing in front of others at dinner parties; as a place for their gentleman owner to settle for a night, occasionally two, to get things right with the world: occasionally for women to do the same. Here is my hideaway and next door is his. We sometimes go in through his front door or more often he comes into mine and we hide ourselves away from the world, sitting and drinking cocktails or more often, in bed drinking cocktails. And within the next few hours I learn everything he knows and who had told him and things about my own family that I would never have been told and never should have believed from a third party.

For those few hours he is mine.

Chapter Twenty Seven

The traffic was surprisingly busy on my way down from Town, but the drive was nevertheless enjoyable and with the top down I was able to enjoy the wind through my hair. The Medway towns were their usual grubby selves but I'm now in open country on this lovely, straight Roman Road to Faversham there's nothing to match the fields of Kent.

Now, I know you'll be thinking – hang on a moment, she was travelling by train and handsome just now. What I have failed to tell you is that Maggie was parked at Bromley awaiting my return. Parking in Town is increasingly difficult. I have to plan!

You'll remember Ospringe just outside Faversham. I'm hoping to meet Tommy before my next encounter with Frank who, let's be honest is getting a bit of a pain in my side. He's not earning the money I've given him let alone any more that he will no doubt be asking me for soon, but I shan't give any to him, Jenny's worth more than all the hours Frank puts in and Tommy beats them all.

'Evenin', miss, I 'eard you coming down the lane even over all this clatterin'.'

'Hang on, Tommy I'll just get Maggie off the road in case anything else wants to get past.' By the time I've turned the ignition off, Tommy's standing next to the door ready to open it and help me out, he's a real gentleman behind all the grime and swearing. 'Thank you, young man, where do you want to take me today.'

'This way, miss.' There's hesitation then, 'Please.' Then his toothy grin as he rubs his grimy hand up and down on his unwashed trousers that are dirtier than his hands and are full of holes so that most of the time he's rubbing his legs with little success in cleaning his hands. Still, it's an effort and I appreciate that he's trying to help me and that he recognises our class differences. He's holding his hand out for me to hold and how could I – or anybody for that matter – not take it up so I do and give it a little squeeze which is lovingly reciprocated.

'Where are we going, Tommy I really do have to go and see Frank later and not too much later?'

'That's all right, miss, he's out and won't be back for at least an hour and Jenny's got her young man up there although none of us believes that's really what 'e is.'

'What does everybody think he is?'

'Dunno, some sort of spy is what most of 'em is sayin' but I aint going along with that until I knows more. You know what I'm like, miss, I wanna be sure.'

'Quite right too.' You have to admire such high morals in a young boy who'd just as soon steal the purse from your handbag if you weren't watching unless, of course, you were a friend.

Tommy leads me from where Maggie is parked towards the old swing bridge and turns right towards the Creek itself before then left again along a much narrower path than we have just traversed. 'Tommy?'

'Nearly there, miss.'

I can see Joan Saynor's garden where it comes down to the waterside and begin to wonder whether that is our destination. Stonebridge Pond is getting closer and closer and I can't resist it anymore. 'Are we going to that bit of grass over there?' I'm pointing directly at the waterfront and there can be no doubt to which garden I'm pointing. He's gone quiet. 'Well, are we?'

'What if we's were, miss it don't matter does it?'

'Well, that rather depends on what's going to happen when we get there.'

'We're going to see the old lady what lives there, and she'll give us tea and cake – and biscuits if we're good, miss.'

'Does she know my name?'

''Course not.' He's shaking his head as if there is no reason in the world why Joan Saynor should know who I am – whose Tommy's guest is this evening – even if he had told her my name.

'I know the lady, Tom its Mrs Saynor isn't it? Why are we going to see her?' He's looking at me with those huge soulful eyes of his because I have spoilt his surprise, my surprise that was going to make me so grateful that he could have another ride in Maggie but almost as importantly, a surprise that would get me a lot more information. He's obviously worked hard at this because his mouth is turned way down at the sides and he's hanging his head so low that his hair is almost touching the top of his boots. 'Tommy, it's fine, I like Mrs Saynor and I'm very interested in what she can tell me, and it won't be anything she's told me before you can be sure of that. How did you find out about her?'

171

'Hard work, miss, 'ard work. Some of my contacts 'elped. Cost me a bit it did.'

Not the most subtle of hints but I'll see what Joan has for me before I decide on how much to give him. 'Don't worry about that, Tommy I'll sort it out with you later.' We'd stopped for our brief financial discussions, but he grabs my hand again and off we go – him directly in front so that I have little opportunity of which way the narrowing pathway is turning or which holes I have to step over. Eventually we land on Joan Saynor's lawn and walk respectfully up the grass towards her back door. As we pass the apple trees – where the blossom is just hanging on and we can see the small apples forming – there's a sound from the conservatory and Joan Saynor is soon walking towards us.

She speaks to her informant first. 'Hello, Tommy dear have you brought me another one of your friends to see me for a little chat?'

He nods. 'She says she knows you Mrs Saynor, ma'am.'

Joan starts to talk and raises her head to look at me, seemingly unaware of my existence until now. 'Does she dear, I don't… think so … I.'

I smile at her and tilt my head to one side. I'm never sure why one does that but it's sort of asking a question without speaking at all or finishing a sentence that requires something more than just the implied question mark. I'm never sure but this just seems to be an appropriate time for the former.

'Don't you ,Joan, are you sure?'

We're hugging each other now, much to Tommy's consternation as he watches us with a complete lack of understanding.

'We're friends, Tommy, don't worry it'll be fine.'

'Come on in, Alicia it's so lovely to see you in such different circumstances and don't look so worried, Tommy come on your cake, biscuits and tea are waiting for you up there just as always.' She points towards the cottage. He grins again – I just love that toothy grin – and follows us up the lawn to the patio where his tea is laid out on a low table fashioned from pails and planks of wood low enough that he can sit on the ground. 'Tommy likes his meals in the open air, don't you, Tommy?' He has a mouthful of cake and his manners ensure that he nods in reply. 'Our refreshment is in the conservatory where there are chairs with clean cushions!'

Joan has prepared a wonderful high tea for us anticipating that I – or whosoever walked up the lawn with Tommy – would be missing dinner. She's right, I am getting a bit peckish despite the full lunch I demolished almost six hours ago since when my level of exercise, however enjoyable it was, is unusually high. There are cucumber sandwiches, scones with jam and just a little cream and what looks like the most enjoyable fruit cake, the recipe for which I would see as a must if I actually did any baking which I don't. She's pouring tea without even asking whether I would like some sugar – although that would be showing off and inappropriate – and then a dash of milk, the genuine stuff, not the dry powder of the lower classes.

'Well, what do we have here?' She's lifting her cup of tea to her lips while waiting for my reply.

'I'm not really sure, Joan. You were presumably expecting someone to whom you could impart some important information to whom Tommy could pass on for due credit and remuneration. The intermediary – as I think we would call them – would expect that the information would be something I, in my capacity as investigator, would find extremely interesting and useful. Whatever the information, it would be received anonymously.'

'Exactly.'

'Then I'm afraid I don't see the current situation as any different – except that the anonymity element is missing. In fact I think we're better off, because we can actually talk about what you're going to tell me rather than me simply getting some bare facts. I expect Tommy will be paid handsomely for his trouble and I shall continue to trust his information as before.'

'I think you're probably right, my dear except of course some of what I'm going to tell you might be more sensitive now that we know each other. If I were giving it to Tommy to pass on to – as far as I'm concerned – to a complete stranger the detail, well, the details might be phrased differently and their meaning somehow distorted.'

'Now look, Joan, this is silly, just tell me what you were going to tell Tommy without any alteration, and I'll take it as it is. The benefit, as I said, is that after I've heard it and thought it through I can ask you any questions I might have. Now, come on, please tell me what you know…'

Chapter Twenty Eight

It has taken me less than half an hour to get from Joan Saynor's garden back to Maggie and on to my usual parking place under Frank's office. His car is not in sight but as I round the corner to his office I see Jenny's car parked as it usually was, partially hidden in the shadow of a burgeoning oak tree: the acorns will fall on stony ground and come to nothing as, I fear will the oak itself. The long days mean that there is no need for lighting until well into the night which means I can't tell from down here whether she's still in the office or not but it's really too late for me to get entangled with more chatter, Joan may have been, possibly a huge help and it's best to leave things now until tomorrow morning when Frank will certainly not be available for discussion.

The town is quiet as I drive past the Town Hall then up the High Street; at the top of the hill I have to wait at the level crossing. The railway station is on my left and because I still have the top down I watch and also smell the steam falling from the train that's waiting at Platform three to leave for London. The whistle blasts and I marvel at the power of the engine pulling the coaches out of the station. The huge wheels are spinning and if I were a boy I'd know why – and I'd know how the train is ever going to get going, how it's going to get a grip on the railway line before it leaves the station and passes over the road crossing on its long journey. But good heavens, all I want to know – just as I'm sure you do – is when my waiting will be over, and I can get on over the crossing to head up the Mall and on to my temporary home.

Corners is in complete silence as I stop the car at the front of the house and turn off the engine. I'm looking up at the darkening blue sky and I suppose if I were a poet I would already be compiling some rhyming lines with which to wow the crowds but I'm not and have no real interest in anyone who does. My mind is constantly on other more tangible things, like planning a murder and getting away with it or not. I can't help smiling because this would be a perfect place for a murder; Agatha Christie would love it but as it is I'm here to solve the mystery of Alan Broadoak's death – at their bridge table, no less. I approach the front door and its opened by reliable John.

'Good evening, Mrs Matcham I trust you have had a pleasant evening.'

'Dear, John yes I have thank you, more pleasant than I might have expected and I have returned home with lots more information surrounding our dear Mr Broadoak who, it seems was not the pleasant, quiet and unassuming gentleman everyone seems to think he was.'

'Indeed, Mrs Matcham was Mr Spillett of some help on this occasion?'

'We mustn't be talking about this, John as you should know by now all of my findings I must keep secret although you might be able to help me with something soon. Has anything exciting happened here this afternoon and evening?'

'Detective Inspector Drabble called this afternoon with some more questions that seemed to be the original questions put a different way, at least the ones he asked me were.'

'What about the others?'

'Mr Charles was extremely annoyed; Miss Patricia was crying when I last saw her, and cook was flustered because Inspector Drabble arrived shortly after tea when she was supposed to be preparing dinner.' He's smiling as he mentions cook's reaction.

'And you, John? How did your questioning go? What did he ask you?'

'Oh, where I was during the afternoon, what I was doing during the afternoon and all the preparations and during dinner.'

'And?'

'And then who was with me while I was preparing the bridge room; who had access to it; how long had it been empty before they got into the bridge room and how long they had been playing.'

'An awful lot of questions to – if you'll forgive me – to someone who is, after all, only a butler. Was there anything else?'

'He wanted to know if I watched the game and who left the room if anyone did; was it a friendly game; who was winning and how was it going particularly leading up to and immediately before Mr Broadoak's death.'

'I explained that I did not play, nor indeed do I know how to play bridge, I can only guess at what happened at the end of the game. The rubber I believe they call it.'

'Yes, yes they do and what did you tell him happened at the end of the game – I'm sorry to have to ask you so many questions at this time of night but I'm sure you realise that it will save time later when I need to speak to you again, further on in my own investigations. I can't have the police getting ahead of me now can I?'

'It's not a problem, of course it isn't. I told him that Mrs Saynor had left the table briefly, while Mr Broadoak was playing a hand – the one which turned out to be his last – to go to powder her nose, but that she returned almost unnaturally soon after leaving. While she was away I straightened her chair and I recall picking up a handkerchief that she had dropped on the floor. I was walking behind the seated Mr Charles to collect the drinks tray to take round to everyone when she returned. Naturally, I replaced the tray on the sideboard and went back to help Mrs Saynor sit down and to get herself comfortable again. I had just left the room and closed the door when I heard a muffled scream and some talking from the card room. Naturally, I went back into the room to find the situation as it was just before I telephoned the police station and Dr Hudson.'

'Nothing else?'

'I recall he asked what I had seen when I opened the door after I had heard the screams. He wanted to know how the room was set out.'

'And what did you tell him?'

'All the players were standing in the places they were sitting when I had left the room only minutes earlier. There was some mention about Mr Broadoak dying after going three down in a six spades doubled, I think it was, yet he and Mrs Saynor still won the rubber,' he pauses as if unsure about what he had said to the police and then continued, 'Does that make sense? It would only be what I said they had said because I don't understand the significance of anyone being three down. And his, Mr

Broadoak's nose hit the Ace of Spades when he hit the table.'

'I'm not sure that the three down is significant and the Ace of spades, if it's a trump card, is supposed to be some sign of death depending on what you believe. That can't be relevant either although from what little I know about any card game is that it would be unusual for the ace of trumps not to have been played until the end of the game. Perhaps him going three down and still having the ace of trumps in his hand before he dropped it on the table and then landed on it when he died and him and Joan Saynor still winning the rubber is more significant. It would be if I were Charles or Patricia who would know what was happening, the effect it had on the game and the effect it had because they were playing for money!'

'I don't see how that could happen and even if it did it surely can't affect your investigation because that's about who killed him not about the playing card he died on. Oh, and they do play for money but for mere trifles I believe.'

'Sorry, John I mustn't keep you any longer you've been very helpful. Goodnight.' We had remained standing throughout my questioning and he had been specifically helpful with more detail than I could have hoped. I stepped forward and despite myself, kissed him lightly on his right cheek. 'Goodnight.'

'Goodnight, madam.' He held his hand to my kiss for a few moments as if savouring my gratitude before repeating: 'Goodnight.' He turned and walked towards the closed hall door and with his left hand on the door handle, turned back to face me and once more held his hand to my kiss.

I hear him locking the front door as I walk towards the stairs, he is locking all of us in to keep us safe, I wonder, as I climb the stairs and hear his footsteps becoming louder and then more softly, disappearing below stairs towards his pantry.

It has never occurred to me until now, that it might take so long for him to answer my questions or more importantly to tell me what had happened during the police visit. It seems that nothing of significant interest was gained and none of our information or our plan of action was given away. There was something about John's – testimony I suppose you'd call it – that seemed contradictory though at this stage I can't remember what.

I have no need to follow him and so remain standing in the dark, chilling hall with half a dozen dead ancestors looking down as if questioning me; why won't I let this drop? When did this event occur? What reason do I have for continually asking questions? Where was Alan seated exactly? His chair had its back to the hall door. It wasn't close to the door because there had to be room for John or, indeed anybody else to come in without bashing against someone or something, but it nevertheless had its back to the door. That meant of course that Patty was facing the door and would be able to see anyone entering the room – if she was looking and had not assumed that the person was John or another member of staff who might move easily around the house.

Four hall chairs, unimaginatively called 'Hall Chairs' and so designed as to ensure that nobody who sat on them would remain in the hall for long with their hard unwelcoming solid wood seats stood stoically where no doubt they had been placed dozens of years ago. Their backs were built at exactly ninety degrees to the seats which resulted in the construction being quite intentionally most uncomfortable. Despite knowing this, I walk to one opposite and but ever so slightly to the right of the door into the card room and sit down. Over the years, my back has become slightly bent so that to sit against the hard back was not easy and it takes me a while to get comfortable.

Comfortable–ish I can now see the card room door and wish I had opened it before sitting down, it is after all, the centre of the whole mystery although only of where the murder appears to have happened. I have yet to establish why, with what and when. I can see no other way of carrying out the murder than by poison and therefore Tommy's assumption has to be right. So we know it's poison, Tommy appears to know – or thinks he does – which poison it was and who supplied it although his source either doesn't know from whom or won't tell Tommy but I'm counting on Frank or Tommy to get that piece of information for me. There are so many ifs and buts and maybes it's impossible to see the wood for the trees. I need some fresh air and to avoid disturbing John again, I head towards the back of the house.

I continue through the rear passage to the kitchen and on until finally I reach the back door. It too is locked but in this instance it's easy to deal with because a key hangs on a hook just by the door, clear for all to see. It is still there tonight and I unlock the door to the outside. I'm hit by the heat, the thick oily, suffocating heat, the sort of heat that tells you to go back inside making sure to keep the heat out. But I don't, as I never have.

Chapter Twenty Nine

I passed a restless night and while in the more lucid moments of my waking hours attempted to complete as many pieces of the jigsaw for which I have gathered pieces. There were few enough pieces and few that were interlocking. John had confirmed the location of all the players with only Mrs Saynor leaving the room at any one time, in fact only Mrs Saynor leaving the room at all. It's hard to imagine that she would murder one of her opposing pair other than to spite her hostess with whom she knew Broadoak was having an affair. Perhaps it was a warning to Mrs Whitten that nobody was untouchable and that she could be next thereby freeing Charles Whitten in the marital stakes. Was Mrs Saynor capable of such intrigue or is it only investigative people such as myself who may find a causal link between murder, beneficiary and perpetrator? I need many more question mark jigsaw pieces. Many more.

Breakfast is a drawn out, solemn affair with no more than two customers at any one time. Cook has provided a veritable morning feast of hot and/or cold courses many of which have been ignored. To show willing and appreciation I attempt to partake of as many courses as I can manage. Cook, standing back waiting to refill any dishes where and when required nods towards me, showing appreciation of my efforts, which she might have seen as a gesture for my buttering her up for questioning later. The thought has crossed my mind.

While I sit working my way through a portion of fried back bacon with a fried egg and fried bread, my father enters, sits at the head of the table and signals to cook to bring him his normal elements of breakfast. I watch with fascination as she delivers first orange juice, then mixed fruit with cream and finally toast. It seems a remarkably meagre meal for such a pertinacious man, so little with which to maintain his stature.

'Good morning, Alicia did you sleep well or did your investigations give you such ghastly nightmares that you became fretful, disturbed and so extremely tired when you came down for breakfast?' He sneers as he speaks, clearly disingenuous of my enquiries.

Defiant in my response I lie. 'Good morning father, I slept extraordinarily well thank you which I believe is considered to be a sign of a clear conscience.' I continue to attack my bacon while waiting for his response. A silence harder to cut through than my bacon, lasts a full minute before it ends with one of his chuckles acknowledging defeat.

'What do you plan for today? Who – as they say – is to come under your cosh or are you giving yourself and the rest of us a day off?'

'Investigators never have days off, father as I am sure I have told you before. We are always looking for clues, considering comments and others' questions and for those things upon which no comment is made or questions asked as I say, always on the job.'

'Must be hard work all that personal stuff.'

'It can be, particularly if those to whom questions are asked limit their answers to the specific rather than expanding their response to include related matters. Do you see?'

'I suppose so, my dear.'

And with that he pats the corners of his mouth with a napkin rises from the table and leaves. My glance to cook shows a mutual disagreement with his actions. We exchange glances and I leave the table allowing her to remove the dirty crockery and other pieces so that John can set the table for lunch when the time arises.

I use the telephone in the hall to telephone Frank's office and establish that Jenny at least will be there if I went straight away. I drive through the town as fast as I am allowed without a nasty policeman stopping me for going too fast and am soon parking in front of the offices. In Tommy's absence I must trust Maggie and hope that none of the boys do anything they shouldn't. I walk up the rickety stairs and find Jenny alone at her desk, working hard on what Jack has left for her to type.

'He's not here.' She looks up at the door to Frank's office.

I look at the clock on the wall 'It's a bit early I expect.'

'Tea?'

'The usual, thank you.' She goes to the kettle and re-lights the gas. It doesn't take long to boil which suggests that she knows the routine well. 'Will he be long?'

'He won't be in till nearly eleven I think he said, but then he didn't know – I'd told him you was coming.'

'It's really you I wanted to speak to anyway. I no longer trust a word he says. Thank you.' She carefully places the tea on the end of her desk and moves some typing out of the way.

'Just in case you spill it.' She says.

'Now, is his lordship making any progress?'

'Not really,' she holds up her hand to pre-empt my inevitable question:

'Why on earth not?'

'Dunno. You can see the last report he's going to have ready for you today. Here it is.' She passes me a slim sheath of paper most of which comprises the opening pages stating the aim of the report and, at the end, the now usual ending stating that more work needs to be done before any definite conclusions can be made.'

'That's as much use as, as a fiddler's elbow.'

'A what?'

I'm certain that my frustration shows, 'Never mind, it's pointless that's what it is. When is he actually going to come up with anything I didn't know?'

'He says that you know most of what he finds out, so what's the point of him doing what you're doing already.'

'He has a point. He has a point. Perhaps what I should do is give him the particular questions I need answering. Do you think that would work?'

'It might. It's worth a try.'

'Has he actually found out anything this time?'

She looks at me as if I was asking for the crown jewels. 'A little possibly but we don't actually know what you know, so it's a bit hard to know, isn't it?'

'Just tell me what's in the report, then I can see if there is anything.'

'Okay, well he knows that that policeman – whose name he can never remember – is going up to the house to ask some more questions, but he doesn't know when.'

'Heavens! I know that and I know the answers to the questions too. His name's Drabble by the way, Detective Inspector Drabble. What's next?'

'He thinks he knows who supplied Tommy's contact with the drugs in the first place but not who he sold them onto.'

'Well, who is it?'

'Not sure you'd know him, he's one of the South Creek Gang - Arthur Gildbert, not a man to be trifled with.'

'But the police would know him?'

'Yes, but they'd never get him into prison, they stick together that lot and would give him alibis and all sorts to stop that. He'd be squeaky clean when the police got hold of him.'

'But they'd know, so that means nobody is responsible, because he would successfully deny having it.'

'Anymore?'

'Apparently they now think it's a man who killed him.'

'And I suppose tomorrow a baby boy did it, in other words they haven't a clue and that's it? That's all I get for my three pounds ten shillings?' All of my time spent on friendly chats with Jenny seems to have been thrown away on this one episode, none of which is her fault. I sit and wait for her reply for which there was a short delay.

'He says he needs some more money to pay off the people who grassed on Gildbert otherwise he says that all hell will break out.'

Now I need to repair the damage with her so that I can try to get what information has been gleaned. I can't help but sigh because this is beyond a joke. 'How much this time?'

'He says in his report that he doesn't know, but on a little piece of paper he wants me to clip to the front of the report, he says you'll know and that it's twice as much as that.'

'He wants five hundred pounds? He has to be joking he must be joking.'

'He said you say that and to assure you that it's not for him it's for the people –

'- the people who gave him the name of the person – I know, I know. I'm relentlessly nodding by the time I've calmed down. 'He'll have to take a cheque.'

'I'm sure that'll be okay. I'll ask him when he comes back. Thanks.' She's smiling and at the very least I feel I deserve a smile. Five hundred pounds is a hell of a lot of money just to find out who killed somebody who isn't a member of the family and only the bridge partner of my little sister. I shall have to recover the costs, not because I need the money but it's the principle I mean crikey another five hundred pounds. 'Would you like another cuppa tea?'

'Please, then we can have one of our little chats and put all that nasty business about money behind us. You must have something interesting you can tell me, and I am a bit thirsty and I'd prefer coffee today if that's possible.'

'The report doesn't give the full story, as you expect. What I've told you is right – all that stuff about Gildbert and the gang – he'll never go to jail let alone be hung for it, that's the way things are nowadays, the gang control everything.' She's almost shouting from the kitchen so that I can hear her over the steaming kettle and then its whistling. 'but he hasn't told you everything. They've also found out that word is that the murderer is one of the household. So, your family.'

'What? Are you sure?'

'Yeah, horrible thought isn't it?'

'Does the word on the street say who?'

'No, not yet but someone'll grass in time and then it'll all be out, and your investigations will be at an end and you can go home. Proper home I mean – up in London somewhere, isn't it?'

'Yes, north of London actually.'

'Oh yes, someone mentioned that, Frank probably or possibly your friend from Chapel House – George Hind is it?, I don't listen to anyone else well apart from my Ron, he's good at picking up stuff. Stuff that Frank doesn't hear about.'

'How does Ron know this stuff whatever it is?'

'He works in the brewery, all sorts of stuff he sees and hears usually at lunch time or breaks they have. All very odd, I don't understand it.'

'Well, anything he can get will be welcomed, of course.'

'I'll tell him to make notes.'

'He needs to be careful if anyone finds out –'

'I know, I already told him that.'

'Now, here's your coffee, enjoy it before Frank comes back and tells me off for talking to you.'

I am leaving Frank's offices in a much better frame of mind now. Something to go on, that I can get confirmed by my little friend Tommy who will no doubt be standing by or sitting in Maggie waiting for a ride after he's told me what he's found out. It might be very interesting.

Chapter Thirty

I leave Jenny musing on the discussions we have had, wondering whether I will actually stump up the five hundred pounds and honestly, at this stage, I'm not certain either. When I get down the stairs and push open the rickety door to the street and to my car Tommy is, indeed, waiting for me and is sitting on my car's bonnet, from which he immediately dismounts. After strict admonishment although whilst smiling, I have a sensible conversation with him during which he confirms everything Jenny has told me. This is an unusual state of affairs but in a strange way reassuring.

During our deepening conversation he is very close to giving me the name of the poison but holds back for some unknown reason and he will not be persuaded. What he has no idea about is the motive and opportunity for what we are now absolutely certain was the murder of Alan Broadoak. I must have those as well as the means before I can put the package to Detective Inspector Drabble although the poison, or at least the fact that the cause of death was poisoning would be a good place to start. He assures me that such information can be obtained even though I can't understand how. He tells me not to worry.

I always find that when someone – whoever it may be

– tells me not to worry, I immediately start to do just that. This instance is just such a situation particularly as the person assuring me is a young street boy albeit a highly intelligent young street boy.

After so much confirming information I have to give my street urchin a ride in Maggie. He thoroughly enjoys his treats and asks, as he always does, what I now need in order to give him another ride. Well, I'm not sure and say so.

'To be honest, Tommy I'm not sure what I need to know next. I will need to know why Mr Broadoak was murdered, but that is almost certainly down to me if what you and your sources tell me about the murderer is correct. I already have some ideas, but they needn't concern you – at least, not at this stage – and then how he was murdered. How he was murdered might be easier to establish if I knew what the poison was and where it had come from. No, where it had come from is less important than who you gave it to you and who you passed it on to.

Without that information, Tommy it's just about impossible for me to find out or work out how he was murdered. Different poisons are given in different ways and I need to know what it is, do you see?' I am getting more and more upset – not upset, more enraged – by the whole thing and am yet again wondering how I let myself be talked into this. It was Patty, it's always Patty and I sometimes wonder if I shouldn't name her as the murderer and that she's just seeking attention in the knowledge that she won't be caught or if she is I'll keep quiet about it and the whole thing will go away. I can't for the life of me think why she would think that, it's never happened before and trust me, it won't happen again. Tommy has already begun his response.

'I can't, miss, I promised, and I can't break a promise to the Gang – neiver of vem. Not ever. It's more'n my life's werf. miss. Please don't make me…'

'Tommy, I can't make you and even if I could, I wouldn't because that would make me like one of the gangs.' He looks down and silently sighs, I assume in relief. 'However, if I ask you something and you don't answer so that I can work out what the answer is that would be all right, wouldn't it? You wouldn't be telling me, would you?' He shakes his head.

'Good we'll make sure nobody can hear me so that we don't give them any chance to catch us out, okay?' He nods. This might become irritating after a while but if I'm successful Tommy will have been instrumental in solving the case.

We're still touring the outer edges of the town having turned left towards the seaward end of the Thames. As the hops fade we wind our way towards the relatively lush grazing meadows surrounding Herne. Tommy remains quiet, his lips sealed as he watches a landscape go by that he had never seen before nor even dreamed of, he had no idea that such places existed. The Creek has nothing but mud, grass and water and they're rarely at the same time. Then we slide past the Seasalter levels emblazoned by their prolific crops of teasels, sheltered by reeds and grasses seeded at the streams' edges, their mix of pinkish purple and white flowers livening the countryside for miles around. He's still silent and I'm hoping he's trying to decide whether his helping me is more important than keeping quiet and risking trouble with the gang. I can't help him with that decision, but I expect he'll be in trouble just having the information in case he will tell me in which case he might as well tell me! If he does, tell me, I'll do everything I can to protect him, but these gangs have eyes and ears everywhere. I don't know how he will decide

'I'm sorry Mrs I can't say anything even by nodding or not nodding, I was told that what I was told in secret from a mate who I trust and owe favours, I can't grass him up, not even for you. Sorry.' He looks up at me, his big brown eyes starting to water as he knows that by sitting in my car he will be punished by the Gang because that's what they do – punish you as a warning to others.

'That's okay, Tommy, I understand, and I hope that the Gang understand too. Understand that you have told me none of their business and that there is no need to and that they must not punish you. You don't deserve it when you have been loyal to them and the person who let you into their secret.'

He smiles, knowing that even by saying what I have, will not stop them giving him a beating at the very least. Knowing that we might never see each other again and that this might be his last ever ride in Maggie for whom I shall have to find another minder he looks away and I wonder if he's having second thoughts about telling me now that he's acknowledged he will get a beating anyway. This is all so stressful that I've almost forgotten what it is I'm wanting him to tell me and then I remember, it's a crucial part of what I need to know, and his help is by far the fastest way of getting it. I'll release him from his torment and say I have someone else who can help me, and he shouldn't worry any more. He's still not comfortable and is happy when I agree to drop him off in Whitstable where, he tells me, he has friends who might be able to help.

He stands to get out of the car, then turns and gives me the biggest hug ever and I cry, floods and floods.

Chapter Thirty-One

Now that we have established that poison is the murder weapon – although I'm not sure whether you can really call it a weapon nevertheless – I must talk to Dr Hudson again. He was quite dismissive of my suggestion before but I am confident having excluded all other means that this is the one whether he likes or not.

In deference to his occupation and the appointment system he operates, I telephone his secretary who, after a brief delay – when she was presumably consulting Dr Hudson – I am allocated an appointment for 3.15p.m. Today!

The doctor was clearly put out by my request for further questioning and so I determined to dive in: 'Dr Hudson, Mr Broadoak was murdered by poisoning.'

'And just what do you expect me to do about it? The body has already been released for burial because the police are confident that it's a heart attack so how have you come to a different decision?'

'Perhaps I have looked at it from a different angle, perhaps because there is no pressure on me to resolve the death or arrive at the 'correct' decision I can look more carefully, more dispassionately – no, that's not fair on Detective Inspector Drabble,

I have no doubt that he has carried out his job perfectly – but as a member of the family – I'm sure you can understand.'

'Miss Matcham…'

'…Mrs.'

'I beg your pardon, Mrs Matcham I'm sorry but what you have said convinces me no more than did your previous so called justification, if you want to stop the burial of Mr Broadoak, you're going to have to get some other authority after that is, you have convinced them of the need for that action.'

'May I ask you two or three questions in a hypothetical investigation?'

The doctor looks at his watch and then the clock on the wall, satisfied that they both tell the same time he continues.'

'Very well, Mrs Matcham but you will have to be quick, I have a patient due in fifteen minutes and my patients must not be kept waiting.'

'Thank you.' I take a deep breath as meanwhile he bows his head and picks up some notes to read while I am talking.

'If someone was being given a drug for, say, low blood pressure and that dose was exceeded what would happen?'

'You know what would happen, the patient would become ill.'

'And an excessive dose would kill them.'

'Of course.'

'With side effects?'

'Possibly. He or she might suffer all sorts of things, it depends what the drug was and how much the overdose was and how they react to different drugs.'

'But they could die.'

'Well, yes.'

'And there are drugs that will kill without risking any side effects or symptoms and cause death instantly, or almost instantly.'

'Mrs Matcham, I can see where you're going with this, but it won't work, I can assure you.'

'Why?'

'Mr Broadoak was not taking any medication – none – well that is only the morphine I prescribed and mentioned earlier and the miniscule dose of Potassium Chloride he had been taking for many many years to help reduce the pain he was suffering as a result of shrapnel wounds to his arm and lower body. With the appropriate authority you are welcome to look through his file to check but you will find nothing.'

'Is it possible to buy any such a drug in a chemist?'

'No.'

'On the Black Market perhaps?'

'Possibly I suppose, but obviously I have no control of that, and I can see no reason why Alan would have gone down that route without consulting me first. Now, please, I must attend to my living patients.'

'Of course, thank you, doctor you have been most helpful.'

As I approach the door I turn, 'Just one more thing, doctor,' I wince as he looks up from what I take to be a patient's notes 'would it be possible for you or one of your other patients to acquire and/or store from their own prescriptive drugs sufficient of a – let's call it 'a killer drug' – to use against someone without you noticing?'

'Look, miss –'

'Mrs.'

'Mrs Matcham,' spoken through gritted teeth, 'I think you're taking this meeting of yours a bit too far. I have answered your questions without fear or favour, I have tried to answer them fully, clearly, accurately and understandable to you such as is within my power, I cannot but feel that with this question you have overstepped the mark and are seeking answers to intrusive questions for a particular patient which I have already told you I should not do. However and finally, for your information our drugs cupboard is securely locked and any drugs removed for any of my patients are clearly recorded, there is certainly no way in which any patient could acquire large stocks of any drug however powerful, nor is it possible that any of the patients could, under their own steam, obtain access to the cupboard for acquiring the drugs and further I have no patients for whom I have prescribed potassium chloride for whatever reason,'

His voice is rising in strength and volume, 'now please get out of my consulting rooms and do not return!' He has spoken without drawing breath and now draws fresh air deep into his thoracic cavity bringing life back to his whole body. He does not smile. In the short period I have known him I have never seen him smile, sneer perhaps but not smile, he takes his own life and that of his patients extremely seriously and I commend him for that.

Dr Hudson's village rooms are situated towards the northern end of Upper St Ann's Road which you may remember, is considered the posh part of town, where his patients are able to come and go virtually unseen, their privacy preserved. There is no doubt that if I were to stake out the rooms' car parking area and list those comings and goings, I would be able to discover who has consulted the venerable doctor and with what frequency but frankly I can't be bothered. What I need to do now is to obtain approval to have the burial process stopped and a new post-mortem carried out by an independent pathologist before our Mr Broadoak is buried for good and in addition to the normal report, the forensic surgeon must be instructed to search specifically for any sign, however small of potassium chloride.

Now we seem to have our poison, or at least one of them.

Chapter Thirty Two

It is Monday and there's still no sign of rain. We have had the hottest summer and the longest period without rain since, they tell us, records have been kept. Apparently the downpour we had a couple of days ago wasn't really any help for the farmers or anyone else because the rain came down in too short a period of of time! That aside it has been jolly hot and terribly dry. The streams, rivers and reservoirs are largely almost without water and even my darling Thames is at an all-time low, revealing parts of the riverbed and what it holds never before seen by members of the public. Still, providing it doesn't stop us doing anything, that's all right, we're still really getting used to a country without war and don't want to have to worry about one without water as well!

Breakfast has been tedious as usual but after the now customary exchange, I have decided that I really should catch up with Cook for her view of the situation now that I know more than before I talked to her last and have heard nothing more about brother William. Before I leave the dining room, I take 'Cetta to one side and arrange to visit the kitchen after she has had time to clear away breakfast.

The full, hot sun has disappeared behind some cloud

although probably not for long and because of the time it takes 'Cetta to clear and prepare, I have a little time available to walk down the lane towards Faversham. The freshness with the light cloud cover is wonderful, I take deep breaths and smile almost savouring the smell as if it is a long-lost fruit. The thirsty plant life is desperately attempting to draw in more than their share of any moisture there is going and I can see the ubiquitous hops turning brown before their natural ochre green almost as I watch. I'm sauntering along the road without any great time pressure and with no particular destination in mind. I am enjoying the quiet countryside and after a while turn a left-hand bend to see the cottages which line the lower most left side of the lane before the Dover to London road.

The first two of the cottages – Laetus – is owned and occupied by members of the family and we shall come back to the events which determine their development and characters in a later volume. But for now I must return to the current problems at Corners and to see 'Cetta.

I turn and cross the lane only to be missed by one of the cars that rarely travel through Brogdale. The hooting horn suggests that the driver is of my acquaintance, but I can't think who or why they wouldn't stop if they were.

My step towards Corners is faster than my outward visit because after my ramble I am running a little late and with recent problems over timings, I live in fear of upsetting Cook's lunch time arrangements. I use the tradesmen's entrance which amuses 'Cetta and gets us off to a good start. She offers me a chair and after my walk I accept willingly. She must have seen

seen my perspiration soaked face and offers me a cold drink of barley water which I also accept and from which I take a swig before starting with the questions.

'Thank you, my poor old throat was parched, it's jolly hot out there.'

'Cetta smiles and says: 'They say it's something to do with the sun. I reckon they're right, don't you?' and now we both laugh and any delay that I might have caused by my tardy return is long forgotten.

'Sorry to bring this all up again but last time we talked you told me about how the menus were arranged – who decided what they were going to eat, in which order and –.'

'They was al'ays in the same order, madam organises the same course you see.'

'Yes, sorry, of course. What we didn't talk about is who actually prepared the food, who put the different parts together and who laid up the plates. Whether there was ever a central dish for people to take their own food – '

'Oh no, madam, everyone was served everything. Nobody ever had to take any food theirselves. Never.'

'But we do at breakfast.'

'That's a different meal, madam. Not at lunch and dinner. Well, possibly at lunch but definitely not at dinner.'

'Okay, right, so who prepares the different bits of the courses: the pies; roast the potatoes; shell the peas; top the carrots; clip the blackcurrants; hull the strawberries; roll and shape the pastries – that sort of thing, there must be lots and lots more – who does all that stuff?'

'That's me, madam and there are lots more; me mostly. That's why it takes so long an' I 'ave to keep to me timings and numbers of people eating and not 'ave some odd people turnin' up late when they 'avent said they's goin' to.'

And there's me thinking I had been exonerated but I suppose I deserve the stare - almost a sneer - when she finishes her rant, at least I have the information.

'And presumably you also prepare the serving plates, all those wonderful decorations.'

'I do miss, yes. Although when there's a special menu on, I usually gets help from some of the girls down at the Chapel House and if vat's not enough, there's usually on odd one or two from the other Whitten houses down the lane.'

'Laetus and Wilberholme you mean.'

'Not so much Laetus, them ladies give their maids enough to do to keep their poor girls busy day and night, so mostly from Wilberholme.'

'I see. So how many were there here on that Saturday night, the night when —'

'When dear ol' Mr Broadoak died.'

'I think we can safely say after what you told me last time and what I have discovered since, that he was neither a 'dear old' or that he 'died'. He was a 'randy lecherous old man' and he was 'murdered'.'

'Oh my goodness, madam, what a thing to 'appen, are you sure, yes of course you're right. What a tadoo? Even if it is how can you say such a thing about such a lovely, lovely man?'

To my surprise, she stops kneading her pastry and sits down, whimpering into her handkerchief sniffing rather loudly. I wait until the poor women collects herself and stands up again before I continue:

'Unless I find out to the contrary because it's true, but you

201

mustn't go spreading any of what I've just told you around the town or even between the girls, even John, that must be our little secret.'

'Of course, madam.' I knew she wouldn't and in fact I only told her because I knew just that. Once it gets around the neighbourhood who knows what or who might come out of the woodwork either in the northern area of the town or, more likely, down around the Creek. Especially around the Creek.

'Is there anything else, madam, only lunch is coming on fast towards us?'

'May I say that you seem to have been particularly close to Mr Broadoak, 'Cetta. Your reaction when I said what an unsavoury character he has turned out to be you almost cried. Is there something you want to tell me?'

She remains silent for a moment, looks across the table not exactly at me, more sort of past my right ear to the mantlepiece where I remember there is a collection of this and that. She ignores them and seems to have lost all interest in the kitchen block where the partially kneaded dough is beginning to crust over and a saucepan on the Aga behind her looks as though it's going to add more unwanted heat to the kitchen's climate when it boils over. She shifts her gaze towards me, sniffs again (a nasty habit which should be outlawed) and takes a deep breath.

'Well seein' as you want me to keep your secret I want yous to keep mine.' She continues to stare at me, and I nod in encouragement anticipating with a degree of certainty, what I think she is about to say. 'When we were very young – still at school like – me and Mr Broadoak, Alan, were classmates and after a while we were sweethearts and I used to have pictures of him in my bedroom – in the drawers of course, not standin' anywhere.'

'Oh, I see.'

'No miss, you don't. Before the Great War he asked me to marry him and we was engaged the day before he was shipped out to goodness knows where. Well, o' course lots of things 'appened to sweethearts during the war didn't they and when he got back he dumped me and married some other floozie. I didn't know who she was or how they met, one time when he was home on leave I expect, when 'e didn't tell me I expect. But he broke off our engagement – though he did say he was sorry – and blamed it on the war. I stilled loved him though. It was fate what brought us together when first I ended up cooking for Mrs Lavinia who by then had married Mr Whitten. Alan soon got rid of his tart and I knew that he had lots of affairs but we was still sweethearts.

'It's been a long time after that since Alan started playing bridge at Corners. I hadn't seen him or heard anyfing about him and even when we saw each other again I don't think he recognised me, but I remembered him. Him as the one who broke my heart.' She stops briefly to dab her eyes which have been watering for some time. 'And then stories started to come down through the girl's chattering. I'd always known he was a bit of a lady's man, but it didn't matter, I still loved him. So, whatever happened before whoever it was murdered him, I won't have a bad word said against him. He cheated on me, but I forgave him, I always forgave him, because I stills love 'im see?'

'Oh, 'Cetta, you poor thing.' Despite everything I feel compelled to give her a cuddle and walk around the enormous kitchen table to do just that. She's shaking, crying her eyes out and between the sobbing and deep breaths she alternates between 'because I still love 'im and I'm sorry miss, you shouldn't have to do this, I'm sorry'. This is going on and on and, bizarrely, I'm starting to worry about lunch being late. I have no idea what to do to get the food ready and I'm trying to encourage her to carry on. 'Come on now, 'Cetta what's past is past it's probably better that you throw yourself back into your work and to remember the good times you had with him rather than what's happened this last week.'

'Yes, miss you're quite right and I must get on, everyone'll be wanting their lunch and the pastry isn't even ready for the plum pie.' She almost sniggers now, sniffs again, stands up, faces the table and ploughs her hands into the pile of even more heavily crusted dough. She looks up at me and smiles. 'Thank you miss, it's very kind o' you to listen.'

'That's all right, 'Cetta, I'm sorry I'm going to be an awful little piggy, but do you mind if I ask you just a few more questions?' She shakes her head. 'Were there any girls helping you on that Saturday?'

'Just Florence and Daisy both of them from Chapel House.'

'Have they helped you before?'

'Yes, madam well, Florence 'as but Daisy's only recently arrived at the house. Their Cook says she's good at what she does and that she came with good references from the Allderttons over The Mall.'

'And you trust them do you? The girls that is. They're not likely to have put anything in the food that they shouldn't have?'

'Not without me seein' 'em.' She shakes her head fervently, her curls almost beating her face as she does so.

'Okay, thank you. So they served the food to the sideboards and then to each of the diners at the dining table.'

'Yes, with me too. We did all of it together. We shared it all out between them and then when they'd finished we collected the dirty plates and once we'd cleared it all away we brought up the puddings and served them too. Jam roly-poly as I recall.'

'What about the plum pie, like today?'

'Oh that's for the servants' dinner later.' She winks.

'And the wine? Presumably, John looked after the sherry, wine and champagne?'

'Not the champagne, they didn't have any, at least not that week I don't think and I thought it was strange at the time, now I comes to think about it...'

'No champagne?'

'No, madam. Not unless one of the gentlemen took some up.'

'Was that unusual? Not to have any I mean.'

'Yes, madam it was, especially for a Saturday bridge game. They usually have champagne at table followed by port in the card room. That week they must have gone straight on to the port. Strange isn't it when you think about it? Yes. No champagne unless as I say – '

She's pondering over the options, whether there was any champagne and if so who brought it to the room and then who got rid of it. Between us we've opened the proverbial can of worms. There might be some irony here if Alan takes the champagne into the room unaware that the poison is meant for him, or there was no poison and I'm over thinking everything.

I say 'Yes, interesting, but John poured the sherry, wine and port.'

'Not the Port, madam, that was warming in the card room, Mr Whitten takes charge of that and would have corked it and then passed it to Alan, sorry, Mr Broadoak to pour his. The ladies might have had some too, it's not unusual nowadays is it, not with this new world and new wild lifestyle all you young people get up to nowadays. I dunno.'

She looks at me and I see her broad smile, a warm smile as if to say, you are lucky young people, I wish I could have done all that sort of thing before the war. These new dance crazes are coming over from America and all the jazz music are starting to liven things up. And she's right we, the fortunate few, are having a jolly good life after the war, but we're also living under the threat of another one as we all are and must make hay while the sun shines.

'You can't really call Mrs Saynor, my mother and my sister, young, surely. Patricia perhaps but not the others.'

'Perhaps not, but then these things spread don't they.'

'Yes, 'Cetta they do. Now, Master William. Can you tell me anything about him? I know he's my brother and all that, but I see him so rarely. What's he like and how often you see him?

'Well we don't see him very often, madam. As I said before he usually only come for more money and sometimes to have his dirty laundry washed or to have a decent meal.'

'I expect you give him a food basket before he leaves don't you? Even if that's not what he came for.'

She looks down at the floor guilty as charged. 'I do, madam. The boy must be starved out there all on 'is own like that.'

''Cetta, he's not a boy, he's thirty seven and is quite capable of looking after himself. What's more he's quite capable of working and if he did that instead of all the gambling I keep hearing about, he'd have a better lifestyle and plenty to eat. So why did he come here on that Saturday? Is it usual for him to come on a Saturday?'

'I don't know, madam, I don't think about it at the time. But now you say, I think it probably was, when all the others are playing bridge. And as I say, he'll be here for one of those things.'

'Does he have anything to do with any of the bridge players except my father and sister of course.'

'I've heard, heard it mind you, that he does, did, gamble with Alan and borrow money from him from time to time. But I doesn't know any of that for sure madam. It's only what I've heard, and I find it hard to believe that of Mr William.'

'Oh I don't find it hard to believe, 'Cetta, believe me it's not at all surprising. Thank you. Is there any other gossip about my brother? Anything at all?'

'Cetta picks up the thread again, 'No madam except that he keeps in with unsavoury company, particularly likes the ladies, but then he always had an eye for the girls as you know only too well, madam.'

'Yes, 'Cetta, I know only too well. Now, I must leave you to prepare lunch and I'm afraid I shall not be here to enjoy your cooking. So only three I expect. Anything special on the menu tonight?'

'Not tonight, madam, no. Sorry.' She smiles and I feel I have made a friend. I turn to leave the kitchen and hear the front door slam shut. It sounds like father returning from wherever he went in the morning so I shall step aside and use the servant's stairs

Maggie is waiting patiently for me outside the front door.

Chapter Thirty Three

Father's study is one of those rooms from which we were barred during childhood whether he was in there or not. In this context, childhood means from birth until aged twenty five. The age limitation caused an air of wonder or perhaps suspicion, I can't remember which although I do remember my mother knocking and entering without introduction on the occasion of my twenty-first birthday when she felt he should make an appearance and greet my friends. Her action was, I remember, to have the opposite affect and for her, his insistence on a demand for another meeting – a reprimand – when the house was once again empty. Fear was the greatest power that he dispensed to all and sundry. But to be fair his furies passed quickly and if any of us were summoned to his study he would probably either have forgotten why we had gone to see him or calmed down so much that he was prepared to forgive us. A visit to his study was therefore a demonstration of control more than anything else.

I knock on the study door and it is opened as I anticipate by John, the not so old family retainer. The procedure has begun.

My father's study leads off the hall but unlike the other

rooms, there is an internal lobby before the room itself large enough for four people, one of whom is most invariably John. There is an inspection viewer in the internal door so that even when John has announced the name of my father's visitor (or on very rare occasions visitors to the house), my father can carry out a viewing of the person as a further – superficial – assessment of the individuals suitability for his time.

The lobby walls are lined with red, padded buttoned leather from the ceiling to the dado rail and square walnut panels from the rail to the skirting. In the modern age it looks ridiculous particularly as the study walls are similarly decked. The design does of course, provide a quiet, insulated place from which sound can neither escape or intrude and I'm sure that here we have the reason for the meeting's location. In turn it suggests that what we are to hear and discuss is for my ears only, except that John remains stoically silent in front of the door as a means of providing further protection from intruders. He has already checked the other two doors that lead from the room one with an inset glass panel in the top half of the door affording a picturesque view of the garden and the other, fully timbered, to the house wine cellar.

'Mrs Alicia Matcham to see you as requested, sir'

It took only a few minutes for father to open the door and to welcome me into the lion's den.

'My darling, Alicia, come on in there's no need for such formality, John.' He smiles (my father that is) it's not John's place to smile in these circumstances but as I walk past him, I smile unkindly, testing. He remains impassive.

'Now, where would you like us to sit?'

'I really don't mind, father you choose.'

Predictably he chooses to sit at his desk in the large, walnut 'captain's' chair with its ghastly brown, buttoned, cracked, leather back rest. Mother is forever threatening to have it replaced by something more modern and heaps more comfortable, but he won't have it – apparently my grand-father sat in it for all his working life and my father wanted to carry on the tradition. (I don't see William continuing the tradition in due course, he couldn't sit still long enough to do anything even if he could think of anything to do.) The other thing from his point of view of course is that he sits higher than his visitors giving him a superior vantage point for the discussion. I, on the other hand sat on an uncomfortable, un-cushioned, upright monstrosity.

'Right, so it's my turn yet again, I suppose. Am I first in the second round of you interrogating your interviewees?'

'Father, we've already had the first part of this conversation when I said you would be the first interviewee but things are constantly changing in this sort of situation and although I would like to ask you some more questions now, I may need to ask you even more later on. I hope that won't be a problem will it? These questions are as much confirmation of what I know and what I've learnt already from other people and which might increase the possibility of you being a suspect or, on the other hand reduce or remove that possibility.' Predictably this has upset him and I'm bracing myself for his reaction.

He stands now, knuckles forcing down on his desk, his back arched in aggression and his face as black as thunder 'What do you mean a suspect? How dare you? Who's said that I might have killed my old friend, my old comrade at arms? How could they or anyone else say that I'm a suspect, least of all you? Hah.'

He uprights himself, turns half circle and stumps slowly to the window overlooking the garden.

'Father, please, please calm down. I'm not saying that anybody has said that you are a suspect, least of all me, but I have been told certain things that I didn't know about and which you haven't told me that have been said at my interviews with them, might lead to you coming under suspicion. And anyway old thing, you must realise that everybody in the house when Alan Broadoak was murdered must be suspects. You were all here so mustn't you all be suspects? However unlikely.' I'm hoping that my unusual familiarity will reduce the tension in the room and by doing so will reduce his anger at being called a suspect. Neither I nor any police investigators would tell him that he's actually at the very highest spot on the tree of suspects!

He turns to look at me, his face more a pale red now and bearing a slight, very slight smile. 'Well if you put it like that, of course, sorry my dear yes, of course, you'd better carry on.'

An apology and no rebuke for calling him 'old thing' what is the world coming to? 'I've been told that Mr Broadoak –,'

'Oh do call him Alan we all know – knew – him well enough and anyway it seems silly to be so formal in this situation.'

'If you're sure?' he nods, 'I've been told that Alan was in the army at the same time as you and was, in fact, your batman for a while. Is that true?'

'It is, although I don't see what that's got to do with anything, that's why I didn't mention it. Yes, he was until 'fifteen; he was severely injured during Aubers Ridge – not that that means anything to you I don't expect - and was taken out of active service for the rest of the show…'

'What happened when he left you?'

Of course I know this from chatting to others, notably John, but verification is always useful.

'Staples – John Staples – replaced him and he and I saw out the war together. Good man, Staples, that's why he's here now. An excellent butler too I might add.' He looks up when he remembers John is standing by the door behind me, 'Excellent butler,' and uncharacteristically he manages to raise a smile in John's direction to which I imagine John bowed, gracefully.

I say, 'It sounds as though you lost touch with Alan for the rest of the war, do you know what happened to him once peace was declared?'

'I did not, no idea what happened to the poor chap no, but by chance I came across him somewhere – I forget where or when - ,' he looks up at John in what seems to be a threatening way, '- but it doesn't matter anymore; yes we came across each other and after de-mob, his sort of work was hard to find and so I offered him a job here as my butler. Seemed only fair after what we'd been through together.' He looks up at John again and then back to me.

'Sorry father but why did he leave here as butler? Was it something he'd done wrong, something to upset you?'

'Why are you asking me all these questions about the war? It has nothing, no bearing on Alan's murder.'

'Anything in his past might lead to someone having a motive for killing him. I'm just trying to find out something about his background – background that is further back than when he was playing bridge in our card room, that's all and whether that takes place at the same time or in the same place with you, you're the obvious person to ask. So why did Alan leave here as butler? Had he done anything wrong?'

'Certainly not! No, he was fortunate enough to inherit the family estate from his paternal uncle who had inherited it from Alan's father during the war. A very substantial estate it was – is – too, so he suddenly became one of the idle, rich lucky buggers; we ended up having some mutual friends and occasionally came across each other. I think your mother knew one of her lady-friends who knew another lady who knew him – you know the sort of thing, being a woman and all that, you'll understand – and one thing led to another and he found himself meeting your mother and ended up at another of her bridge afternoons and was soon amongst us.'

His appearance hardens again; I've struck a nerve and feel satisfaction in his hurt after referring to my knowing things simply because I am a woman. How degrading.

'Then, as of course you know, your mother invited him to join our Saturday bridge game.' He avoids my gaze now and looks down as if the loss of Alan has had a greater effect on him than I first suspected. He gets up from his chair and walks again across to the garden door where he stands with his hands clasped behind his back. 'He was a good man. Alan was a good man and whoever killed him deserves what's coming to him. A good man.' He breathes in deeply again and turns to return to his chair. Once he's sat down he looks across at John, 'Wouldn't you say, John? A good man?'

'It's not my place to say, sir. He was one of your friends, a very close friend of Mrs Lavinia I would say that she is better placed to answer that question.' John remains expressionless during his succinct answer, but I feel that I know what he thought of Alan and, for that matter thinks of my father.

'Well, whatever John hasn't said, he was. Alan was a good

man. Is that it now then?'

'Not quite, would you mind if John left us alone, father, please?'

'I have no secrets from John, Alicia, he should stay where he is, and I have no doubt that what he hears will remain in this room.' He looks across at John, who I assume nods in agreement. 'What do you want to ask me?'

This was always going to be difficult never mind with John standing behind me. 'There has been a suggestion that Alan was blackmailing you and –' before I can continue he interrupts:

'Absolute tosh! Blackmail me, whoever told you that? Absolute nonsense.'

'As I say, there has been a suggestion that Alan was black-mailing you because he found out about your black market operations during the war and that you continued to make profit from the black market throughout the war even though he was no longer appointed as your batman. Are you saying there's no truth in that?'

'Of course not. no truth at all.' Interestingly I note that while I was asking the question and during his brief response, his avoidance of John's eyes and the tension between them is palpable.

'There we are then, I think that's all for now, thank you. Sorry that some of those questions were so hurtful father, I had no idea they would be.' That, as we all know, is complete and utter rubbish but in some respects his reactions were perhaps surprising. I did think that John's reply and otherwise stoicism were most impressive.(He has for some reason now left the study, but I shall make a point of thanking him later). And now another surprise – father turns and is approaching me with his arms open. We give each other a big hug, me because I got what I wanted and him because (and I'm guessing here) he got away with what he did or didn't do during the war. We shall see who comes off the better later on.

Chapter Thirty Four

The content of the forgoing paragraphs suggests that it was only my questioning that occupied my waking hours. This, obviously, was not the case.

During most mornings father would take the dogs for a walk alongside the chalk pit. The path made his shoes and the dogs' feet acquire a bright but grubby – or muddy and sticky if it had been raining – white a covering of chalk. Chalk hasn't been quarried there for several years now and it must have looked a bit strange from an aircraft – a blob of white in the middle of all the green fields. I remember we had to be careful walking along the track because there were no fences or railings to stop anyone falling over the edge. I suppose that would be an alternative murder – to push your victim into the quarry. Nobody thought about the danger, we simply walked or skipped – I remember Patty and me skipping – along the path which ran gently downhill and through a farm. I think the farm's name might have been Whitehill Farm for obvious reasons, but it made no difference to our outings.

Through the farm we had no choice but to walk more slowly and down a short muddy lane, over a small river bridge with stone walls either side and then another short, but narrower lane to Water Lane which brought father and the dogs to a junction of decision. Our village church was on the left and where we went every Sunday. Funnily enough, the Sunday school was in the village school further up Water Lane, following father's alternative route on the right towards the main Dover to London road. I remember stories of kids (us included) falling off the road into the floodwater, although the floods didn't happen every year. This year the drought has carried on for three months up to now and although there were baby showers the river was running dry. The paths were all dry which meant that they weren't slippery and the roads were dusty and there was certainly no sign of any water in Water Lane!

I always got a bit bored by now and went to sit on the bench seat by the church gate, but father kept on going towards the London Road. At the junction with the London Road was his favourite building in the town. The Maison Dieu had been one of his major archaeological projects and now held many of his finds from the Roman period.

He was a difficult man to love although I know, we know, that he loves us dearly and we try hard to love him. We do in our own ways. He was always very firm with us when we were younger and gave us no quarter if we were heading in the wrong direction. I think that's why Patty and I have turned out so differently and I'm sure being the stronger helped me through childhood and my formative years. I left home after a wild argument with him about my wanting to marry Gerrard with whom I had had a wild, exciting, intense three year love affair. My intended was considerably older than I but despite Gerrard's wealth and position in society, father was resolute in his decision that I must not marry him. But I did and at the tender age of eighteen I married my thirty five year old lover and we debunked to London. It was all jolly exciting, especially as we had mother's approval. All this drove a wedge between father and me, especially when Gerrard died soon after our marriage and my second husband, the lovely Oliver, died even sooner. I was clearly not meant to be married although doing so had left me with a not inconsiderable fortune! Now I am an independent lady providing a service principally to the family but to others as well. I'm not sure that he approves even now, even though Patty still lives at home and brother William is forever looking for handouts.

But I'm working on it.

Chapter Thirty Five

As I leave father's study I almost bump into John, who I later learned was on his way to the breakfast room where we all had lunch. Although it was an inferior meal in the context of meals, he was required to supervise the table preparation. Bumping into John was never an unpleasant experience and in this instance by toppling my papers from my arms, our encounter was even longer and therefore more enjoyable. While we were both on our knees gathering this and that together we manage a brief kiss and a smile. When we stand up Cook's standing behind me and I can sense her disapproving look burning through my body. Anyone would have thought that she thought that he might have had hopes for her. It was never going to happen, and I have no fears on that score. John falls into butler mode and wipes away an imaginary kiss on his cheek.

He coughs before a light rebuke, 'Mrs Matcham, do please excuse my clumsiness. I didn't see you coming out from your father's study hidden as you were by the doorway.'

'John, please don't worry and it's easy enough to sort out the papers; anyway, it'll give me a chance to re-read what people have said so that I can see who killed whom and who is likely to be the next victim.'

'Next victim, miss?' 'Cetta sounds scared more than worried and any concern about any relationship between the two of us is long forgotten.

'Well, there's often a second if not third victim, in those fiction stories and often in true life as well, or so I'm told. Once the killer has the taste of blood on his (or her) lips or their fingers they want more; it becomes like a drug they've become addicted to.'

'Well, that's terrible. But Mr Broadoak was poisoned not stabbed nor nothing, there was no blood.'

John steps in casting me a brief look of despair, before directing a response to 'Cetta. 'I think Mrs Matcham is using the word blood in a figurative manner 'Cetta, meaning it as the taste for murder – the simple satisfaction of killing someone.' 'Cetta nods her head in a possible understanding.

Then she says: 'I expect you saw a lot of that in the war, you and Mr Whitten, people wanting to kill more than one person.'

I can tell that John is frustrated by the simplistic transition and I now leap in to save him voicing what's on the tip of his tongue. 'That's not exactly the same 'Cetta is it? Armies are there to kill each other because it's a war and that's what happens in war. So the same person may have to kill more than once because that's what they have to do, not because they want to kill more than one person. In fact,' I say once more to save John's frustration exploding in 'Cetta's simple face, 'in fact, lots of soldiers, when they have killed once, feel unable to kill again even though they're told they have to.

'Do you see, it's different? And in fact some soldiers are so affected by the killing that the get sick and have to be sent to the army hospitals and some of them are even sent home.' I look across to John for confirmation and to bring him back into the conversation from which he had been so keen to escape earlier. I look up but am unable to see him. It's possible that he has had to go to answer the telephone although I didn't hear it ring. 'John?' I hail him loudly and he soon returns as if he had simply been standing behind the scenes to absent his part in that part of the conversation. 'I was just explaining to 'Cetta that some soldiers have to be sent home from war because they get ill after killing someone. I'm right, aren't they, John.'

'Yes, madam that's quite correct. Some are, indeed sent home to hospital.'

'Cetta nods in agreement although still with a puzzled look and tightly screwed eyebrows, making her look angry rather than understanding. 'Like orders is orders I suppose.'

'Exactly.' I watch John's shoulders relax and he flashes me a smile in appreciation, although I mentally file his brief absence in my 'what to ask John later' folder.

'Cetta starts up again: 'So, after all that stuff about the war, who does you think'll be next then?'

'I've no idea yet, 'Cetta. Once I find the killer, it might become obvious that I or we should have known who it had been all along. Then I'll have to find the hard evidence the police will need for a conviction; but until then everyone must keep a wary eye open.'

'Oh right, Mrs Matcham I'll do just that.' With which she turns and scuttles along the passageway to her kitchen. John and I cruelly enjoy the collection of jokes and misunderstandings before parting in our respective directions, he possibly wondering if I had noticed his absence and me wondering why he'd disappeared.

Chapter Thirty Six

There are five of us at lunch: mother, Patty, myself, Dr Hudson and George Hind. While I can sort of understand why the dear doctor is here, the arrival of darling George Hind is a complete mystery. Father is noticeable by his absence and I can only assume that George was a last minute guest to satisfy Cook's need for clearing the food she's prepared, for her animosity towards waste.

'No father today?' Stating the obvious I ask the assembled at large, although fully expecting mother to answer.

'No, dear and before you ask, I'm not sure – in fact have not the faintest idea – where he is. Dear John scoured the area close to the house and called for him across the lawns but without success. I can only assume that he has decided to launch himself into one of his stupid hobbies and has become so engrossed that he's forgotten the time or is unable to hear the lunch gong or John's call.'

George looks up at me and – albeit in a somewhat scathing manner as I would have expected from the others – pre-empts our question: 'I know that many of you will be surprised to see me, but had Charles been here I am sure he would have explained – although of course, there would be no need as I

223

would not be here!' He guffaws when he's finished his little speech, not realising where it would end when he began. 'As it is, I must leave it to him to make the explanation at a later time or date and enjoy my lunch which, I have to say, is the best lunch I have ever seen.' He smiles and looks at Lavinia who returns his smile with a bland meaningless equivalent. I can rest easy, there is clearly no relationship between them. Nor indeed should there be, but my investigations have revealed so many assignations that I can't be sure who is being unfaithful with whom.

Gareth Hudson often joins the family for lunch as there is frequently or has been, something wrong or about to be wrong with one or more of them and it's useful to have him around, on the spot so to speak, rather than having to call him in from wherever he is enjoying his Sunday afternoon in peace and quiet.

Despite the fact that we are all enjoying lunch, he launches into the matter of the times.

'You'll all be interested to know that the new post-mortem report has been completed and apparently Sodium Phosphate was not the primary cause of Alan Broadoak's death; in fact, nothing to do with it at all. Well, I say nothing at all, that isn't strictly true. It was one of what we call a cocktail of drugs: Pentobarbital a fairly new drug discovered by someone (whose name escapes me) 30 years ago which renders the victim unconscious; Pancuronium one of those drugs used in South American arrow poisons and then Potassium chloride (Sodium Phosphate) which causes a heart attack. But it's the combination of the three poisons that caused poor old Alan to collapse without any warning, convulsions or shaking. Nothing. Just death. Well, you know what I mean.'

My mother is somewhat squeamish, and I'm surprised that it's taken her so long to say: 'Are we sure that to discuss such matters is quite appropriate at the lunch table?'

Dr Hudson says: 'No, of course not, sorry, we'll wait until we have finished eating, but they've found – oh, yes, sorry.' The sight of mother's raised hand not more than twelve inches from his face reminds him of the agreement he made only seconds before.

John brings in the desserts comprising sherry trifle or bread and butter pudding with custard or as it comes in, there is, of course, the inevitable cheeseboard to follow and so I choose the lighter sherry trifle but everyone else lumps for the bread and butter pudding, dutifully served by John leaving the custard to be poured by the diners. I was pleased to see my bowl filled with sherry trifle no doubt in part to nobody else having any and I returned his generosity with a broad smile.

'Thank you, John. I shall enjoy each spoonful as I watch the others chew lightly through their puddings.'

Mother says: 'Well, Alicia it's Sunday so is there some chance that you will be leaving us all alone this afternoon; or do you have one or more of us in your sights intending to baffle us with questions you have already asked but using different words, trying to trick us into saying something different so that you might trick us into admitting that we are the killer?'

She isn't wrong about the questioning and now that we know the cause of death – or at least the probability of the cause – I will obviously be asking additional questions. My mother can be well, very, you know, challenging!

'I thought we could have an afternoon off and look forward

to afternoon tea, dinner and bridge. How does that sound to everybody?' It's bound to sound good and I think I've gained points from each and every one of them. Although not everybody seemed to like the idea and I wonder why.

'Dr Hudson?' I really can't leave this until later.

'Yes, my dear?'

I hate being called my dear by people outside the family, so he's on a downward slope from the start. 'Forgive me, but you are a GP and, indeed our GP, but you've given us a very detailed result of the Post-mortem or at least of the drugs used.'

'Yes, my dear.' He coughs and his oversized belly wobbles as if its pleased to go on what might seem like a short walk, in anticipation of the ongoing movement.

'I only ask because as the family investigator I want to be sure of the cause of Mr Broadoak's death before proceeding.'

He replies, bristling as he does so: 'Well, I suppose it's true that I have merely read the report and quoted as best I can what it contains. I can claim no deep knowledge of these drugs, where they come from, for what purpose the murderer might have used them or in what proportions. I can only extrapolate from it says in the report which I'm sure can be made available to you if you so wish.'

He looks across at Mother for agreement, which she must have given as he continues, although its essentially waffle trying to justify his fees. But he launches into another speech as further justification:

'As I was saying at lunch, Sodium Phosphate was the first suggested poison because it could easily be somewhat bizarrely absorbed through Alan Broadoak's eye drops. The second guess – yes, guess, because some of these poisons are not easy to identify, only small quantities can cause death and we don't know whether it was given to the deceased, Eserine that is, in small doses or in a larger dose. But it comes from only a small part of the world – Nigeria I think it is – and is difficult to obtain, a large quantity may have been difficult to obtain. The killer is trying to make it hard for we doctors because it's almost impossible for any of us to find out anything about it and we've also considered Mercury given over a long period, but it is difficult to imagine how it was administered. The surgeons are continuing their research and a cause will be found. Once it is, we may well have our killer.'

At the end of his repetitive foray into the truth of the perceived drug cocktail used as the murder weapon, he looks at me with a well-practised smile. I bet I can read his thoughts:

'There you are, I've told them what I believe and with my reputation in the community and relationship with the family – as I am sure you're aware – they're bound to agree with my assessment of the situation and what degree you will have information from the post mortem at the very least several points ahead.' Or something similar!

Okay so now he's backed into a corner, on the back foot as they say. He has control of the situation, but we can't have that.

I say, 'You are very kind, Dr Hudson I'll talk to the pathologist so that he can release copies to me and all the other interested parties to avoid any delay while waiting for them to each ask for a copy.' I turn away from my adversary and intentionally dismissively decide to speak to mother of Dr Hudson and his last, somewhat pompous speech.

He says: 'I'll see you both later.'

He must know what I'm going to say and has decided he

doesn't want to hear it. He knows that I'm right. He doesn't care. At last he's out of hearing distance and I can see that mother is finding the whole thing too much, generally too complicated so I try to keep it short.

'Mother, he didn't say anything about how those drugs worked. I know you want to find out how Alan was killed and who did it, but we do have to investigate all these things further. Ok, my love?'

'I know, dear, but it's starting to upset me and I'm afraid if all that talking, and questioning happens and if they start saying anything to me I shall start to get all confused and that won't help anyone will it? You'll look after me won't you? Dr Hudson has never liked me, so he'll put me at the top of his murderer's list. But I didn't kill him. Alan I mean. Honestly. You do believe me, don't you dear? Please, you must.'

She no longer presents herself as the efficient, welcoming lady of the house. She no longer has any degree of control and she is at anyone's, everyone's beck and call, and will agree to anything put to her. She couldn't kill a dead spider let alone her bridge partner and lover.

I certainly believe that she believes she didn't kill him. At least not on her own. I hope to God she wasn't involved or that this isn't the most impressive, successful bluff of all time.

Only time and Detective Inspective Drabble will tell.

Chapter Thirty Seven

'Come in.'

The voice sounds frustrated, uncooperative and as though the speaker really has no time to talk to me, although I have given nothing to indicate that I am here to discuss the latest findings. As I step into Leonard Drabble's room he doesn't look up but simply points at the empty chair facing his desk and the only surface that isn't covered with files or random sheaves of paper. I dutifully sit and wait for him to bring his head out from a file the contents of which seem be thickening as each minute passes.

'Yes?'

A grunt, still no sign of recognition. I must use a more powerful perfume next time, but I clear my throat for the time being.

'Good morning, Leonard how are things going? It looks as though they're getting you down.'

He doesn't deserve any more of a welcome.

'Yeahsss, I'm trying to get your family sorted out and I'm getting nowhere. I suppose you're going to tell me that that's why you're helping me and that that's why you're here.'

'It is and I am.' Now he gets a smile, an 'I've got you right where I want you' smile and he knows it,

'Okay, I give in. Just tell me who did it, how they did it and why and I promise to buy you lunch.'

I raise my eyebrows. 'Lunch?' I pause for effect. 'Not dinner?'

He sits down hard on his chair with a much more welcoming smile on his face than I think I've seen for a long time. 'Okay, dinner. Whether my expenses will stretch to it or not, it'll be my treat. A real treat to get rid of all of your family files off my desk and back on the floor for some unsuspecting constable to sort out and file. I reckon you'll have earned it.'

'Thank you and I'll certainly have done that. You've had the PM report I assume and read it from cover to cover, so you'll know that we know – almost certainly – that Alan Broadoak was murdered by poisoning (there's a surprise) and that it was by using a lethal dose of a Potassium cocktail of drugs. How it was delivered remains unclear. Although by injection is the most effective, by mouth would have worked just as well in conjunction with the small Potassium Chloride pills Alan was taking for his weak heart and, it seems, his war wounds. Not only are we uncertain of how the drug was delivered we have no idea who murdered him. I have my suspicions but none of them can be backed up yet and to reveal them even to you is likely to confuse the investigation even further.'

'Interesting, I too have my suspicions about who killed him, but I don't want to tell you for the same reason. Well, Mrs Matcham you seem to have everything under control and heading fast towards a conclusion. I must ask who your principal suspect is.'

I shake my head not wanting to give in if nothing else. He's staring at me and he is a policeman after all, so I give in. 'Well, okay, I suppose top of my list is my Father and/or somebody instructed by him to carry it out, but I'm really not sure who those people are.'

'So, two of them you reckon, no wonder it's complicated and to be honest it seems as though you've really made no progress at all.'

'Oh I have – in my mind if nowhere else, as I said, I don't want to say anything because it's still a bit confused. It's probably two of them but I can't be sure it's two of them and that's why I am reluctant to tell you anything further. If it is Father, I'm honestly no closer as to what his motive is, although again I have my suspicions.'

'So, why are you here taking up my valuable time?'

He's laughing. We're both relaxed, enjoying the short break between trying to solve our murder mystery and anything else he might have on his desk. His is an intense business and everyone needs a break now and again even a short one like this.

'Well, Leonard,' I'm smiling as I move slowly towards him as if speaking to a wayward child, 'to make sure we don't waste our valuable times we need to keep each other up to date as we originally agreed. To summarise where we are; it helps to tell somebody else, somehow it helps.'

'Right, I'll need to say goodbye, I'm up to my armpits in another murder, a drowning in the Creek but definitely nothing to do with your lot and not your sort of stuff at all, before you ask. Go on, you carry on independently, just tell me when you're nearly there, I have to keep the bosses in Maidstone satisfied that I'm making progress!'

'Thanks, Leonard you're a star.' He comes around his desk and as we shake hands I pull him close quite easily and give him a peck on the cheek. His ease of movement almost wanting, showing a willingness is slightly disconcerting. Now, as you'll remember I'm not averse to a bit of flirting and indeed the odd kiss here and there, but I have never considered that Leonard and I – well will almost certainly not, you know. It's just that in this situation that sort of thing helps to oil the wheels as they say. It doesn't mean that we're going to leap into bed, just as I appreciate what he's just said and that we're more friends rather than business contacts. It helps both of us. Up to a point.

'Nice perfume.' He notices, perhaps he needed something to happen before mentioning it.

'Thank you. Glad you like it. It's new this year, it's called 'Distinction' if you want to buy your wife a spray, but I warn you – it's a bit expensive.'

'Money isn't an issue – I don't have a wife.'

'May I be so bold as to ask why?'

'She died; eight years ago it is now, in that railway accident outside the station. A bad year, lots of us lost our loved ones; mind you it brought a lot of us together working through the rubble looking for our wives or our husbands, kiddies – that was the worst – all the time clearing everything away to get the trains running again. I shall never forget 1925. Sorry, you didn't want to know all that, but perhaps all this,' he spreads his arms across the floor-covering of files 'the work's helped – something to do, you know? Nobody to go home to. Not anymore.'

As he speaks, and tears well up in his eyes I move forward and give the poor man a dangerous hug. I'm guilty of bringing memories to the surface when there was no need, all because of the high cost of my perfume. 'Sorry, I shouldn't have mentioned it – the perfume – sorry, Leonard.'

'It's not your fault, I try to keep it bottled up – you know – personal stuff, it's not supposed to affect my work.'

'It'll be our secret and I shan't mention it again.'

As I relax my hug and begin to move away we give each other a smile and I kiss his cheek again, this time with more affection but still nothing romantic and I hope I haven't gone too far.

'Look, sorry, Alicia, I really should be getting on before anything else comes through the door to distract me'

'Yes, and I'm late for an appointment with Frank Spillett – not that he would have been on time anyway!'

Both of us force a laugh as I open his office door and I walk through to the general office. I get no looks from the detectives as I suspect they all know what has passed between us during our meeting and I wonder if it happens on a regular basis, whether he sees his office as an interview room for another wife. In which case I am insulted. As I walk towards the front door, I make a mental note not to wear that perfume when I'm going to meet Leonard again.

Chapter Thirty Eight

Pentobarbital – made from early 1900s condemned unconsciousness.

Pancuronium – used by the South Americans in their arrow poisons.

Potassium chloride – induces a heart attack.

Eserine – discovered in the early 1930s specifically in Nigeria and neighbouring Gold Coast in West Africa; recently available in the UK and paralyses the heart

The cocktail is used as a lethal injection in the Americas.

After my emotional meeting with Leonard I'm not sure if I can cope with anything else today, least of all talking to a common gumshoe (as the Americans would say), but I might see Tommy and/or Jennifer and either would brighten my day.

I leave Church Street – the seemingly danger road as far as Tommy, who is very wary and mistrusting of policemen, says – and I drive along East Street towards the town centre and the Town Hall and have to stop at the traffic lights at the bottom of Preston Street on my left; I can see only the north end of the town hall and I mention this in such detail because during my, as always short, wait for the lights to change to green, out of the shadows provided by the International Stores from the ever brightening sun, a small figure leaps into the passenger seat.

'Wotcha miss, sorry if I surprised you, but I couldn't miss a chance to see you and I'd heard you were inside the cop shop so here I am.'

'I confess I'm not surprised,' I say letting off the hand brake and gently moving the car forward following another sports car, 'anybody jumping into my car would surprise me, you could have been a thief or even worse a killer, but it's no less than you, Tommy, my best mate.' I turn briefly to look at him and see that his cheeky grin has spread from ear to ear presumably at my calling him 'my best mate.' 'So what is it that is so important?'

'I wanted to stop you before you got any furver.'

'But why? Look, I can't stop here, not in the middle of the road.'

'You'll 'ave to drive into Middle Street, over there,' he points and I follow, 'You can stop vere long enough for me to explain what's happening. Please, miss

'Right, right, if you say so.' Much to the annoyance of the driver in my pursuit I signal to turn right giving less notice than one is supposed to. I drive slowly along the cobbled lane past The ODEON Picture House and stop in what Tommy is confident is 'the middle' and I ask why he's being so particular.

'We needs to try 'n' make sure vat nobody knows we're 'ere.' His dialect becomes more pronounced the more concerned he is about our predicament. His breathing is becoming heavier, showing greater concern. The more worried he's getting, the more am I.

'Come on Tommy; you've scared me half to death, you've

made me park in a narrow lane where the police could penalise me for doing so and now you're talking as if we could be murdered at our next breath! Our friendship could suddenly cease to exist if you don't say something sensible to relieve the dreadful terror I'm beginning to feel inside.'

It's clear from what he says next that he's heard little of what I've said and understood less. He's been concentrating on what's happening around us and trying to work out whether we're safe long enough for him to explain. He's decided that we're safe.

'Sorry, miss, I had to make sure we was safe.'

'And are we?'

'Yeah, for a while anysways.'

'Right, come on then, spit it out.'

'The man's at Frank's. It aint safe for you – for – us to go there while he's there.'

'The man?'

'The murderer. The man you're chasing after.'

'But, Tommy that's wonderful. Excellent. We can go down there, solve the mystery and catch the killer at the same time. He'll tell us how and why he did it and I can go and tell Detective Inspector Drabble and then I can go back to Bletchley.'

'You aint serious, miss. We can't do vat. His strong men will kill us before we gets anywhere near 'im and we'll end up dead before we even seen 'is face. You're mad; worse.'

'I know, Tommy, I'm afraid I was playing a trick on you but we might at least be able to find who's down there.'

This is a situation where we need Leonard's help. Leonard and all the forces he has at the police station which I understand are not very many! He's said I need to give him notice of a 'raid' as he called it and at the very least I need to get more information from Tommy before we can decide what steps should be taken next.

'Sorry, Tommy you're right of course. Firstly, who is 'the man', presumably you mean the murderer, the actual murderer not one of his henchmen and not the one who bought the poisons.' He turns out that he still thinks only one person was used.

'Poisons, miss?'

I don't think I've seen Tommy's face showing what, I think, reflects panic.

'Yes, we now know that it's likely that at least three different poisons were used to kill Mr Broadoak. They were bought separately and then mixed – we don't know where – to get the right mix before they were given to Mr Broadoak.'

'Vat means vat I's been given duff information. 'less all free was –'

He's lost in thought now, he's been betrayed, and his troop of informers have let him down. Badly. I can see him trying to recover his position, it's possible that his mate has sold all the poisons to whoever it was and had premixed them so that the buyer had only to decide the method of administration. If this was the situation it can be recovered. I can see his brain, crunching the alternatives searching for the next step. Firstly, how he can get the situation checked and fast. He looks up at me as if I can help with the first step and I shrug, I have no idea what to do next.

'I'm sorry Tommy, I don't know what you're thinking about what or about whom so I can't come up with any clever solutions,' He looks up at me, puzzled. 'ways out'.

'Oh, no miss, I know. There's no way you can help me now – not at the moment anysways. I'll just 'ave to be careful and let you know what we need to do next.'

My new priority is to find out who we need to avoid and Tommy must know otherwise he would not now be panicking. He is out of the car now and creeping further along Middle Street to an area which I think is called Court Street. Honestly, there are so many little roads and narrow streets that I'm surprised anybody can find anywhere they want to go. I watch him, resisting my strong urge to call out to find out what he's doing. For a few minutes that seem like hours nothing has happened. He's keeping crouched in the corner where the two streets join. He can presumably see into the main road ahead in the same way that I can see his grubby backside. After an even longer wait, he turns and runs in a funny sort of way crouched while he's running. Very funny. I don't wait for him to get back in the car.

'Tommy?'

'Ssshhh.' He puts a grubby little finger to has grubby mouth. 'Sorry, miss. I just seen 've man what's bought the drugs who's down there doing more business – he spends all 'is time buyin' and sellin' drugs. Vat' what he does.'

'So whoever it is must be going to murder somebody else.'

'Most likely you, miss if they think you're getting close to finding out who murdered your Mr Broadstaff.'

'Broadoak, Tommy, not Broadstaff.'

'Yeah, right, does it matter?'

'I hadn't thought of that, he might be going to murder me?' A shiver runs down my spine as my investigation takes on a whole new dimension. My gosh, how can I possibly carry on while I'm having to watch my own back while I'm watching someone else's?

'Tommy, what can we do? What can you do?'

'Don't worry, miss, I'll get done what needs to be done, I promise. You don't need to worry. Leave it to me, 'vere's no need for you to worry and I don't fink any of your friends or family will be involved – not yet anyway.' He's almost grinning, I've never seen such a wicked grin and now's not the time for grinning.

'I'll ignore the last part of what you've just said about family and friends except, have you actually been told that someone in my family is involved? Or, heaven forbid actually be the murderer.'

''eaven forbid, miss?'

'God forbid; surely not; the very last thing I would expect.'

'Oh, yeah, right – heaven forbid, miss.' He winks and shows me one of his face splitting grins harbouring two sets of blackening teeth and I think he's just added another expression to his lexicon.

Chapter Thirty Nine

'Right, Tommy, why did we have to stop in Middle Street and go nowhere near Creek Street? I understand dear boy what you've just told me about the man buying and selling drugs, but did we have to stop? What's happening at Frank Spillett's offices because that's where I was heading?'

'Word is that the drugs used was a mix of – an' let me off if I gets the words not quite right, miss - Pentoburial; Pancratium and Tassium chlorive and somefin' that's a new one – Eserine? Does they sound right?

'Pretty much, you're a clever boy Tommy. I know about the second two, Pancuronium freezes the body so no part of it can move or show any pain or convulsions. Mr Broadoak didn't show signs of any convulsions or pain so that explains why, when he died, he simply fell forward. Potassium Chloride is a well-known drug for causing death by causing heart attacks. In small doses it gives relief to the sufferers with weak hearts or low blood pressure but if the weekly dose is increased over a long period a heart attack is likely to occur. So that's what actually killed him – what caused him to fall forward? We know that he had low blood pressure and was prescribed Potassium Chloride as a treatment for that, so the murderer had an easy way of killing him but needed to cover the normal side effects associated with the overdose of Potassium that Broadoak was going to be given.'

His eyes were glassing over, but I felt I should go on because it might help him understand how complicated and dangerous all the drugs were and why. He was quite bright, so I carried on regardless.

'Pentobarbital I don't know about, but I expect it kills people.' He laughed. I had his attention again. ' So why stop here today?'

''Cos Frank's involved and I don't know what he does.'

'So is this why Frank was reluctant to take me on as a client. Most of his income comes from drugs and the investigations for people like me get in the way.'

'Yeah, vat's why I needed to keep an eye on you, you and Maggie here. You don't know vese parts like I do and I didn't want you hurt.' Another grin.

'I must move on, back into the real world, Tommy and I'll presumably see you when my car needs looking after again.' I've finished with all this complicated undercover business and I'm not sure how much I should have told Tommy although the rest of the complicated details I've kept to myself, when, what and why. He doesn't need to know what I know and how complicated and dark it is, but it's all underground ages away from where we simply wonderful people are, and our lives must go on. So, if I go to see Frank or Jennifer or someone else I shall go away and see them. I shan't consider that I might be murdered. Heavens No!

I leave Middle Street and the surrounding merry-go-round of

lanes, turn into Quay Lane and park my car outside Frank's offices as usual. There is no reason to suppose that there's anything afoot. There is as yet no sign of Tommy anywhere and I shall have to trust to good fortune that nothing happens to Maggie in his absence. The front door to the offices is open and I can hear raised voices at the top of the stairs. I can't hear the subject which has caused the rumpus but I proceed up the stairs and by the time I reach the top, the shouting has stopped and Jennifer is sitting at her desk looking very unsettled and on the verge of, or barely in control of the end of, a period of tears. Her face and especially her cheeks are very red, and her eyes appear large in their sockets.

'Jenny, are you all right?' It's a ridiculous question but it's one we all ask when faced with a distressed person. She looks at me but appears to be so upset that to make any movement or to even say anything is impossible. I can hear Frank shouting in his office and watch Jenny's face for any sign of the cause. There is none and I sit next to her in an attempt to protect and encourage her. The door opens and Frank bursts out of his office looking more dishevelled than usual. He looks briefly at Jenny and then turns his attentions to me.

'What the hell are you doing here woman? You're not due a report this week and even if you were I've nothing to say to you, so you might as well go and let us get on with what we were doing.' His temper is subsiding.

'I'm sorry but I am concerned about my friend, Jennifer here and I will wait until she has regained her normal state of composure before I do or say anything else.'

'Things, things have gone wrong. I must sort them out I – '.

'We'll see you later.' I glare at Frank and indicate that he should leave. He goes back into his office and slams the door shut.

Jennifer and I spend the best part of quarter of an hour with her snivelling and trying to explain what had caused the rumpus and that Frank was involved in something that she didn't fully understand and that she was reasonably sure Frank didn't either.

I say, 'Jenny, we've established that Frank hasn't prepared a report for me nor has he for some time and in fact it seems he's changed his mind and doesn't really want me as a client. It sounds as though I'm making it too complicated for him' She nods, appearing confident that our meetings will soon come to an end. 'I'm not sure that he has provided information worth the initial amount of cash I gave him, but we can probably ignore that complication.'

'I think he probably did do enough work to start with, Alicia and he definitely wanted you as a client, but I agree he doesn't seem to be too worried now. I'm not sure why.'

'Perhaps we need to try to find out what's caused the problem.

'All I know is that he's just taken on another new client who I'm sure is tied up with one of the Creek Gangs – that could certainly be worrying him.'

'I'd be worried if they were one of my clients. He won't be able to release information to anyone and especially you; a bit like I told him to do except that what I didn't do is threaten him with death!'

She laughs, at last the spell has broken. 'Tea?'

'I thought you'd never ask.' I squeeze her hand and let her go to the kitchen.

'So, what did you really come here for? An update on his

work for you? Like he said there isn't another report and to be honest I don't think he's done much on your case for a long time.'

'Right, now tell me what you know. Please.'

She passes me the steaming tea and before sitting down, closes the door at the top of the stairs presumably in an attempt to make sure that we can't be overheard by any unexpected visitors. 'I can only tell you what I've overheard round and about and what I've picked up from the street. You'd be best to talk to Tommy for that local gossip. I know that this new client is a faceless, nameless specialist killer taken on by the South Creek Gang.

'This killer, he brought the poison with him there's been no buying or selling as far as I know in this office, so I don't know what all the fuss is about. I heard somebody say something about a Gold Coast, but I'm not sure where or what that is. The street says the killer is American, but it may be that he (or I suppose it could have been a she) came over to give it to the killer and tell them how to use it. But I'm not sure about that. Tommy would know, he has contacts in both gangs. Plays it dangerous does Tommy. Whatever is going on is bigger than most of the drugs and murders are. Everyone's scared stiff. We haven't seen him for a couple of days.'

'He's fine, I hope he's watching Maggie at the moment. So, we're no nearer to knowing who actually killed my mother's friend or why.'

'I did hear something to do with your father in the war but then everyone knows the story about him saving your John's life don't they so it can't be that. Some of them say that your father owed the murdered man money and couldn't pay it back or didn't want to or something. But I can't see your father killing anyone for anything can you? He's a lovely old man, forgive me for saying so.'

'No, I can't either but then he's my father so I'm not really the person to ask. There must be some truth stuck in the middle of all that stuff somewhere. Thank you Jenny, I mustn't take up any more of your time. Thank you. Now, you look after yourself and if you want to telephone me at home, at Corners that is, you can. Oh and another thing, he's not 'my' John' by the way. That seems a bit harsh because sometimes I very much feel as though he is, but then why should the streets know that.

All she does is nod and start to shake and then says: 'No, Mrs Matcham of course he isn't so the street must be wrong.' Now she grins and I feel slightly embarrassed that the street might not have anything better to talk about.

'Don't worry Jenny, darling, he won't do anything to you, but telephone me if you're worried. Okay?'

I stumble down the stairs holding what passes for the hand-rail, out into the bright sunshine and find Tommy is pretty much where I left him but is now sprawled across 'Maggie's' bonnet again as usual. 'Thank you, Tommy, would you like another ride?'

'Ooo, yes please, miss. I's looked after her and given 'er a quick polish whiles you were up 'ver.'

'Come on then, let's go.' There's a slight breeze coming up the Creek as we drive into the face of the incoming air flow, down along Creekside as far as the turning for Seasalter. 'Do you fancy a longer ride today?' Without waiting for a reply I drive towards the reed beds and the stony beach of the sham-bles that is Seasalter. With the breeze in our hair I felt that we were running away from my father and heading towards an illicit weekend in Margate. It was great fun and I turn to look at Tommy sitting smartly next to me. 'Are you enjoying your ride, Tommy?'

He in turn looks at me, we're facing each other, and I raise my hand toward his cheek wanting to touch him but of course I manage to resist. There's never any question of me approaching him in that way – I'm not that sort of girl – but perhaps more importantly, I don't want to risk losing his help in building a case to find the murderer. Even though it was barely more than a twitch, I could tell that he'd seen my hand move towards him, 'I'm sorry, Tommy, I don't know what came over me I was never going –.'

'That's all right, miss, I know how these things work and I knew your hand would stop where it did. It's one of them fings, I look so much older van I am so…'

'But I'm sorry nevertheless I should never even have crossed my mind, I suppose it's just that you remind me so much of someone I know in London.'

'D'you love this bloke, miss?'

'I don't know, but you look so much like him. Sorry, it won't happen again. Come on we must get back and on with our plans.'

He smiles one of his enigmatic smiles, I turn Maggie around and we sweep back to Faversham.

Chapter Forty

M y summarising

There is now no doubt whatsoever in my mind – as I'm sure that there is not in your mind - that Alan was poisoned, possibly by drinking or by injection shortly before they began playing bridge. The end of the evening's game came at the conclusion of a rubber at which he died. There is an indeterminate time lag before the barbiturate takes effect, the length of that time delay is irrelevant as long as Alan goes into the bridge room rather than wandering off anywhere else. He would have gone into the card room immediately after dinner, bridge players are determined human beings and once they have agreed a time to begin, there is little that will alter that decision!

While I know pretty well who the killer is, the timing of the murder and the means of the murder; the source of the drugs is unknown but to a large extent that's irrelevant, at least in terms of the guilty party or parties and the motive – perhaps the most important of the element of the killing – has yet to be clarified

Mother is unlikely to be the murderer: she is too feeble, and she was having an affair with Alan. There's no obvious motive unless she has suddenly become jealous of Charles's affair with

Joan, but it's been going on for so long this is unlikely.

'Cetta hasn't got a clue about anything but cooking and gossip. Her affair with Alan was many years ago and bears no relevance to the current situation. It's impossible to imagine there is anybody who could consider possibly their affair to be worthy blackmail or jealousy.

George Hind is in business with my father but I've looked into the company's financial records and there are no complications or difficulties involving either of them or any loans or wrongdoings in the company which Alan could have been involved with that might suggest a motive for dispensing with him, nor have I uncovered any affairs between George and any member of my family or close friends that could tie into a reason for murder.

Dr Gareth Hudson is the most able to get hold of the drugs but if he did why is there so much additional drug activity in Creek Street? He wasn't anywhere near Corners when the lethal injection or dispensing of the drug was given. I suppose he might have persuaded someone else to give the injection but that's extremely unlikely. And why would he want to murder Alan unless the latter was aware of any wrongdoings by Gareth that Alan had uncovered. My investigations show no evidence of any such wrongdoings.

Patty is unlikely to have been desperate for me to come down from Town if she were the killer. Her level of innocence is not entirely to be believed but I can see no evidence as to why she should murder Alan, even if she had found out that Alan had found out something that Father had done and for which Alan was going to blackmail him. The police and Gareth had already written the whole thing off as a heart attack so why should she stir things up unnecessarily? Nor would she have any means or knowledge of how to find the drugs. And most convincingly (though still hard to believe) Patty and Alan were lovers.

Joan Saynor would be extremely unlikely to murder him as she has no motive – they were lovers after all – unless Alan had discovered her affair with Charles and that he was blackmailing Charles and she wanted that to stop: she had easier access to the drugs than most of the other suspects because she lives on the banks of The Creek but it is doubtful whether she had the contacts although she does know Tommy albeit not necessarily who he really is – or at least there is no evidence that she knows…

That leaves just three people who could have killed Alan: Father, John and me! So, on the face of it any one of the three of us is the murderer or we have provided a reason for Alan to blackmail somebody within our little group and that one of us therefore murders him or someone who cares for one of us murders Alan to prevent him taking any action.

I have reached a point of uncertainty in a serious sequence of motives based on who knows what about whom and whether Alan knew of the motives and had decided that the wrongdoers were worthy of blackmailing.

To say the least the situation is complex and even now, I'm not sure that I have summarised the situation correctly. Of one thing I can be sure and that is that I have not summarised the situation clearly enough for you to understand. Suffice it to say that it's Father, John or me who is most likely to have murdered Alan Broadoak or caused him to be murdered.

The following pages follow that assessment.

Chapter Forty One

For my entire life I have believed my father to be an honest man; an upright citizen; if not on a nationwide analysis); a considerate employer to his company workforce and to our domestics; forthright certainly but also fair. As children we – or at least I – thought of him as stern although perhaps serious, strict and a little harsh would describe him more accurately. He was – is – a Christian of sorts and we always went to church every Sunday; with such frequency that we had a pew put aside just for us, an inheritance I have since found out as a leftover from the Lord-of-the-Manor period in history. His belief did not prevent him going to war in 1914. He returned from the war as an atheist and yet still insisted that we went to church. We were always led to believe that he fought in a number of campaigns, gained a number of medals and was mentioned in despatches on several occasions and we have no reason to disbelieve what we were told and not infrequently reminded of. He retired from the army at the rank of Colonel and still insists on being addressed as such by everyone other than his family – our family!

We know that during action, Alan Broadoak was father's batman and that they became what you might call close friends then, when early on in the war Alan was invalided out of the services, John Staples was appointed in his stead. Similarly, on de-mob they continued to be friends and as such, Alan was appointed butler here at Corners until he inherited his own estate and was replaced by John who remains our butler to this day. Dear John. I love him dearly. His relationship with my father is less obvious than was Alan's. They were close friends despite their difference in rank, but since John's arrival here, at Corners their relationship has been erratic. It varies from one of absolute devotion to, at the other end of the scale, unfettered hatred.

As a bridge player, father's interest began before the war and he carried playing – to his distaste they played for money – throughout his spare time in the mess. When he returned home it became one of his favourite pastimes, second only to eating, drinking and playing billiards. Oh, and walking. He had developed a great belief in keeping fit to the extent of a brisk walk every morning along Chalk Pit Lane through Ospringe and back to Corners via the London – Dover road. He was a reasonably good billiards player but had never been a particularly good bridge player although his powers of concentration and a determination to win were great assets. He was, however, unforgiving of his partner as Joan Saynor had good cause to mention when I had seen her at her house on the banks of the Creek.

The building firm established by my grandfather was once again thriving through no thanks to the destruction heaped on the town during the war. Faversham itself was of no interest to the Germans and their cohorts but the Creek and the gunpowder works certainly were and we are constantly hearing stories of close escapes and great explosions; meanwhile we are all grateful that with the threat of another war, the works have been closed within the last couple of years. The brickworks too were coming into their own, supplying the Whitten building firm at cost while others around them were charged at a good profit.

In short, father was a hardworking, generally supportive father, a presumed loving husband, a good employer who prided himself with good gamesmanship. My father was well to do. He worked hard and played hard. He was a pillar of the community. Why would he murder Alan Broadoak? Why would he get somebody else to do the job for him?

On reflection I can see no reason why I should have ever considered him a possible murderer and I have to cross him off the list, leaving John and myself.

Chapter Forty Two

I have already told you of John's war career and how he connected with my father. It's true to say that he was grateful to father for giving him a job when Alan inherited his estate, but he always harboured the knowledge that he was second best. That he should have been given the job as soon as the de-mob had arisen. He was every bit as good as Alan Broadoak and had suffered no war injuries while unswervingly serving his master throughout the conflicts. He had supported Colonel Whitten in the trenches and carried out orders unflinchingly, even when he sometimes questioned the legality of what he was asked to do.

Colonel Whitten had demonstrated an increasing drive for cleanliness in the trenches. He believed – perhaps correctly to some degree but totally impractical in the battles that encased them – that the effectiveness of his battalions would be improved if the trenches were clear of the dead and dying. Clear of debris.

There had been occasions – only three as John remembered under questioning – when John had received orders to remove a soldier from a trench and when he discovered that that comrade was still alive; very seriously injured and unlikely to live but nevertheless he should be cared for. His CO had reminded him of the order and added that it was more effective to kill him now and move his body. Against all his beliefs, John had carried out the order in recognition of the times when the Colonel had saved his life during a bombardment. Three times he had been saved, three soldiers had he killed under orders. His CO was or at least purported to be a Christian, forever quoting Matthew 5 verse 38: 'an eye for an eye, a tooth for a tooth'; what more could John do.

John has no family; his parents were killed early in the war and his only surviving sibling – a sister named Solenise – had been killed by her husband after a fight with one of their neighbours over a loaf of bread. Her husband was hanged before the means of her murder were determined and wild speculation had gone through the community as to whether the husband had used a knife, a heavy fist, poison or a knife. Nobody knew and nobody would. It took John a while to recover from the shock and then conscription took him over and he was saved by Colonel Whitten who became a father to him and saved his life.

There's no doubt that John owes a debt of gratitude towards my father for his actions throughout the war and giving him a living after the war. He has provided a roof over his head and clothing and belongings until he was able to repay my father by deduction from his wages.

He (John) had few hobbies or pastimes, indeed he would not have had much time to enjoy any: his job and the additional responsibility for being on call twenty four hours a day left little. He did like the odd pint on his day off and betting on the nags. He resisted flirting women although rumours have it that he had been seen with one on a regular basis and if pressed he would find it hard to deny. We had a special relationship, John and me. Our time together, time away from prying eyes and ears was infrequent but we had a structured regular pattern of when we could be alone, and our liaisons were always full of passion and intense love-making. Naturally, we were keen to preserve our anonymity not least since my investigations into Alan Broadoak's murder had begun because any association between us might have called many factors of the murder into question.

Despite our what I suppose anyone else would call a relationship it was really more of an agreement to have sex when we had the opportunity, I had to question him to the same extent and in the same way as I had the other members of the house. Neither of us knew everything about the other and while we were each certain that the other was not the murderer, propriety had to be maintained.

John and I met again in the card room for his follow up questioning.

'John, obviously I know much of your army career, but can you please confirm how it was that by pure chance you found yourself in the same battalion as my father who thus became your CO. After joining as an infantryman my father appointed you his batman in March 1917 following the repatriation of Alan Broadoak – my father's then current batman.'

'That's correct. Your father had saved me from severe injury and saved my life on three occasions while others lay severely injured and dying in the trenches. He was very loyal to his men and particularly to those who obeyed instruction by him unquestioningly. I always felt that we had a special bond during the latter parts of the conflict and obviously I continued to show how grateful I was when I came to Corners after Mr Broadoak vacated the position.'

'Have you felt, or do you currently feel any animosity towards Mr Broadoak? You have always appeared to have been second best – my father's back up if things went wrong or when Mr Broadoak vacated the positions unexpectedly. Nobody would blame you if you held a grudge against Mr Whitten for treating you the way he has.'

'But if I bore or bare a grudge against Mr Whitten and I had murdered somebody, surely I would have murdered your father not Mr Broadoak at whose door one could not attribute any blame. Far from it. It is my understanding that Mr Broadoak recommended me for the positions before he left both occupations,'

'I suppose so, although his making the recommendation I fear is untrue. The police have been right through your father's documents and records and see no reference to your change of jobs, even to the extent of having an incorrect date for your beginning as butler here at Corners, Now we must talk about the events of the night in question. It was Saturday 10th of June and Mr and Mrs Whitten were hosting their traditional Saturday dinner and bridge evening. In this instance their guests were Mrs Joan Saynor and Mr Alan Broadoak, correct?'

'Correct, madam but the guests are not always Mrs Saynor and Mr Broadoak.'

This came as a surprise to me as in previous discussions with members of the family and, indeed DI Drabble, there had been no suggestion or observation to this affect.

'There was a small group of players who took it in turns to make up the four, I believe is the correct term. It so happens that on Saturday it was the turn of Mrs Saynor and Mr Broadoak. I am not certain of the guests next week, but I have the details of those who visited last week, although the game was cut short when Dr Hudson had to leave early to care for one of his other patients.'

'If we stay with the Saturday of the murder for the moment: did everything appear normal to be following the usual pattern and timescale? Where you always asked to provide drinks for the players, did they always take the same partners and sit in the same seats?'

'I believe so, madam.'

'Think, John. Think.'

There was no crumpled nose or star gazing at the ceiling or hoes or hums, John simply stood where he was, staring into the distance just over my shoulder. He looked good enough to kiss, to bring him out of his trance, but I managed to remain professional and waited.

'I think, madam the only difference was that Mrs Saynor took a sweet sherry rather than her usual dry. Mr Whitten and Mr Broadoak had the usual port and Miss Whitten continued her sweet dessert wine as usual. I heard talk of cocktails for the ladies as was becoming the fashion, but Mrs Saynor was certain that those drinks were meant to be drunk before the meal.'

And I confirm that to be the case, madam. They all sat in their usual places and they used the usual two packs of cards. Mr Whitten was always the first dealer and he and Mrs Saynor always looked as though they were going to win and suddenly found themselves losing at great pace.'

'I thought you weren't able to play the game, John.'

'That's correct, but I recall the relevant outcomes of the comments made and the time by which they have given up playing. I don't need to know how to play, just what affect the result has on my masters and their guests.'

'And it all went as usual until Mr Broadoak collapsed on the table. From what you say, you were in the room all the time. Yes?'

'No, madam. I was present most of the time but there was an occasional break from play at the end of each rubber and during the following period of play it was necessary for me to replace the bottles and prepare drawing room for entertainment when the game had finished.'

'How long were you away from the game?'

'No more than ten minutes, slightly longer if – forgive me – I needed to visit the lavatory.'

'As you say, all things ran as normal.'

'Going back to the previous Saturday, 3rd June. Who were the guests?'

'Dr Hudson partnered Miss Whitten and Mr Whitten partnered a Miss Graham, a lady I have not seen before and for whom I am therefore unable to provide any further information.'

'And again – all was as normal.'

'Exactly so, Mrs Matcham.'

'Finally, if I were to ask you who had murdered Mr Broadoak, whom would you say was the prime suspect?'

'That's not for me to say, Mrs Matcham'

'But let's suppose they insisted – I insisted?'

'Mrs Whitten,'

'You didn't waste too much thinking about that, John,' he looks down as if his haste suggests something he didn't want to show, 'so, why her?'

'Mr Whitten's infidelity and that's despite her own and secondly, women usually murder people using poison as used here.'

'Thank you, John. It's helpful that you're able to speak with such great knowledge of the way women murder poor, unsuspecting men.' He's smiling at me, the type of smile he occasionally shows me, we both standing and move towards each other, embrace and kiss. His lips are warm to touch and, I imagine – I sense – are mine. The kiss brings a shine, a glow to my face as I feel them warming to his touch, reddening as the extra blood floods to my cheeks. I hold the back of his head and pull his hair, gently at first and then more strongly as our embrace becomes more passionate. We are standing grasping each other's body, our heads on each other's shoulder. 'We can't, John, there isn't time and this room is too public. Later, where we meet normally. Yes?'

'I'll be there, Alicia. I'll be there waiting.'

A final kiss and we part, knowing that we should break off the relationship, at least until the mystery has been solved. Knowing that we wouldn't and knowing that as the investigator I was still in control, it was my decision, he was still mine.

Chapter Forty Three

I have now completed my first and arguably the second round of questioning although I seemed to have asked the same questions on each round and I've had either different or additional information. After all that, while the world of innocence and guilt swirls around me, I'm sitting in my first floor bedroom sheltering from the searing midday sun, wondering (as I'm sure are you), that if I was on the other side of the fence and I was asked the same questions what my answers would be, what would be my reactions and if any subsequent action was appropriate. Of course I'm only doing all of this in my head, there's no point in writing it all down, nobody is surely going to read any of my replies.

I'm starting my list and surprise myself at some of the answers, in particular the times and whereabouts of the suspects. Once I slot in my own timings, I'm surprised that there are many instances when I don't have an alibi and of course that worries me, because sooner or later DI Drabble might well ask me the questions and quite rightly, from his point of view, there'll be no assumption of my innocence. That would be awful. When I think carefully, I realise that the reason I have no alibies for great swathes of weeks before the murder is because I was at home in Bletchley and my alibies will be numerous friends and colleagues in Milton Keynes. In Faversham Alan Broadoak is already dead.

My conscience is clear.

I drain the cup of coffee kindly brought me by Concetta, check that my clothes are appropriate and in position – one can't look scruffy even in one's own house, darling, particularly if you're going to interview your father – for the third time. He is not going to be pleased of the need for me to question him again and to arrive looking like well, a servant, wouldn't help matters. Father has never been a slave to fashion as fathers rarely are and although he appreciates everyone else's short skirts and dresses and particularly our set's partying and plunging neck-lines, he is less admiring of his own daughters' fashion choices. Patty always tries extremely hard to dress drably whereas I carry on regardless. Today however, I have made an effort and my bobbed hair and high neckline reveal merely a pair of in date heavy drop earrings and matching necklace all, of course, in solid silver. He would expect nothing less. I am stifling and have no doubt that that will become obvious to all but him.

Never mind, I can see him in the distance heading towards me with determination and I suspect he will still comment on my short dress.

'Hello, Father, out for a stroll - Mad dogs and Englishmen – all that sort of thing?'

'What? What are you talking about girl?'

''Mad dogs and Englishmen go out in the midday sun.' Even you must have heard of that: Noel Coward, from that show a couple of years ago. You must have done, you silly old thing.'

Notice that I have successfully mis-directed him, so that he ignores my skirt. Such attributes as the ability to misdirect are extremely useful when explaining things to people or pointing things out.

'Stuff and nonsense all this new ... anyway, I hear you want to talk to me again, about Alan. What else can I tell you?'

'Well, I pretty much know what you were doing around the time of the murder, but I'd really like to hear a bit more about your time in the war.'

'The war? Whatever for? That ended years ago. Talking about ending years ago my darling – why on earth is your dress short, firstly it must be very cold – which it isn't because even I can spot a heatwave when there is one – and secondly possibly more importantly it shows far too much of your legs.'

I've failed – I must make a note to practice.

'I know, obviously, but you were both there and I wondered if there was anything that happened during the war that might throw some more light on his murder. I am not saying that you murdered him of course. More importantly as you put it, these dresses are all the fashion and might even get shorter. It depends on what the designers think they can get away with. I don't expect you to understand, Father, but they're not cold and the shortness attracts the opposite sex.'

'Young men you mean.'

'And women.'

'Women?'

I pause whist he takes in the horror of women together. 'Yes, if they're jealous and want a closer look.'

He coughs for no apparent reason. 'Anyway, of course I never thought you'd be accusing me and well, I don't know what sort of thing you mean by extra information. But I suppose so if you must.'

Confusing him now, I expect him to give more away than he really wants to. 'Just start at the beginning and stop in 1918.'

'That'll take forever, you can't want it all – can you?'

'We've got all afternoon.'

'Well, oh all right then, here goes…'

Don't worry, I'm not expecting you to have to sit through it all. It took all afternoon and half of the next day before he'd finished and sat back in his chair looking as though the weight of the world had been lifted from his shoulders. He looked satisfied, triumphant and exhausted, despite the overnight sleep. What you need to hear about is the time when poor old Alan was shipped back to Blighty and John Staples took over his job.

'… We'd pushed on – still in Nigeria – as part of the West African Frontier Force and I was booted up to Colonel.'

'Well done.'

'I deserved it of course.' He flashes one of his rare smiles.

'I'm sure you did.'

'For the first time, I was given a batman. It took me a while to get used to having someone running about after me doing jobs and so on, pretty much as I ordered him to do. That is when I first met Alan Broadoak. Keen chap he was, infantry, no rank but willing and hardworking, nevertheless. After a while we became friends, I suppose you would call it. Not in a-let's-go-to-the-mess-and-get-soaked sort of friend but in a more relaxed master and servant way. He came into my dugout for tea, for the odd chat when things were quieter – that didn't happen very often.'

'What did you talk about?'

'All sorts of things but don't ask me now what they were: how many men we'd lost and how many had been shipped back; how many replacements we desperately needed and how many HQ were going to send us. Mainly about the locals how they kept changing from one side to the other so that it was difficult to know whether we should shoot them as the enemy or welcome them as recruits. Bloody mad time it was. There were hundreds of the damn things and actually, I was lucky to get a white chap as batman, a lot of my fellow officers were landed with natives who couldn't even speak the lingo.

Anyhow Alan was with me, I don't know, I suppose from mid-1915 to Christmas 1916. Then he took a bullet in the arm early 1917 which our medic sorted out and he carried on. Later in the year he took some shrapnel in both legs and was invalided out. Sent back here to Blighty. It took a few days to get him back, but our John Staples was brought in to replace him. To my surprise he was even better and fell into the job easily. He knew what to do and when and why I wanted something in a particular way. Amazing. Anyhow Broadoak was shifted out and I never saw him again until he was asked to join our Saturday evening bridge dinner followed by a few rubbers. He'd learned to play in the forces of course, but it was a different sort of game then – all done for money, cigarettes, saucy postcards and chocolate. It took him a while to catch on, but he was soon into our game and made a rather good partner for young Joan Saynor. Ended up playing little Patty of course.'

'Did you get together to talk about the war.'

'No, never. It was over and we had won. It was a war to end all wars and we had no wish to talk about it. It was gone, long gone, years past and forgotten. Thousands of men died fighting for their country, we must remember them but not the war itself. Even now, all these years later we acknowledge comrades when we come across them, but it's become an unwritten agreement.'

'That must be difficult, all those stories of campaigns and the battles won and lost.'

'It was sometimes, but Alan and I had never talked about it, even when we were alone with nothing but our memories and a bottle of port.' He laughs now, not at the action they had seen but the two of them sitting calmly drinking port, equals in a world that had suffered so much.

'And what about women?'

'Women?'

'Yes, women. Two chaps together you must have talked about sweethearts back home. Wives back home. Friends of the troops behind the trenches. That sort of thing.' I risk a cheeky grin to lighten the load.

'Well, of course they were mentioned, bound to be. As you say all lads together behind the lines.'

'But not much misbehaving of course, you were married.' I start one of those knowing winks we use all the time now, but decide against it and, I think, stop just in time.

'Of course not. No. We er…'

'No.' He seems somewhat embarrassed and I won't push him

any further. Thank you, Daddy darling. You've never talked about it before and I can see why now. Thank you.' I put my notepad on the table beside me and go over to give him a hug. He shies away at first but succumbs quite quickly, appreciating for the first time perhaps, what it means to have a daughter.

Changing the subject he says: 'Are we all done here at last? I think I just heard the lunch gong?'

'We are, let's go in before it gets hogged up.'

Arm in arm we stroll into the dining room only to find we're the first. John is still checking that the cutlery and glasses are in the correct places, even though I have told him time and again that such times are in the past and we should just sit down.

'John, what have I said about all this fuss and nonsense?'

'I remember, Mrs Matcham, forgive me.' As he speaks he casts a knowing eye at my father, reminding me that he will never change and all the time my father's in the house we will do things his way. I smile and nod trying to remember that I mustn't say anything again when father is with us.

As is so often the way, lunch was uneventful. The rest of the family joins us and because my chat with Daddy has been so personal, nothing more was mentioned except Mother chimes in with:

'Well, dear did the interview with your father reveal anything useful, any deep dark secrets?' Mother was clearly concerned about her relationship with Alan being discussed and Patty stopped talking to father because she is concerned about her relationship with Alan being revealed, while blissfully unaware of our mother's.

I trot out my standard speech: 'You all know that I cannot say anything about the discussions I had with Father, anything and everything said at any of your interviews is confidential – you wouldn't want me to reveal things said at our own little talks discussed over the lunch or at the dinner table would you?' I look at Mother and Patty consecutively and see that both are shaking their heads, quite vigorously. There's a surprise.

The brief encounter concluded, my parents and Patty leave the table, permitting a short, quiet time for me to be alone with John so that we can arrange another 'chat' in his pantry. 'I have some more specific questions to ask you I'm afraid.' He doesn't look afraid.

Five minutes later I am knocking on his pantry door which is partly open. He opens it enough to allow me into his private sanctum and then closes it firmly in defiance of anybody else's attempt to join us.

'I only have one question this time.'

'So you do really, have an actual genuine question.'

He's pulling my leg or more likely he wants to. 'Just one really, before we can settle down in peace and have one of our chats. It is about your time with father during the war."

'Oh not that bloody war again, I've told you all I know. Isn't that enough? I thought that was all behind me, behind all of us who served, and you keep on dragging it up.'

'I'm sorry, but it was and still is a large part of everyone's lives. I can't ignore it. When I was talking to Father earlier he mentioned how you easily fell into the job that Alan had been doing – better than Alan himself and that he was incredibly pleased were his actual words. Now as you know only too well, my father isn't known for giving praise and certainly in that mega-demonstrative way. Can you shed any light on why he might have thought that you were so wonderful?'

John is staring at the ceiling he is clearly wondering what to say. The question doesn't seem to have embarrassed him, not shaken him as I thought it might. 'John?'

'Sorry, I'm not sure why he would have said that. It's true that I didn't find the work difficult where Alan had found some of it particularly hard. And I suppose I might have done some things differently and that he liked my new ideas. But I can't think of anything in particular and he never called me amazing, but then I suppose it's not a word that we used in those days. Sorry.'

'Not to worry, it's just what he said and the way he said it. Perhaps he was just surprised you fitted in so well. How soon after the war did you get together again?'

'Oh, not until 1925 I think it was – around the time of that horrible rail accident near here. I was helping to clear away the bits of broken carriages and the rails with what machinery we had; a nasty job it was too, we never knew when we might find another body and there weren't enough firemen, police, engineers and the like, so the rest of us from Faversham and around had to muck in. Me and a mate of mine had just finished lifting some twisted seating (fortunately empty) when I heard Colonel Whitten's voice. He was ordering people around left right and centre,

I knew his voice instantly and afterwards wasn't surprised that he had assumed responsibility for one section of the track. I turned around but he didn't recognise me at first, not until he looked down and saw me climbing across some rubble towards him. Styles, he called out, then grabbed my hand, we embraced – which he suddenly seemed to realise was most inappropriate – and we exchanged means of getting in touch. You could have knocked me down with a feather when nearly a year later, I got a telephone call from him inviting me up to Corners for lunch. He offered me this job and here I am. He said he knew I could do it because it was just like being a batman really but without the deaths and with clean cutlery and china. I remember him laughing when he said that. You couldn't make it up really.'

'No, I suppose not. Did you have anything to do with Alan Broadoak either during or after 1918?'

'No, nothing, not until he was invited to come here for bridge a few months ago.'

'And what about during the war?'

'Not really. We were only together with the Colonel for a couple of days and then, when they had enough room, Alan was shipped off home. Is that everything? I can't think of anything else you'd need to know.'

I get up and sidle across the room to give him a huge hug and one of my most powerful kisses. He's groaning, writhing under the pressure and I can feel him pulling me towards him. He sits on the bed and I join him. It's only a matter a minutes before we're naked and writhing about again under a different pressure. We make love, passionate love as though he has never been with a woman before, although I know he has. We separate and I lay in his arms while we both smoke, soft swirls of smoke making love above us, intertwining as we watch them rise to the ceiling.

'I should be preparing the table for dinner.'

'Yes, you should and if you're late I shall complain.'

I'm not sure that that's true actually. I think you could make up the story he told, and it wouldn't be that hard to do, but I let the subject drop. I think I have enough information now at least, sufficient for my objectives.

We get dressed slowly, lovingly and before I leave I kiss my index finger and touch his lips. 'Not so long before next time.' I feel more desperate than he does and maybe I am. We'll see.

Chapter Forty Four

You'll be thinking by now that I have forgotten all about Jennifer, Frank and Tommy and I can understand your concern. At the time of my family interviews (the larger part of which have been recounted on the forgoing pages) it seemed more important to establish the question of who carried out the murder, one of the consequential benefits of which was discovering why the murder took place at all. It is now time to discover the manner of the murder – although I think we can all agree that it was by poisoning – to the extent of how it was carried out and the source of the poison. This I am convinced is the forte of the afore mentioned assistants.

I arrive at Creek Road in time to see Frank's car disappearing around the corner at the bottom end of the lane no doubt heading for the bridge. As if by order young Tommy arrives following his smile and I wonder where he's been hiding, waiting for my next visit and I almost feel guilty although there's obviously no reason why I should!

'Mrs Matcham, it's time you was back 'ere, you 'aven't been for a while now. I fort you'd forgotten us. Well, forgotten me anyhow.'

'How could I possibly forget you, Tommy? Are you okay?'

'Of course, I know how to look after myself. The Creek keeps me cool if I get too hot during the day.' He continues to smile, 'and there's been a lot going on the last few days, if you know what I mean. She's up there if that's who you're wanting; her boyfriend 'asn't arrived yet and Frank's off to his latest lady friend I think so he'll be a while.'

'Thank you, Tommy. Will you – '

'Look after Maggie for you, of course, Mrs – I've been missin' my driving out in her. She's lovely!'

'Ok then, I'll see you soon.' I feel he deserves a kiss so rather than giving it to his head – I shudder at the very thought – I kiss my hand and touch that on his head. He seems to know what I'm doing and shows his appreciation by one of his smiles.

It's actually only two or three days since I climbed the creaking stairs to Jennifer and Frank's offices. I wouldn't have expected anything to have changed and Jennifer's cheery voice was soon offering me tea and a biscuit once she could see that it was me and not a forgotten client wanting their report. At the top of the stairs, I am surprised to be met by her boyfriend, Ron who was sitting comfortably in 'my' chair.

'Oh, hello, I'm sorry young man, I've forgotten your name.'

'Ron, Mrs Matcham. In fact Jennifer and I were just talking about you and she was saying that it was a while since you visited her – or Frank. Are you here on business? Or just a friendly chat?'

'Business, not that it's any of your concern.'

'Oh but it is, Mrs Matcham, it is.' He winks at me which I think is completely uncalled for and inappropriate. 'Okay, I'll leave you to it and I'll see you later, darling.' I assume the final notation was directed at Jennifer and completed as he began walking down the stairs.

'Bye.' Jennifer calls after him. I sense that they've been talking about something other than their private lives.

'That's the second time I have encountered the gorgeous Ron when I suspect you should have been working. It's none of my business of course, but was he here on security matters or purely to excite you?' Cheeky but girly seems appropriate despite our backgrounds.

'As you said to Ron, Alicia: 'business, not that it's any of your concern'. You already know that he's responsible for our security so that should be all you need to know. Now then, we haven't seen you for a while, I thought Frank had upset you for some reason – no reports probably!'

If that's how she wants to play it, I'll retain the information and we'll proceed. 'I've been carrying out deeply searching investigating questioning of my immediate family. It hasn't been fun believe you me. Anyway, it's only been two or three days at the most.'

'Four actually, not that it matters really.'

When anyone finishes or immediately prior to finishing a sentence with the word 'really' it always means that they believe it to be otherwise and/or there is something potentially sinister lurking in the background. Dr Hudson's 'you're fine my dear, really,' means that I do have something wrong with me that I need to sort out and that there is something about which I should concern myself although it's unlikely to be critical.

'In other words, something important has happened about

273

which I should know. Like Frank finding the murderer or has found a good way of finding it out. Yes?'

'No, but something important yes.'

'Go on then sweetheart.'

'He thinks he's discovered which poison was used and probably where it came from.'

'I say! That's fantastic, does he have a report on its way to me then?' It's hard to sound that enthusiastic when you already have the information at your fingertips, but confirmation is always welcome!

'Er, no, he's waiting till he's sure where it came from before writing to you. But I can tell you if you like.'

She must be teasing, surely she's not stupid enough to hold it back from me. 'Come on then.'

'He's not sure what it's called on the street and he's working on that, but the original name, the proper name, is Eserine. Frank's not sure but he says that your Dr Hudson should be able to find out, or if he's the murderer he'll know already, what it is, where it comes from and what it does – although of course we know what it does – it kills people! I suppose you could try asking Tommy to find out if you don't want to get Dr Hudson involved or that pet copper you've got at the Faversham station.'

'I don't have any pet copper at Faversham or anywhere else.' That's not strictly true but he wouldn't be able to help in this situation. 'I'll see what I can find out; it's another part of the jigsaw. It's getting quite good fun now, isn't it?'

'If you say so, Alicia, I'm really not sure I could call it fun. You should see the state Frank's in, he's been beaten up at least a couple of times, his car's been scratched and cut about and had crap tipped in it. He's not happy and expects you to pay him some more cash, it's been a nightmare.'

'If he has done a good job at the end, he'll certainly get the rest of the cash, as you put it. If he can show that he's suffered in some way by getting the information, I'm sure I can find even more cash! You've certainly been very helpful so I'll certainly make sure that his business and both of you will be well rewarded, don't worry. Does he think there's much more he can do, he's been very elusive, I've only seen him once or twice since the day I appointed him.'

'He's wanted to try to keep a distance between you and him so that it makes it easier to get the information. If they think he's passing it all on as soon as he gets it, they'll clam up and he'll get nothing. If he can keep his distance and time between getting information, there'll always be someone else to blame if it starts a gang war and nobody wants one of them.'

'No, I quite understand that. So what about your boyfriend where does he fit in? His face has told me that he's part of it even though we've only spoken once before, what is it he provides again?'

'Security, he tries to keep the hitmen away from these offices so that I don't get hurt, Frank doesn't get hurt, not in here at least and the offices themselves are untouched. You've no idea what they're like. Especially if one gang thinks it's the other who's done whatever it is they think has been done; whichever individual has done something. So, for example when Frank found out what the drug used was and the likelihood of who used it, the minders would have been all over our files like a swarm of bees to find out what information we've got them if Ron and the others hadn't been here.'

'I see.' Most of it, but there's nothing I could do, even if I could speak to Frank face to face. I need to be careful not to get Tommy caught up in all this, he's given me lots of information - I suppose they could have fed him duff information, but I don't feel they have. 'I think I'll go down and see how Tommy is. It sounds as though he's pretty well in the thick of it.'

'He is, and he's only a boy really.'

She grins, knowing full well that there is no report and never will be, he won't be putting anything in writing which will make it almost impossible for me to prove all my theories to Leonard Drabble when the time comes and I suppose that actually that time has already passed because I should have told him who I suspect of the murder even though I don't know for sure.

Tommy is standing dutifully by Maggie when I reach the bottom of the stairs and he leaps into the passenger seat when I wave him to do so. 'Any trouble while I was away?'

'No, miss. One or two of the kids but overwise quiet – none of the gangs. It's quiet times, like I said before.'

'Seasalter?'

'That'd be great.'

And we're off, the warm wind blowing our hair while we both admire the never changing view of the fields, only the weather makes them look different and with the drought still slowly killing off the less resistant grasses and hedgerows the main change for the last several weeks has been from lush green to dirty brown. We drive in silence along one of my favourite routes back to Faversham via Herne. I'm not a silent creature by nature and am the first to break the quietness of the wished for gentle showers.

'And what do you know you can tell me that I haven't already found out? What do you know that can bring my investigations to a close? we're a long way from solving the whole thing but I expect Jennifer told you that the poison was Eserine. What she almost certainly didn't tell you was that it comes from the Calabar bean which grows almost exclusively in West Africa, particularly Nigeria.'

'She said nothing about vat, and surprising 'cause its important.'

'I suppose she might not know that.'

'If you hadn't guessed, miss, I fink Frank might be doing his own investigation which is why you've had so few reports. He's using your money to pay for 'is own investigations and who he'll sell the information to. The opposite gang probably.'

'Well, my darling boy, I hadn't thought of that, really I hadn't and as you say, it would explain about the reports. Of course it also means I can't trust a word Jennifer says and it's likely that a big chunk of what she's already told me is lies.' The bitch.

That is undoubtedly true but there have been many occasions when Tommy has agreed with what that cow has told me, so that means that although he's giving me this 'I'm a good boy I am' come-on he's lying too. So, sweeties, I've heard it all before and it's all down to me as it always is.

Chapter Forty Five

The clouds are typically low as I park in front of the police station and behind what I believe is Len's boring, black police issue car – as boring as I can imagine. As usual, the station waiting area is deserted but I soon see a familiar face and after a few 'hellos' am seated in Len's office as boringly brown as his car is black!

'So,' he says encouragingly and with a higher degree of enthusiasm than before, 'have you solved our murder yet? Can you pass me a folder of proof and punishment as you promised? Who is the murderer, when did they do it and with what and why? That's all I need to know and we're away.' He sits back in his chair, a broad smile splitting his face, displaying teeth of a colour not unlike that of his office walls. He does have the courtesy of not smoking whilst I am in his presence but despite a lecture from me when we first met about the dangers of smoking, he is obviously still as they say 'having a fag' when I'm unable to see him.

'I'm afraid I'm not quite there darling, everyone has been telling me lies, even your friends from Special Branch – so what chance do I have? What I do have, is a good idea who the murderer is but not enough proof just yet to give you their name. What I am certain of is that Alan Broadoak was poisoned by a drug cocktail most of which was something called Eserine.' The most important point here is that there was no reaction from him when I mentioned Special Branch.

'Not come across that one before.'

'Nor me, but then it's only recently starting to be used in this country. Apparently it comes from something called the 'Calabar' bean whatever that looks like, and frankly who cares, but the most interesting things about it are one, it's easy to grow and two, it's grown pretty much exclusively in West Africa and mainly in Nigeria.'

'Why is that so interesting?'

'My dear Detective Inspector, do I have to do all your work for you?' I'd better smile now in case he thinks I'm genuinely annoyed, I can see that he did but has now smiled in return! 'Who do we know that, during the war, spent time – quite a lot of time – in Nigeria?'

'Well…'

I simply can't believe that the names don't slip off his tongue and I'm not going to wait: 'Alan Broadoak, Charles Whitten and John Staples. We've written out Alan's heart attack so that leaves the other two.'

'Interesting.'

'Of course it's interesting but I don't know how, when or why. Have you uncovered anything in the way of help in that direction?'

'Nearly there then, but I'm afraid I can't help with anything yet. We've had to slow down a bit because of some major burglaries in the town.' I'm really frustrated but I bite my tongue because I don't want him to give up all together. 'Well,

Mrs Matcham, sorry, Alicia, you've made enormous progress in a very short time and I salute you, especially as it looks as though the murderer is one of your own family, or a member of your staff – one with whom I understand you are having an affair. If I can help in the final touches, please let me know.'

'Thank you for your acknowledgement of the difficulties. Father was always going to be a problem, but John came as a bit of a shock and I do, possibly did feel that I was falling in good old love with him. A shame but there it is. Anyway, I suspect my need for you and your men will be at the denoue-ment when I tell the family about the killer within. Whoever it is, it will cause a stir.'

Chapter Forty Six

THURSDAY 22ND JUNE, LUNCH

The clouds have lifted as I leave the police station which makes for a pleasant top down drive back to Corners. I fancy lunch there but as I have yet to tell Cook I will no doubt be in a lot of trouble when I do. Its only June and yet the trees think its autumn. The Mall is so much lighter as I leave the railway station behind me and head for the London road. I miss the city with all the fun and frolicking, the theatre, the parties, the – the everything and, of course the young men and my young girlfriends.

Although George Hind is wonderfully entertaining and as frequent a visitor to the club as am I, he's hardly one for parties and prancing which means that I've been able to enjoy our regular get togethers in his flat. Here in gloomy Faversham, what is there but the slow moving, grubby, brown creek with its rough, drug ridden banks and in the more civilised area of Brogdale walks in the brown countryside and the odd game of cards and by recent experience an unsafe game of cards at that. Not that anyone else has been murdered or died at any bridge tables since I arrived, not as far as I know anyway.

I'm let off my late request for lunch as Patty has cancelled although nobody knows or probably cares why and Cook had prepared lunch for her so I'm eating Patty's lunch, but I'm sure she won't mind. Father and I are alone at the end of the meal, either by chance or design and I'm going to forge ahead. 'You know the war?'

'Of course I know the bloody war, I was there, remember?. What is it you want to know now?'

'I know, I know, sorry, I was just wondering what you got up to when you weren't killing the Hun. You know, cards – bridge or poker perhaps – chasing the pig – or whatever you called it, I don't know, polishing your gun? Anymore?'

'That's a cheeky question if ever I heard one, my girl. It's all a bit private mainly manly stuff – you know, old boys talking and jokes, not really something I can tell you about now and nothing that will have any bearing on what you're asking; but cards yes, mostly rummy and poker of a sorts – bridge between the officers in the mess but only for 1d a hundred, nothing extravagant mind you, it was a different game to the one we play on Saturdays now.' He laughs as though there were all sorts of variations between the two games, the mess version involving something saucy or at least something that he wasn't prepared to divulge and actually I don't want to know.

The general idea is that what he's given me is sufficient for my investigations. He's still rambling 'A lot of the men were ordinary men remember, no commissions just foot soldiers and in the end as we all know now they were cannon fodder; a ghastly, shocking, disgusting, horrible um terrible expression but accurate, nevertheless. I lost a lot of my men towards the end of it. Bloody Hun. But bridge was not really their thing, John will tell you that, he was there; he was one of the poor bastards; he was one of the lucky ones – but none of them ever had the time anyway, too much killing to do. Too many uniform checks. Too much boot polishing.'

'Boot polishing in the trenches?'

'Of course, we had to maintain some degree of pride and respect. Clean uniform and shining boots as a good place to start. Um, what's, what's this polishing your gun then? I've not heard of that before?'

'It was just something I heard one of the lads, as you call them, laughing about while I was in the police station and I heard some others having a good old chuckle while I was waiting for my informant down in the Creek lanes. I'd never heard of it until then either. Could it be some crude alternative name for another game, something unseemly perhaps I wouldn't mind I mean to say, we're all a bit more broadminded nowadays and of course it may have no bearing on the investigation but what do you think?'

'Er, no idea, my darling girl, now I really must get on, lots to do.'

I sat there as we always did, taking in Father's answers, taking in the things he'd said about the war and things he hadn't, things we hadn't heard before and undoubtedly never will again, I'm only glad that I could feel as though I had witnessed the social aspects of war in the trenches, such as it was. Him an officer. John a foot-soldier brought under the cover and protection equal to that of the officers. He was one of the lucky ones, father had said. I wonder.

I feel I need to clear my head after all that information and turned down several offers of company, not in an antisocial way of course, I simply wanted to be on my own for a while away from the investigation but time to think about them nevertheless. I'll talk to John again next, so that I can try to tie his version of the social life with my father's. I want to discover how different his was from the officers and how his life varied from that of Alan Broadoak. I think I'm getting close to the centre of this case, this murder, but I can't quite get it together – all my ducks in a row I think they call it.

Although I dislike the country and towns, miles outside London and the immediately surrounding villages (I live in one for God's sake) I do enjoy a walk in the country. I can think of no explanation; the smell of cow dung is repellent as is the odour from various hedgerow flowers but taking everything together, for some unknown reason I enjoy it and Corners is a good starting point. I'm off for a walk, some of that bracing Kent air from the North Sea that everyone is always on about that's what I need to blow some of those interlocking cobwebs away. I decide to turn right at the end of the drive and walk along the lane towards Whitehill. To my disappointment there's no wind not even the slightest breeze, just the seemingly never-ending blaze of the sun burning the hedgerows and meadows.

I take a cigarette and my cigarette lighter from my bag. It's a beautifully engraved present from my dearest and much missed, the late Mr Matcham, my dear Aubrey. It reads 'To my dear wife Alicia for as long as I live'. It was the best present he ever gave me and, although his final gift was when he died leaving me an extremely rich widow enabling me to go and do with whoever I pleased, my lighter was his real last gift, a strange, at least an unusual engraving coming as some portent of doom considering that he died only two weeks after giving it to me.

I put the silver gift back into my handbag almost immediately realising that to use any naked flame in the open countryside could be the cause of massive fires across the county. An act that is currently considered and is treated as severely as an act of treason. Quite rightly too.

I follow the lane down a slight hill and have to stand to one side as a car roars past on its way to goodness knows where. There was no suggestion of it stopping as there often is in Town so no doubt the concept of slowing down doesn't exist in the wild west of Kent. Half-way down the hill I stop again to take in a view of the fields ahead. I know I've just been raving about missing London, but I can't argue about the beauty of the countryside. A narrow stream trails its way across the brown grasses while a few cows try to graze. If it was the usual green, the view would show what looked like a carpet with a blue curve running from one side to the other, now it's as if I am standing looking over a desert, a desert of light brown sand towards a narrow oasis of dying trees in front of large sand dunes. It isn't a pretty picture, but it fits well with the long interest in all things Egyptian, the fascination of the pyramids (though here their tops are domed rather than pointed) and what they contain. I've never understood their fascination, but I can now see their beauty, acres of dry sand backed by sand hills and I wonder what secrets are hiding behind these dunes.

You can have too much of a good thing and I've had enough fresh air and deep thought about the beauty of things before and around me. These beautiful things are different from the dreams, the hallucinations, the screaming, indescribable dancing seamlessly followed by the serene all-encompassing glow of the beautiful things in Town. I miss it all, you can tell, I know you can and I've probably let you into too many of my fantasies. But now, now, I need to get back to work and I start to walk back to the house. After a while I pass a newly built bungalow on land bought from the Whitten family during the course of them building Corners and then past my name-sake, Matcham another home built on land bought from what became my family.

When I arrive back at the house, I walk in through the side gate to find the entire family lazing under the few trees we have in the garden. I continue walking towards them as one by one they hunch up on their elbows to say hello.

'Alicia, dear,' my mother has a number of ways of addressing me whichever one she uses means I can tell the mood she's in by the greeting I get and the tone of her voice. On this occasion she was undeniably in a good mood but with puzzling news to tell me.

'Mother?' I nod to the others as I get closer so that I can hear what she's going to say.

'Alicia, dear we have had a telephone call from a young lady by the name of Jennifer – she said that you would know who she was – and she asked me, well, it was John she spoke to actually of course, she asked to be telephoned back as soon as you returned.'

'How did she sound?'

'You'd better ask Joh – oh, here he is you can ask him now. John, how did this Jennifer sound when you spoke to her?' I smile, knowing that I'm never going to be allowed to ask him.

'Well ma'am, she sounded as though she wanted Miss Alicia to telephone her back as soon as possible, but she didn't sound as though it was a matter of utmost importance, more of interest than anything else.'

That tells me nothing but before I have to decide, I can just hear the telephone ringing again. John moves swiftly towards the house and I decide to follow him; in case it's Jennifer again.

I let him pick up the receiver and before he hands it to me, I can hear Jennifer's voice quietly stressful in order to avoid any obvious panic.

'Jennifer?'

'Mrs Matcham,' (always if there's a likelihood of someone overhearing) 'I thought you might be interested in this before your next visit.'

'I'm always interested in anything you have to say – relevant to the case or not. You know that.' I smile, looking at John who has so far thought it unnecessary to leave me alone. He returns my smile and trundles off to his pantry leaving me to talk in peace. 'So, what do you have for me?'

'Well, Frank has just walked in, made a telephone call and then left again.'

'Again?'

'Well, he'd left only a short while before, if you see what I mean.'

'I know exactly what you mean, go on.'

'As you know, I don't listen into his telephone calls because some of them might be private,' I laugh knowing that she always listens, particularly if they're likely to be private, 'I actually missed the start 'cos I was makin' tea but when I sat down again I heard him say somethin' about the delivery of some drugs. When it had been made, where it had been made and who to.'

'Who to?'

'Right. Well I heard him say something about Wednesday last week, other side of the Creek but I didn't hear who to.'

'To – '

'Yeah, yeah, to whom. So I can't tell you anymore, but I thought that might help. Frank repeated what he'd been told and ended up by asking about who had had the drugs. The other bloke said again that they didn't know, except that he thought it might be a woman, quite an old woman he thought, a bit of a surprise. I didn't really want to have to tell you that just in case you'd be here when Frank was, although I know that's unlikely.'

'Interesting, thank you, darling, very interesting. And helpful too. I think. Anything else? Is there a report due?'

Laughing quite forcefully, she says 'There's always a report due as you know, but he hasn't given me one to type up yet and anyway, as we both know they're always a waste of time.'

'True, well I must get on, Jenny another important interview to carry out. No doubt we'll speak again soon. I'll drive down as soon as I can.'

We end our conversation as my mother crosses the hall.

'Who was that, dear? You look very happy, whoever it was.'

'Just someone helping with my enquiries, mother, nobody special.' I lower my head, looking directly at the parquet floor.

'Of course not, but helpful I expect.' I can almost hear her smile as I hear the rise and fall of her feet across the floor carrying her to the sitting room for her afternoon nap.

John opens his pantry door after my first knock and closes it once I am inside.

'Madam?' I glower at him. 'Alicia?'

Now, I smile and sit down in his not uncomfortable visitors' chair. His pantry is one of the smallest rooms in the house, but it's his and only a few of us has rite of passage. Above the door, running the full width there are the seven bells, one from each of the principal rooms in the house and one for the front door, which is larger and therefore necessarily the loudest of all the bells. It can be heard almost anywhere in the house and requires his immediate attention irrespective of what he's doing when it rings.

Although allowed to, he has done little to personalise the pale painted walls, there are only two photographs and the shadow of one which has either fallen or been taken down: a picture of his mother hangs over his desk, next to another of a senior army man in full dress uniform of which I imagine to be of his father. Signs of the third, the missing photograph, are above his bed in such a location as enables him to see the person in the last photograph before he drops into bed after another busy day and goes to sleep.

'I see you've not replaced your missing photograph yet.'

'Not yet.'

'Who was it, anyway?'

'Someone I once knew, someone special.' He looks away obviously embarrassed, a face colour I've not seen him show before.

'Sorry, John, perhaps now isn't a good time, perhaps I should come back later.'

'No, now is a perfectly good time, Alicia.' He's back to his normal self again and shows no sign of emotion. 'Is it about the murder?'

'Partly, yes, just a few more questions; if that's okay, these things crop up after talking to someone else and I've been talking to father.'

'Always the source of questions if I may be so bold. Ask away.'

'It's about your relationship with him, father and with Alan Broadoak.'

'I don't understand. Relationship?' I can't believe he's so dense so, possibly restrained.

'How you got on, how you occupied your time together at the front, how long you managed or tried to meet together, did you have anyone back home; that sort of thing.'

'Right, well, after I joined up, Alan and I ended up by complete chance in the same platoon. We sort of palled up I suppose even though he was your father's batman and so had different duties at different times – I didn't know that at the time. I just had to get used to what I was going to have to do, where I was going to sleep if there was any chance, you know the sort of thing, well, I suppose you don't but you know what you've been told I suppose. And no, there was no one back home. Not then.'

'John it's fine, take your time.' I stroke his arm and shift my chair closer to him. I want to find out about this 'not then' comment. My guess is that it has something to do with that empty photograph frame. I'll get there but now is not the time.

'Well, it took a while to do that, but men were running about all the time. Lots were keeping their heads down or waiting for the order to stand and fire while their friends were being shot or killed and others were carrying the dead and dying to the mortuary and the hospital. It was every bit as horrible as the stories say.'

'But you must have had some time to sleep, to write letters home, to read letters from home, to play cards or...'

'On the front line we didn't get much time, but once we were pulled back for the next lot to take the bullets and canons we did, of course we did, and the letters were very important even though they were all so censored it was sometimes hard to know what had been written. It didn't matter to be honest just a letter from home was enough to know there was someone thinking about us. We'd play poker when there was time making or losing a bit of cash as we went along. I think I was up a full five bob by the time it was all over, it helped pass the time.' He looks away from me to the window and his eyes glaze over, I can see that answering my question has taken him back to the bad times, times he didn't want to remember.

'I'm sorry to have to ask you my love but is there anything else?'

He came back from his memories: 'Sleep, that's about all but it was sometimes too noisy to sleep even though we were dug in away from the front. Horrible it was. Horrible.'

'And if you don't mind me asking, how did you become father's batman? How did he pick you?'

'Even now I'm not really sure. It was a long time ago, memories fade, even those sorts of memories.'

'What do you mean 'those sorts?'

'Of the war.' I nod, realising what a stupid question it was.

'It was late 1915 if I remember correctly, perhaps early 1916. I went back to my dugout which was next to Broadoak's. He was crying – not unusual for a man in those days – and told me that his mother and father had died in a German raid a few weeks before he found that he was being shipped back to

Blighty. You know, after getting so badly wounded they couldn't sort him out at the Stationary Hospital – though what he was doing back at the mess I don't know. He been hoping to see them of course it had been ages; very upset he was, you can understand,' I nod consolingly 'so I tried to comfort him. There was nobody else anywhere near us to start with.

I talked to him, I held him sort of like my mother used to hold me if I'd hurt myself falling over. And that seemed to work, the longer I held him the better he got and the more we talked, the more he told me about your father and what The Colonel called their special relationship. Then we heard someone squelching along the trench and I instinctively let go. Broadoak smiled, understanding, and I was away, to go on fighting the bloody war while he was waiting to be taken home. When my whole family was bombed out it had the same effect on me, and he'd consoled me as I did him. Troup movements meant that we didn't see one another for a while and then one day out of the blue, I was called to the Colonel's quarters.'

'You had no idea why?'

'I was told that Broadoak had at last been sent home and apparently he wasn't expected to return. It seemed that he'd told your father that if he ever needed a new batman then he should seek me out as his replacement. So he did and here I am, I couldn't refuse. And anyway it was much better than being in the trenches full time. As it turned out your father's Mess was so far from the trenches that I actually billeted in the cellar of the enormous house where a dozen or so officers lived. Occasionally I was sent to the trenches with instructions for future troop movements, but otherwise I was relatively safe. I never found out how Broadoak happened to be injured, or why he couldn't return.'

'So you lived a life of luxury.'

'I suppose so. Sort of.'

'Definitely. And after the war?'

'It was long after demob, your father spotted me while we were clearing the chaos of that railway crash on the London-Dover line the City end of Faversham platform two – you must remember that.'

'Of course I remember it. I read about it in the papers of the time. I was at home of course, but news does find its way from the south to north. So what happened between you and father when he spotted you?'

'We had a chat and he offered me the job as his butler and here I am. It was only after I'd brought my kit and some other things that someone had saved for me from my bombed out home, that I discovered I was replacing Broadoak again.

'As simple as that.'

'I heard through one of my old buddies that Broadoak had mended, had left his job as The Colonel's butler when he inherited a large estate in Sussex somewhere, lucky sod. It was only a matter of weeks ago really that he turned up at your mother's bridge party – she had no idea of course; my father hadn't ever talked about him or that Broadoak and I were – you know. It's just the way it goes. That's how I became you father's batman after all.'

'I suppose so. How did Alan react when he started playing at the Saturday game and found you waiting on him?'

'It was funny really, he gave your father a queer sort of look, a strange look, but he seemed okay. He kept teasing me and making the odd remark to both of your parents about how I had served in the trenches when I wasn't serving the officers and now I was in service again but that he was amongst the idle rich. It didn't seem to matter that he'd got there simply by chance, by being injured and I'd had to work my ... off to get where I am and that's only by chance. He kept quite a distance between us which wasn't difficult, nor I have any cause to speak to him outside of the Saturday meal or subsequent game. He was a bit odd around your father although I can't deny that there did seem to be a friendship developing between him and your mother.'

'Friendship?'

'There were rumours of an affair but that's all, tittle-tattle.'

Chapter Forty Seven

I feel that I'm making good progress on the interview front but not much more on the source of the drug that actually killed Alan or how it was administered. Jennifer's recent telephone call suggests that Frank is making progress but has no real plan to prepare a report for me detailing his findings. In fact, I'd go so far as to say that he's been an almost waste of space and that Jennifer has been far more helpful without being paid, at least not by me.

It takes little more than ten minutes to drive from Corners to Frank's office and that's where I'm heading now. The skies are starting to darken so I, like the rest of the population start praying for rain. There are no signs of umbrellas and nobody has any real concerns about getting wet and even if it did rain, we'd all be so pleased to see it that getting wet would actually make our days. Tommy is waiting outside Frank's office as if he were expecting me. He doffs his cap.

''afternoon miss I was expectin' you, Jennifer said to expect you about this time. She said she telephoned about something yesterday she knew would sparkle your appetite or somefin' like vat. Shall I look after Maggie for you as usual? Are you expectin' to be long? Frank's not due back for a couple of hours yet, so you've plenty of time for a cuppa with Jennifer.'

'I'm not sure, Tommy, just keep an eye out for anyone who's likely to cause trouble generally, or damage to Maggie. I don't suppose you've got any information for me have you?'

'Don't fink so, they're getting closer to finding out where the poison came from and where it went, the difficulty is tracking where it went from the collection down 'ere to whoever took it up to the big house. But I think that still has to be down to you.'

I leave Tommy watching a youth who's heading towards him to do who knows what and to be honest I'm not worried as long as it doesn't affect me or the investigation.

Jennifer is sitting at her desk typing a letter or even a report. Although she's a secretary I realised long ago that I've never seen her actually typing before. She nods me towards her visitor chair, and I sit here marvelling at the bizarre office walls, or rather what's on the walls. The room is lined with wooden panelling and stuck over it are photographs, newspaper cuttings, posters, letters, magazine cuttings and other, similar detritus much of which can have no bearing on any of the cases under Franks so called control. Sitting here I wonder what he actually does, I mean does to earn a living, it clearly isn't detecting, no self-respecting person would hire him – although I did, but that was family. I'm wondering how our parents could have got together to do business and while I'm reaching the conclusion that I shouldn't even be trying to work that out, Jennifer's finishes whatever she was working on and has disappeared into the kitchen. She returns with the traditional mugs of tea and sits down.

'There's no more since this morning.' she says. 'What I told you on the telephone is all I heard which was that there was some drugs arriving and being collected last Wednesday either sent by or delivered to a man or woman but we're not sure which or what the actual drug was – we're all assuming it's the poison for someone to murder this bloke of yours – Eserine wasn't it?'

'Firstly he's not my bloke as you so crudely put it and secondly, I reckon we're further ahead than that. I think I've identified the killer I think, no I'm pretty certain, why the man was murdered and if the killer is who I think it is I think I know how. We just need to be sure of where it came from and the form it was in. I'm assuming liquid for use by injection. Anything else would be difficult to administer. Any guesses?'

'Obviously, Frank is involved somewhere, probably collecting it from the dealer and passing it on to the murderer – possibly today. It is Thursday morning isn't it. Could be either the actual murderer or the one with the brains to organise the killing, I suppose.'

'Again, any ideas?'

She continues: 'Assuming it was Frank who collected the stuff he'd need to pass it on quickly because he thinks the cops are on to him, so it must be someone he sees more often than most. That's not easy to know because he's so often out of the office and I don't know who he sees but I've suspected for a long time that he's up to something and more recently I've been worried that it's drugs. There's more of it about nowadays and it can make people a lot of money for whoever sells or buys them. Frank has no investigating clients – apart from you – so he has to be getting his money from somewhere. I've always expected

297

he was in with the gangs, but he was around here a lot more in those days, well that was only what, ten to twelve years ago. He was still working on the normal detecting work some days. He even gave me reports to type up then! His earnings must have been more from his detecting and it actually paid the bills. I reckon the drugs started by Frank using and enjoying them and then, later, he took on some of the buying and selling. I only pick up things from Rob. You remember Rob?'

'I remember Rob. What about Tommy?'

'Too young and too innocent.'

'Do you believe that, do they have to be older than he is then?'

'Yeah, I should think so. They'll be brought up the Creek on the barges and taken off before the genuine cargo is unloaded. There's plenty of chance for that to be done and plenty of gang members to do it. They probably take it to a room in one of the hop warehouses, normal people stay out of those when they can because the smell is so strong. Any smell from the drugs would be absorbed by the smell from the hops and they could divide it into smaller packages for distribution, they wouldn't normally sell it from the warehouse it'd be too risky. But I'm sure Frank is one of the loading sellers and that he's one of the ones who sell it on onto the street traders. They then sell it on again to their customers. They're usually people on the market stalls or the gypsies who come down for the picking seasons or are passing through to somewhere else. I dunno, it's all very complicated.'

I'm sitting here and wondering whether Frank is the first man we need to worry about – or at least he's the first one whose name I need to check in my investigations – the police can take on the crooks earlier up the chain, I'd never have a chance of tracking down the barge owners. What intrigues me is the amount of information that Jennifer has about the drug trail in Faversham and how that fits in with Alan's murder. I have to ask. 'You seem to understand an incredible amount about the local drug trade, my darling; how is that, or am I being silly and out of touch because I'm too busy enjoying myself with the end result up in town at our wonderful parties?' I'm not entirely sure that I should have divulged my own use of the drugs but I'm hoping to show that I have an understanding of what Jenny has to put up with and what Frank is doing.

'I knew it, it's people like you and the crowds you mix with who are buying the stuff and using it at the wild parties you all enjoy every evening and weekends in your posh houses in the city and in the country. You probably know more about it than you think I do or at least the effects of them. You'll certainly know more people who use them. Most of the stuff for your friends in London will start from here, it's easy enough to get it up the road. To be honest I thought that you were a user first off, but I didn't know of course.'

'Wow, that was a bit of an attack.' I stand up and walk slowly towards her. She's shorter than I am and the fact that I'm actually looking down at her in body and understanding is not missed by either of us. She has stood bolt upright during her tirade but now her shoulders are drooping and her hands wringing each other in embarrassment; she was staring at me before, but her gaze is now through her watering brown eyes.

The change in her demeanour is staggering, from flagpole to wet washing. I put my arms around her and squeeze her gently, comforting and lovingly; we've been good friends over the last few days, and I hate to see her like this. 'It's all right my little sweetheart, have you been talking to that boyfriend of yours? From what you say Frank is in it up to his neck but probably only in the early stages of distribution.' She manages to shake her head even though its buried deep in my chest. She sniffs – a dreadful habit which doesn't endear her to me anymore than do her tears.'

'Frank knows a lot about what goes on in the docks, in the barges and a lot about the people. He reckons Tommy is involved somewhere but I've already told him that he isn't.' She looks up at me, sniffs again causing me to shudder while she drags her arm under her nose. Until this incident I have thought her a discreet young girl always willing to help whenever she can, who wants to drop poor old Frank in it whenever she can. Now I can only describe her as a snivelling youngster, what a fall in grace. 'Look, my darling girl, can't you take the rest of the afternoon off? Is Frank due in later today?'

She shakes her head, takes a small step back and with a deep sigh says: 'He said to take tomorrow and the day after off this week. He said he was going to be away and wasn't expecting anyone to call him on the telephone or to be dropping in for a chat. He said I couldn't do anything so I might as well be at home.' She sniffs yet again but uses the other sleeve this time.

'Well then, I could take you home if you like and you don't need to come back until Friday do you?'

'That'd be ever so good of you Mrs Matcham, sorry, Alicia. Are you sure it's no bother? Not out of your way?'

'I wouldn't offer if I couldn't do it. Tommy will have to wait for his ride today or he could come along for the ride too if you don't mind.'

''Course not, I know he likes his rides, he earns them after all.'

I wait for her to do what she calls tidy up, although the result seems jolly well the same as when she started. We walk downstairs, her following me so that she can lock the door. As expected, Tommy's standing dutifully by the car. We agree that he'll come with us and I turn the car round before we roar off towards Oare where Jennifer lives. Through more tears she tells us that her mother died a few months ago and that it hasn't been easy living in the house on her own after so many years. I don't suppose it has.

I park outside number 45, she gets out, thanks me for the lift and says goodbye to Tommy. 'I can't let you go into an empty house my darling. Stay there for a minute, Tommy can you look after Maggie for me, I'll settle poor Jennifer in and be back soon – we'll go off to Seasalter afterwards and have an ice cream if you like. What I was going to do can wait.'

Inside number 45 its dismal and cold. There is no refrigerator in the kitchen, but a bottle of milk stands open in a bowl of cold water on the table next to a cut loaf of bread and a plate of – I'm not sure – dripping I think they call it. Of course kitchens aren't my strong point, 'Cetta looks after us at Corners and John sees to my other needs; so kitchens are a whole new adventure but based on this one, it's one I could well do without. It appears that my presence alone is sufficient support and she soon has a kettle on the gas with two cups and saucers next to a rather garish teapot. We sit down to drink and I wonder how Tommy is faring outside.

It's almost half an hour before I can leave Jennifer and I find that Tommy is running around the car trying to keep warm

– we're alongside the Creek and a surprisingly strong, North Sea breeze cuts through the heat being experienced elsewhere. He says he's sorry, but that he actually went across the green to the Álbion Tavern for a half pint of Shepherd Neame's best.

'You deserve it, Tommy come on, to Seasalter and ice cream; I think I might have one this afternoon too. I'll look in on Jennifer later, I expect she's asleep in bed by now.' He nods and looks around as we wind through the roads to his favourite spot and what is becoming mine too, one I shall remember for the next time I come down from Town. The cool breeze off the sea and an ice cream is just what's needed in this heat, what more could we want.

Chapter Forty Eight

When eventually I leave Maggie on Corner's drive and walk a little unsteadily towards the front door, John opens the door before I can reach out to the bell pull never mind ring the bell.

'You look somewhat weary, Mrs Matcham, are you all right?'

'No, John, I have had a very trying afternoon on the other side of the town with a young boy and my private investigator's secretary while attempting to gather information. I need one of your special pick-me-ups to settle me down.'

'Of course, madam. The rest of the family are on the terrace, would you care to join them, and I shall bring your drink out to you?'

'I would, John, what a wonderful man you are.' I manage to pull myself to my full height and give him an affectionate peck on the cheek, anything more intimate would be inappropriate and reprehensible if viewed in such a public place. We both know that and refrain at least for the time being.

'DI Drabble telephoned while you were out, madam; he asked if you would telephone him on your return.'

'Did it sound urgent?'

'I wouldn't say it sounded urgent, madam but I did get the

impression that he was keen to speak to you as soon as you returned.'

'Thank you, I will telephone him after I have finished at least one of your fabulous refreshers.' Another peck and I walk through the house to the terrace where my tiresome family are relaxing in the ubiquitous sun sipping John's various concoctions without a care in the world.

One thing I hadn't expected, and one which John hadn't prepared me for was that Dr Hudson was also sitting on the terrace having been called out for one of mother's headaches, which he diagnosed as a slight attack of sunstroke. I could have told her that but whatever he gave her has worked well enough for her to be sitting in the sun once more. Dr Hudson has insisted that she sit in the shade and that just because there has been so much sun doesn't mean that her constitution is now used to the heat.

Although the family ignore me, Dr Hudson stands, takes off his hat and offers me his deckchair. 'Mrs Matcham, good afternoon. Do. Please. Sit.' I accept his kind offer and he moves to a less comfortable chair beside me.

'Thank you, sir.' I make a point of smiling at him, excluding the rest of them. Petty I know, but that's how I feel at the moment, 'Perhaps I could ask you one or two technical questions before you leave us – before you return to your surgery that is.' I cannot miss an opportunity like this, however squiffy I am.

'Of course, we could go inside now if you like, out of this wretched sun.'

And we do.

'Last time we spoke, doctor I recall we had agreed that Mr

Broadoak had been poisoned by injecting Eserine.'

'Eserine, yes, although I don't think we had agreed by injection. It was either that or by being spread in his food. I think I said that Mr Broadoak had been prescribed Eserine by his own doctor – Doctor Poach I think his name is but no matter – following the hospital's recommendation to use it in order to relieve the lower back pain arising from the injuries he sustained in the war.

I believe the dose was particularly low but had worked incredibly well. I had no experience of the drug until Mr Broadoak moved here – in my area of responsibility so to speak – and asked for a continuing prescription. It is an opiate which should only be used in small doses of course but, like any opiate it can become addictive and in large doses will cause death. I do now believe that Mr Broadoak died due to the accumulation of his regular dosages and a huge overdose of Eserine. We must look at the post-mortem again. Look closely at the detail: the amount Broadoak had been prescribed and what was in his bloodstream when he died.'

'No, of course, I understand. I think we can agree that the drug was injected in the large final dose in the bridge room though, there seems little doubt about that.'

'Well, yes, although apparently the time delay before it having the desired affect varies depending on the size of the dose and the size of the victim. Broadoak was not a small man, but he was already taking a small dose so was perhaps more susceptible or receptive to a large intake than a small one. I don't think any of us knows apart from – as I said just now – the pathologist. They can detect incredible information from the body nowadays.'

'The pathologist and, of course the murderer.' I know this is a bit of one of those corny old statements, but it should at least summon a response from Dr Hudson as to whether he was involved and to what extent. And yes, I'm sure there was a twitch. Not enough for him to be the murderer but enough to know he was involved, inevitably he would be supplying or being aware of the drug coming into the house.

'Do you have any idea how Eserine could be obtained here in England or perhaps imported from Nigeria? It seems almost impossible that anyone else would know what it was or how it worked?'

Hudson shrugs and neither of us is any further forward. 'Let us continue drinking these powerful cocktails John has prepared for us shall we? For the time being at least.' He peers over the top of his spectacles as if to say, 'don't you think you've had enough for today, young lady?' But he's not my father, at least I don't think he is!

He says, almost slurs. 'Yes, let's, they are rather potent aren't they. I feel quite squiffy as I believe you say.' He giggles which somewhat negates what has just been inferred, but he has confirmed the what, when and where. Near enough.

While we gulp our way through these scrumptious cocktails, my mind is straying to other things, my wobbly mind that is. It comes to the decision that it is time to see Drabble again. Surely he must have been able to gather more information possibly more than I can expect, so between the two of us he must be about ready to make an arrest. I have a feeling that it is going to be a bit uncomfortable when I tell him almost everything I've discovered. I should probably have updated him sooner, so I try to come up with reasons why I hadn't.

It's only now I remember that yesterday John said he'd had a message from Drabble asking me to telephone him on my return and although John '...wouldn't say it sounded urgent...' I should telephone him without further delay. I telephone, apologise for my tardiness and agree to meet him the following day at 11.00 o'clock.

John was right of course it didn't sound urgent.

Chapter Forty Nine

Here I am fresh faced and bushy tailed standing at the Police Station desk.

'Is DI Drabble available please?'

'Good morning, Mrs Matcham, if you'll please wait a moment I'll just go and see.' Being known by name by the duty desk policemen is either reassuring or insulting depending how the words are spoken, but I rise above that and pull my body up to its maximum, stunning height. Never let it be said that I am unaware of my features or place in society.

Drabble appears from the line of offices to my left, he is walking in a surprisingly straight line while reading a file – at least a number of gathered papers or something. This is a major achievement and in other circumstance might be applauded by his colleagues but to me it shows indifference to my standing in his reception area, its verging on insulting.

I draw his attention to my presence as his awareness seems to have strayed. 'DI Drabble.'

'Mrs Matcham, please, I think it best if we have our discussion in my office.' He lifts the wooden barrier and directs me to his office, the location of which I know only too well, it's where we have had many unsuccessful and pointless meetings.

His politeness is not as usual, and I make a point of saying so.

'You seem somewhat preoccupied today, Drabble is something amiss?'

'My apologies, a mere trifle, a point of clarification. Now, am I right in hoping that your presence means you have made strides towards a successful conclusion in your investigations?'

'DI Leonard Drabble, I do believe I have. The last piece of the jigsaw has now fallen into place, all that remains is to put it in the box, so to speak. Into jail.'

'Well done, Alicia. Excellent. I believe that I too have solved the case and that we can apprehend the murderer.'

'Let's hope we have reached the same conclusion.' We exchange stares, worried that we haven't but as mine is the correct one, it hardly matters. We discuss our research and findings; questioning and interpretation; opportunities and application. We agree that there can only be one person responsible for the murder and we must tell the family in the traditional fictional style before identifying all those involved and then naming the murderer himself. .

There is little more to be done. Drabble asks if he might join me in Maggie for the triumphant drive to Corners while two of his men are following in the van in which the culprit will be taken away. I ask if I might make the explanation of how we reached the result of our investigations to the family while he simply makes the final arrest. It would make it more personal and increase my fee. We agree just as we turn into Corners drive. Drabble had telephoned ahead to gather the family, associated guests and staff together in the drawing room, it was the largest room in the house and allowed chairs for most of the gathered company to be seated during which I anticipated might be a long announcement...

John had clearly been waiting for us in the hall and opened the door as we approached from the car.

He welcomes us and says: 'Mrs Matcham, Detective Inspector Drabble, I have gathered everyone together as requested and have taken the liberty of furnishing each of them with a drink, I hope that is acceptable.'

I smile, one of relief that we are just about there but it's Drabble who speaks. 'I think so, John, in these circumstances. We might be a long time; I'll just have water - being on duty you see.' At last he turns to me - no police manners, naturally - Mrs Matcham?'

'Oh how can I refuse another of your wonderful cocktails please, Johnny dear, I'll have a large one with extra grapes.' John winces at my calling him Johnny dear at least he does in public it's a sort of private, giggly, usually a drunken sort of name, but then I soon will be. He nods and turns to walk back to his Pantry; now comes my giggle and I sense Drabble looking at me.

When we enter the room all eyes turn to look at us. Had I not been in similar circumstances before I could see how the situation would be disconcerting as it is Drabble and I stand side by side until the buzz of conversation has abated.

Chapter Fifty

The drawing room is an ideal location for me and, indeed, for Len Drabble to confront the suspects. I have faced such groups before, and the confrontation held no concerns for me. How Len Drabble will respond I have no idea.

I give an understated smile and begin: 'Thank you all for joining us this afternoon.' I now point to Len Drabble as many of the assembled won't have the first clue who he is. 'This is DI Drabble from Kent Police and the senior officer at the Faversham Area. We have been helping each other with our investigations in fact, I think it would be true to say that we have worked together on the case. Yes?' I turn and look at Len who smiles and nods his head in agreement, he doesn't say anything, but I can tell that he has scanned the assembled family and located the face of our perpetrator. He has officers posted at all the doors and potential exits from the house and garden to catch the murderer should he or I suppose she choose to make a break for it.

'In consultation with Dr Hudson, and the pathology report, we have established that Alan Broadoak was poisoned on Saturday 10th June and that the lethal dose of Eserine was almost certainly administered before the game started, although

311

the murderer was not particularly concerned at the time of Alan Broadoak's death. The efficacy of the drug varies depending on the size and standard of health of the target and, unusually, the fact that Mr Broadoak was already taking a small dose for his back pain complicates the matter further.

'None of these things worried the killer, all he or she wanted was for Alan Broadoak to die at some point during the weekend. We think that for Alan not to die during the meal is interesting and may well mean the drug was administered by using one of the later courses of the meal, in all of which Alan indulged substantially.' I look heavily at 'Cetta to see if there is any reaction to the not very well hidden accusation. There is no noticeable change in her stance or the look on her face. She remains as ragged as normal and simply returns my look with a smile.

'We understand that while the principal drug used was Eserine, two other drugs were used to create what is called a cocktail of drugs and the murderer knew what he or she was doing. As my sister knows because she was unfortunate enough to be sitting opposite him, Alan's death was silent and slow. We all know that the murderer must be a member of the family or one of their friends or servants here for the regular Saturday game of bridge. The murderer is in this room.

'Alan Broadoak was obsessed with women, spending time with them, toying with their feelings and their relationships with other family members and having rampant sex and all in secret. He collected names, notches on his bedpost as some would say – or wherever such people keep count of their various partners. I have been surprised to discover just how many affairs exist within the group of people in front of me. Many, perhaps all of you should be ashamed of yourselves soaking up this new, free lifestyle that has emerged since the war and taking it just a bit too far. What Alan's affairs did was to create a list of partners, a longer list for him to blackmail others within the family and of reasons to kill him.' It is interesting just how many women are looking around the room trying to count up who was having who and when. Were any of them having affairs with him at the same time?

"Cetta, I mentioned the meal as a cause of Mr Broadoak's death. We have been unable to find any evidence that you had the opportunity or the motive to carry out the murder. The only aspect of the meal to consider is that two others had an involvement. Mother usually comes down to help you decide upon the menu but this fateful Saturday, Patty came down and made a couple of changes you wouldn't have expected your mother to make and then William arrived unexpectedly not just for money as usual, but for the first time, to be included in establishing the menu for the meal. Did he want to watch Alan Broadoak die; did he want to make sure that his poison would work? It's too much of a risk. But I'll come to you, William in a minute.

'Joan Saynor has been a friend of my mother for many years and, indeed a friend of my father since he became one of the Saturday four. Lavinia can have no reason for killing Alan because he and she were having an affair. Indeed she was one of the last people who would want him dead, except that at the same time Mr Broadoak was having an affair with Patty, my sweet but not so innocent, naive little sister. Arguably, for this reason mother should have killed Patty or vice versa although it appears that neither knew of the other's affair.' I see them exchange looks almost out of sympathy than anything else. 'We will keep them on the list for now because poisoning is the preferred method of choice for women, whoever they're going to murder.

'Patty, my darling Patty. I know you called me in to investigate Alan's murder, to prove yourself right, that he had been murdered and that he hadn't simply died of a heart attack – which was quite likely with his history of a weak heart. If you had killed him it was a big risk not to accept Dr Hudson's cause of death, but then you were probably wanting to have the glory of doing something big and important belying your perceived persona. You wanted people to know about your affair with Alan to show that you weren't a little girl anymore, that you were a grown woman with a sexual appetite. That you could commit murder even if it did mean that you'd be hung for doing so. Patty, you silly girl.'

She says, 'But Ali, I didn't do it you must believe me, I'm not that stupid, I wouldn't have risked you investigating his death if I'd killed him, you're right. I can't believe that he and mother were having it off at the same time as he was with me and anyway, he was my bridge partner, why would I kill him? And that other thing about me and mother, it's just horrible, disgusting. He could have just been walking from one bedroom to another in the same house.'

Quite understandably she shudders at the very thought. She didn't have it in her whatever she might want people to think. She sighs and at the same time – somewhat unexpectedly – so does mother although and I anticipate a little *tête-à-tête* later, comparing notes is on the cards.

'Mother, Lavinia, I'm sorry to say so, but I think you're

rather outside the group.' She's nodding, knowing what I'm going to say next. 'I know you had an affair with Alan, but that was before Patty came along and you had only broken off an earlier affair with Alan immediately before your marriage to my father although as we all now know, you began another affair with Alan some years later. For what it's worth I don't believe that there is any doubt as to Patty's fatherhood, but that's for another time.' This causes a short intake of breath around the room and somewhat darkens the atmosphere.

'Now, coming back Joan, Joan Saynor, you've been my father's bridge partner for what is it – four or five years? You have no obvious reason to kill Alan Broadoak. Except that you were deeply in love with him – in fact, as well as your affair with my father, you were having an affair with Alan, weren't you.'

She nods and tears run down her cheeks as she looks down at the carpet. I knew of the affair as did several others but not all of those gathered in the room.

'It was horrible,' she sniffs, 'I was sitting next to him when he slumped onto the table. I watched him, his body bend slowly … horrible.' Now, as she breaks down and can say no more, everyone appears to understand her reaction or lack of reaction when, two weeks ago, she did nothing but sit in her chair at the bridge table and stare at him. Now, everyone knew that they were clearly more than just bridge partners.

'I'm sorry, Joan, but I must go on.' She nods in agreement 'You were equally as jealous of his affairs with Patty and my mother. But for you to kill him is illogical, you'd as sooner kill my sister and mother because you would then you would have Alan to yourself.

'So, ladies it was all about having sex with the dead man as far as you're all concerned and hell of a lot of it so it would seem. So, there you have several motives for killing each other yet the same motive for killing Alan Broadoak if, as I assume, that he was blackmailing one or more of you. But I/we don't think he was.'

Len Drabble taps me on the shoulder and tips his head towards one of the constables standing next to him. 'Sorry, Alicia but this man's having difficulty keeping up. Any chance you could slow down a bit?'

I say, 'Of course, but I think we've nearly reached the end of the lady suspects, so your man has plenty of time to catch up before we get to the men. Now, one lady in this room remains a suspect and as my little sister pointed out right at the start of all this, that's – me!' Titters circulate the room. 'I can see your reactions, but it is only right that I am on the list. In my defence, firstly, I was not having nor have I ever had an affair with Alan Broadoak, one of the few who didn't, but more importantly I was fifty miles away in Bletchley, at home listening to some dance music with my neighbour who'll vouch for me I'm sure. Not only that but I had been at a day early-summer party in Bletchley with my friends and indeed would not be here even now were it not for this investigation. I have a different independent witness with whom I had lunch on the day after Alan's death. A gentleman known to many of you, George Hind from Chapel House just down the road.' I turn to Len Drabble who says nothing but does give me one of his rare smiles…

'Okay, the men. There are only four of you: Dr Hudson, Father, William and John. On the face of it none of you were likely to be the killer but let's look at what I discovered. First, my young brother William, who is hardly ever at home except when he wants money. You spend most of your time in the lower end of town with the drunks and drug merchants. You're a gambler, which is the reason you frequently want money and you have to tidy yourself up before father will let you in the house.

That Saturday, 'Cetta tells me, you arrived in the afternoon, talked to her about the menu and then asked to be added to the table. She guessed you wanted money and you did, but somebody killed Alan Broadoak before you could talk to father which dispensed with or at the very least complicated your chances that day and you were going to have to stay the night to stand any chance of father bailing you out again. What were you doing in the house and to the amazement of the entire household, why had you asked to sit at table? But that aside, why would you want to kill Alan Broadoak? I'm still struggling to find a motive and even though you were here, you stuck out like a sore thumb and would be the first choice for anyone looking for a scapegoat or, indeed be the first person both I or DI Drabble would suspect as the murderer. William? He's never here, and when he is, Alan Broadoak is killed. That's too much of a coincidence for me.

'John, our trustworthy butler did it, the butler always does! What do you think girls, did he? Now for those of you don't know, John and I have a sort of thing going on.'

I glance at John who smiles in return, acknowledging our infrequent but fervent dalliance.

'It's not that serious, but when I'm here in deepest darkest Kent we go into a little huddle when nobody's watching and have a go, you know, we have sex, usually in his pantry but sometimes in my bed: once or twice in Patty's, three times in mother's and once in the kitchen.'

My mother, sister and 'Cetta are beside themselves with horror, presumably firstly that I admit to having and doing such things, secondly that I do it with the butler and last of all that we had chosen their beds and the kitchen table to do it in or on.

'It really shouldn't be such a surprise nowadays, darlings, in fact, it's all the rage at London parties and even one or two down here in sleepy old Faversham.

Patty seems the most distressed though as the youngest I would have expected her to understand. She wails: 'But doing such a thing here in my bed. Or the other places, it's just – horrible to think about. How could you Ali, how could you? I thought we were friends. I thought, I don't know it's just ...' and she's lost for words. It's hard to imagine why she thinks it so wrong, she was, after all, having an affair with Alan Broadoak.

'Well Patty let's all think about you and Alan shall we? I don't particularly want to know where you had each other but others might.' I smile at her and she looks guilty.

'And mother, you had an affair with him too so where did you two become entwined? And I expect you've had more than the one affair haven't you?' She doesn't react and I'm not surprised, having affairs and being married to my father is clearly, understandably a reason for straying and I'll leave them to it.

''Cetta, I know the past is the past, but I doubt that John has fond memories of the two of you rolling around on your bed together and I certainly don't want to think about it for all sorts of reasons.'

I can't help laughing loudly at all three of them, laughing I think as loudly as I've ever laughed for a while, they each look like fish waiting to catch flies. I'll leave them to it. 'Now, John, I can't give you an alibi because I was in Bletchley so what were you doing?' John's blushing now and I feel sorry for him. I don't suppose I should have laid out our sex lives before everyone, but I wanted a bit of fun, a bit of excitement, because I didn't expect to have the chance again and I've already been challenged by Patty of all people.

After a few moments to gather his thoughts he says, 'Well, you know that I was here serving the meal. Nothing more, nothing less.'

'But when I asked you earlier you told me you were in the kitchen, you had access to all the food and you plied everyone with drink, wine, brandy, port. The whole range. You had all sorts of times when you could have put the poison mix into their drinks.'

'But why would I do that? Why would I want Mr Broadoak dead?' He spoke the last few words with less volume as he realised what I would be saying next, about him being second choice to my father. Every time second choice, he could only have a job because Alan had left it when he was shot at or had inherited an estate large enough to swallow up the whole of Northamptonshire or wherever the ghastly place was.

'I'm sorry to say this, John but you were envious of Alan Broadoak. Father had given him two jobs before he had given each of them to you. You were envious of him for being given the job, for inheriting the estate and you were envious of his success with women. 'Cetta and I were the only two women you'd made love to in your life and you're what, late twenties?'

319

Patty says: 'Not everyone has such a rampant sex life as you Alicia, I don't think you should condemn him for that, in fact…' I look at her and then quickly at John again, well I'm blowed.

'You mean you and John? Is this true John, have you been having it away with my sister when I'm not available? You dreadful sluts, oh my God! Now, mother, what do you say to that?'

Father says, 'I'm not sure that you can lay all the blame at John's door or at Patty's, my dear. Your own life is nothing to be proud of is it? And anyway, we're not here to hear about other peoples' lives, enough damage has been done and enough hatred stirred up by your revelations. What people do behind closed doors and with whom they do it is their own affair.'

This is not at all what I would have expected from father, he's not so stuffy after all. 'True, father and I shall come to yours in a minute, but the whole point of unearthing these affairs is to show who has a motive to murder Alan Broadoak. DI Drabble is wholly with me on this.'

Drabble says 'I am, Mrs Matcham, I am. We must determine who had a reason to murder Mr Broadoak, then who did it and how they did it and when. Then actually tell everyone who did it and arrest the right one! I suggest you are allowed to move ahead with this otherwise we shall be disturbed by the need for and the serving of dinner or tea or supper whatever it is you call your next meal in this house.'

He coughs almost as if he were apologising for his comments.

'But, before we move on I must acknowledge the enormous amount of help we have both had from a mister Frank Spillett a private investigator whose office is near the Creek and someone else, one of the smartest young lads who ever existed and who lives near the Creek, a young lad who goes by the name of Tom or Tommy, I think you'll agree Mrs Matcham we would have found the whole investigation significantly harder to draw to a conclusion without them.' There is a short round of applause. 'Now, please I must let Mrs Matcham continue.'

Before I'm allowed to continue, 'Cetta interrupts the flow of conversation: 'There'll be nothin' for dinner if we don't get this sorted soon.' And she has a point.

I continue, nevertheless, 'I agree Inspector, Tom in particular has kept me up to date with what's going on and the various goings on around the Creek drug centre!' Tom, who is sitting cross-legged in front of Patty looks at me knowingly and smiles, his teeth glinting as I have never seen them before. 'Right, so we have William unusually here on the night of the murder but usually living with those ghastly druggies down by the Creek and we have John full of jealousy towards Alan during and after the war. So that just leaves you, father.' I turn to look him straight in the face. All eyes in the room seem to follow mine and are trained on him but he doesn't look like a frightened let alone a guilty man, there's no sweat on his forehead, not a twitch in either eye, in fact he just looks his normal lovely self - intimidating and masterful.

The assembled masses seem to have a mutual strength of reason to blame him, to address their own faults at him and to rid them of his tyranny, a whole range of tyranny directed at each and every one of them. Now they're turning their stares toward me. They look like rabbits caught in the headlights of a car, not knowing what to do but knowing that it will be difficult for me to condemn my own father and remembering that I have exposed the secrets of everyone else's private lives without any sympathy for the people concerned. Suddenly, they look like a box of frogs, waiting to pounce, their protruding eyes large and white with specks of black in the centre.

They look ready for blood and I am ready to give it to them without any care for what he would do if he's guilty and makes a run for it. In a way I hope he does, it will be like one of our fox hunts with the family and staff on foot chasing him across the fields guided by the police and with only one goal in mind, if DI Drabble and his men don't get to him first.

Chapter Fifty One

At least for now father remains seated and I can't help feeling that he's taken a stand against the yet to be voiced accusation, by showing no sign that he'll make a run for it. 'Go on then, do your worst, although I'm not guilty – not of murder 't any rate. No doubt the rest of my short comings will be scattered amongst your friends and family and the staff but that will only serve to embarrass many of you who are standing and seated in this room, we can talk about that between ourselves, in private later. Go on my dear, I'm waiting for you and for my tea.'

I remain standing and walk across to where father is seated. I stand behind the chair and resting both hands on the top of the high back, I take a position which I consider one of control.

'I think we'll briefly go back in time to start when you married my mother in early 1899 shall we Detective Inspector?' Leonard turns to face me and blinks owlishly, nodding slowly at the same time. 'After you married mother I was born six months later while you were continuing an affair with an unknown woman, whose name is irrelevant here. You married mother while still married to this woman – as we'd say now, keep your options open. There is therefore a possibility that I am not your daughter but in fact was fathered by Alan Broadoak, we will leave that for another time.'

Father stutters 'But –'

I continue, 'Just as all that kicked off, the Kaiser had the audacity to help whoever it was kick off a war in the jolly old Balkans; we were soon drawn in to support someone or other and your domestic problems paled into insignificance. You received a commission to launch your army career and then who should come along as your able batman, but simple foot soldier Alan Broadoak. You couldn't believe your luck and soon gained complete control over him.'

'I say are you –'?

I rest my hands on his shoulders and he quietens. 'Then, without any women about and once you had him fully trained in his routine, you forced him to satisfy your obscene desires believing that while sodomy was – and still is for that matter – against the law even in wartime, you would never be discovered and anyway when it was all over, you'd never see your batman again. Broadoak a mere foot soldier was guilty of breaking one of the most disgusting laws that existed and wouldn't stand a chance of persuading the courts that you instigated the crime and his case would be aborted, that it was all in his imagination.'

Again father stutters and coughs 'You can't prove any of this. Stop making up stories trying to make a fool out of me.'

'But that's what happened, I've found a witness. Alan Broadoak's time in the war was short-lived, he was shot and to the day he died suffered from an extremely severe wound of shrapnel. He was shipped back home and who should take his place but John Styles.' Now I point to John who had already hung his head in shame. The experience had been a painful one, physically and mentally but he and Alan had a short time together to exchange notes before Alan was shipped back home. John knew what was coming. Alan had told him what he would be expected to do, sooner or later, and even though John twice saved your life you should have owed him a debt of honour, you continued to punish and abuse him.

'We have two men shamed by their High Ranking Commanding Officer, whatever you were at the time. A good reason as you saw it to murder Alan Broadoak, to stop each of them reporting you to the police or the War Office, whichever it was. John Styles was left alive because with Alan dead he, John, would have no alibi. But of course to cap it all there was your racketeering. You made an absolute fortune out of the black market and John knew. He had told Alan but with Alan dead John had no alibi for either the sodomy or the racketeering. It's true that John is guilt of blackmailing you by holding a list of your purchases and sales through the black market and of the profits you made. Thousands of pounds recorded against you. Something the police and even the War Office might have cause to bring charges. As it was, John let's say, bribed you into giving him a highly paid and privileged job here as a butler.'

At this stage it felt as though the entire room was holding their breath, waiting for the next revelation condemning my father to a clear cut judgement of the death penalty.

'But before you could take any action you discovered that both Patty and Lavinia were having affairs with Alan Broadoak at the same time. There are now four or five motives, four or five reasons why you could have murdered Alan Broadoak, but you didn't, someone beat you to it although I don't doubt that you will be charged some other crimes, murdering Alan Broadoak will not be one of them.'

I feel a huge sigh of relief around the room, although I would have expected some degree of horror that the man who was the Master of Brogdale, Director of a large building company and another company of brickmakers could have committed such heinous crimes and carried out such indecent acts.

I should apologise at this point as I'm sure many of you will be thinking, why on earth is this business of revealing the guilty party taking so long. Trust me, it's worth the wait.

'The only matter you now need to know is how and when the murder was committed. I said earlier that Dr Hudson assures me that Eserine does not act within a fixed period of time however it does have what he calls as an 'active life span'. This means that whoever murdered Alan Broadoak had to be sure that the drug would work during what he or she considered to be the ideal time during the game of bridge or even simply during the weekend. Ideally, Alan had to die between 8.00 pm and 11.00 pm. And he did.

The post-mortem showed an excessive amount of the drug in Alan's body, far more than was sufficient to kill him bearing in mind that he was already taking a regular dose and the pathologist believes that Alan drank the drug with alcohol. Both John and my father had the opportunity to drug Alan's port or wine. This merely confirms that the murderer was one of them and since the pouring of the poison into specifically the correct glass with the minimum possibility of being seen, it's quite clear who is the murderer.'

My father has remained seated during the entire evening but even now makes no further comment or movement, I continue unabated: 'In conclusion, and I think you'll agree when all these glorious misdoings are put before a court, undoubtedly at the Old Bailey, with all the arguments back and forth and the announcement of the opportunity to commit the murderer, I deeply regret that the only person who DI Drabble here can arrest for the murder of Alan Broadoak is our long time, loving and trusted butler John Styles.'

There is a huge gasp from the assembled company and a look of complete surprise from my father who stands up and walks briskly towards me, a huge smile slapped on his face in disbelief. John too, looks at me in complete surprise a look of 'why me?' on his face, as if he was being blamed for a murder committed by someone else, specifically by my father.

I say, 'Inspector, please do what you have come here to do.'

Chapter Fifty Two

Len Drabble is moving towards me to where John has been standing namely next to me during most of the lengthy denouement. John continues to look me closely in the face, the farewell of an occasional lover with anger in his eyes.

It's time for Len to make his closing speech and we both sigh in disbelief. 'Ladies and gentlemen, please may I have your attention for a moment.' My family dutifully turn to face him, a few cough, a few mutter believing all the talking to be over and that they could begin tea.

'Mrs Matcham has told you in minute detail the extent of our investigations – primarily her investigations – into the murder of Mr Alan Broadoak on the Saturday 10th June. Her extensive, substantiated searches have brought us to the conclusion that John Styles is indeed the murderer. But right at the start my superiors in Maidstone expressed concern over Mrs Matcham carrying out an investigation when the guilty party may be one of her own. They asked me to ensure that the decision and arrest is the right one. To make sure that my investigation was entirely independent to Mrs Matcham's, I was unable to tell her. I must now confess that my investigations have been taking place in parallel to those of Mrs Matcham and without her knowledge.

'Quite naturally I expected that these investigations would provide support for the arrest and subsequent conviction of Mr Styles. I was provided with an enormous amount of information from Mr Frank Spillett and young Thomas there…' He points to Tom sitting quietly, leaning against Patty's legs. '…to whom Mrs Matcham has given little credit. Together they and Mr William Whitten have unearthed another sequence of events which is supported by many of Mrs Matcham's collations, but which we three agree is more compelling than those we have just heard.'

The gathering, now without 'Cetta begin muttering, some sighing and those who possess one, look at their watches.

'Please, I'm sorry to drag this out but it is vitally important. We have established that there is a more straightforward sequence of events that reaches a similar, but different conclusion. You will have noticed Mr Styles' surprise and fury directed at Mrs Matcham when she declared him to be the murderer. You will also have noticed Colonel Whitten's relief and demonstration of gratitude to his elder daughter, at being let off the hook, so to speak. Each was strongly suggested to be the killer of Mr Broadoak.

What Mr Spillett, Mr William, Tom and I have established is that it is clear to us that there is a lot more to these investigations than meets the eye. Mrs Matcham has given clear evidence as to where she was and with whom she was talking on the day before and the day of the murder. Mr Spillett has been up to London and Bletchley – quite a nice day out apparently – gaining further evidence and noting the times of the journeys.

'He, his secretary, Mr William and Tom have been talking

to their contacts and friends in and around the Creek – some of them quite unsavoury characters I understand but nevertheless trustworthy, I'm told – and we have come to a different conclusion to the name of a different murderer. I regret to say that, Mrs Alicia Lavinia Sofia Matcham, I am arresting you for the murder of Mr Alan Broadoak on Saturday 10th June 1933, you are not obliged to say anything, but anything you do say will be taken down and may be used in evidence against you. Constable please take Mrs Matcham away.'

I make no expression of surprise or demonstrate any resistance when handled by one of Len's constables. As I am taken away, I hear exclamations and voices of disbelief that I have been arrested let alone actually being taken away, mutterings from some that they really knew that I was guilty all the time, even though they clearly did not. Unfortunately, DI Drabble is correct and I commend and attribute no blame to any of his helpers in their reaching the conclusion they have. I am sorry that I shall in future be unable to sleep with John again or as I had hoped I would – sleep with Tom or drive with him to Seasalter to keep one another warm, huddled against the North Sea breezes and to talk of a myriad of subjects. But it is entirely my fault.

As we reach the door that leads to the cells, I hear Len Drabble being asked the inevitable question – why did she do it? I turn to look at Len and he nods in agreement allowing me to speak to my assembled family.

Chapter Fifty Three

SATURDAY 24ᵀᴴ JUNE, LATE AFTERNOON

'To my family, friends and servants I can only say that I am sorry. Alan Broadoak started his destruction of my family – our family – when he began his affair with my mother. He enticed her, encouraged her, he offered her comfort and he provided her with the long lost sex of her youth. He threw himself at her feet and how could she refuse a young man fifteen years her junior. Then the blackmail began. Mother was – is – married to a wealthy man who has paid large sums of money to keep things quiet.

Three years after the hushed affair began Alan Broadoak started to blackmail father for two thousand pounds a year. The amounts increased over the years and by this year – ten years later – his demand was for thirty thousand pounds and father, having lost most of the family fortune in the Market Street Crash was on the verge of collapse. My plan to kill Alan was resolved to be during the weekend of 10th – 12th June I hadn't fixed the specific date, other than it was going to be sometime around that weekend and I had never known exactly what would happen but when conveniently, despite medical and legal decisions that Alan had had a heart attack, my dear little Patty was so convinced he'd been murdered.

'I am sure you can all see that I had to be the one to investigate his death.

'Until a fortnight ago I had intended to confirm the heart attack theory. I had learned so much about Alan Broadoak's wormlike writhing through you all and just how many of you are having affairs or have secrets from the past had suffered and are still suffering from his blackmail. I resolved to make this – I don't know – this, this – proclamation of my actions. My last good deed to you all.

Much of your ill-doings were unknown to me until I began my questioning and I am terribly sorry for all the skeletons in all the cupboards that I have unearthed but I hope you will understand some of how that happened. Patty's love for Alan was so strong that she could only believe he had been murdered while everyone else was simply glad to see the back of him.'

I look across straight into my little sisters crying eyes,

'You had no idea that he was having another affair, had you my darling?'

She shakes her head and bows it in embarrassment.

'Lastly, you certainly never gave any thought to the possibility that he was blackmailing father. He wasted no time in doing that. His golden goose had come in – is that right? He was, contrary to his image of a soft, kind, helpful and loving gentleman, he was an extremely nasty, spiteful, vengeful and untrustworthy man who had to be stopped and he deserved everything he got.

'My family are the most important thing in the world to me, so I killed him.

'God so help me, I murdered Alan Broadoak.'

There's no applause, no cheering as I leave the room, arm in arm with a policeman held tightly under each. I glance at mother and father the former crying and the latter with his stiff upper lip in full view. I had expected from a few of those present, at least some sign of appreciation, even perhaps some applause but no. I am a murderer and as such I have brought shame and disrespect on the family I resolved to save. Despite my reasons, despite my justifiable murder, freeing so many of my loved ones, they have cast me aside.'

Chapter Fifty Four

While I await my execution or the result of my appeal against thereof, I have laid before you my account of the events that occurred in Corners during the hottest, wettest weeks forever in mid-June 1933.

I trust that you have followed and understand the sequence of events as I have recorded them; the rationale, the whys and wherefores of my murdering for the purpose of saving the destruction of my family.

How and when did I commit the murder of Alan Broadoak? Now that's something I shall leave to your imagination; all I will say is that the answers lie in an old tried and tested family recipe.

For those who come after me, those who may murder other members of my family and their friends and those who unwittingly or determinedly taught me all I know, they will be the subjects of further revealing narratives should those independent but inevitably nasty people of the jury allow me time to write them down.

Finally, I hope that you will at least have sympathy for my murdering of the reputations of not only my father, but of John Styles, my mother and of poor Patty, bless her, who played a large and conveniently crucial part in the tale. Nobody should in any way be allowed to destroy a family such as Alan Broadoak was attempting to destroy mine.

Until next time …

Acknowledgements

Kathy (my wife, confidant, retired headmistress and editor)

Alison Hartley (widely read crime genre reader, retired headmistress and editor)

Roy Penrose, first director general of the National Crime Squad (retired) (Police operational & enforcement advice)

The owners/residents of Corners

Charlotte Mouncey, my talented designer and typesetter

James Essinger, principal of The Conrad Press